"Extraordinary. . . . Captivating."

—*Library Journal* (starred review)

"Harrowing and bleak, ultimately redemptive, this story of family growth and poignant courage speaks to caring mothers, fathers, and all of us who wish to protect our children."

—Louise Erdrich, author of *Love Medicine* and *Tracks*

"An arresting tale of courage and hard-won wisdom."

—*Booklist*

"Beautifully rendered. . . . The gripping chronicle of a tracker finding herself as she looks for others."

—*Kirkus Reviews* (starred review)

"Timely and intriguing. . . . May inspire hope in others, especially women who feel trapped in desperate situations."

—*Publishers Weekly*

"I was captivated. . . . [A] thoughtful and inspiring story of a woman making new tracks for herself."

—Ann Jones, author of *Next Time She'll Be Dead: Battering and How to Stop It*

ALSO BY HANNAH NYALA

CRY
LAST
HEARD

A Tally Nowata Novel

Hannah
Nyala

POCKET BOOKS
New York London Toronto Sydney

An *Original* Publication of POCKET BOOKS

 POCKET BOOKS, a division of Simon & Schuster, Inc.
1230 Avenue of the Americas, New York, NY 10020

This book is a work of fiction. Names, characters, places and incidents are products of the author's imagination or are used fictitiously. Any resemblance to actual events or locales or persons, living or dead, is entirely coincidental.

ISBN: 0-7434-5172-4

First Pocket Books paperback edition September 2004

10 9 8 7 6 5 4 3 2 1

POCKET and colophon are registered trademarks of Simon & Schuster, Inc.

Cover design by Lisa Litwack
Cover illustration by Gregg Gulbronson
Interior book design by Davina Mock

Manufactured in the United States of America

For information regarding special discounts for bulk purchases, please contact Simon & Schuster Special Sales at 1-800-456-6798 or business@simonandschuster.com.

For
Cle Elum,
whose last cry I didn't hear soon enough,
and will never stop listening for again.

And for Stewart,
the best reason I've had for waking up
in a coon's age.

ACKNOWLEDGMENTS

It couldn't have happened without

Tally's crew:
Nancy Berland
Louise Burke
Irene Goodman
Alex Kamaroff
Megan McKeever
Craig Patterson
Amy Pierpont
Stewart W. West

And mine:
Ronni Kern
Pat May
Tali Nyala
Vicki Wilson
Stewart W. West
and the boys
(Coober Pedy, Henry Streator, Cle Elum, Sedro
Woolley, and Abu)

All mistakes are mine.
Some I even made on purpose.

SAR
Acronym for search and rescue,
Rhymes with bar.
Where we usually end up when we're done.

—Handwritten placard on Laney Greer's desk

CRY
LAST
HEARD

DECEMBER 14

They don't tell you the 10 codes will save your life, though they will: 10-4, Acknowledge. 10-18, Backup Required. 10-24, Constant Monitoring.

Or that the 11 codes will drop your heart to its knees no matter how many times you've heard them: 11-99, Ranger Needs Assistance, or 11-44, my own personal least favorite—Possible Dead Body.

They don't tell you a crushed femur looks like milky ice against new snow, or that a child's frozen body mimics the blue peace of sleep. They don't say death has its own smell at thirty below or above, or that it sticks with you for weeks, like an old skin that cannot be shed. Nobody teaches you how to wear it either, day after waning day, and not throw up.

The codes we learned in training. Everything else, we learn on our feet. Over and over again. Until that eleven-cadence gets under our hides, and we feel its shape before it's even called.

How to survive all that is left strictly up to us.

~

It was cold in the house when the bird flew into the windowpane yesterday, and fell silent into the snowdrift below the eaves. Bess had just left, and I was curled up in a chair, surrounded by toys and wrapped in her favorite afghan head to toe, staring sightless out the window, dreading today.

I've been dreading today for three years. It came anyway.

The thunk made me flinch, and started the pain in my neck, so I went to the door and stepped out, sock-footed, retrieving the stunned cardinal—why, I can't say. Do not know. Dying is the way of all things. And then I went back to my chair and just held its limp, cooling body, quiet inside. There's no raging in me anymore. Two years of that's made me tired.

"Tired is as tired does, like pretty," my grandmother used to say. That's all well and good from over there where you sit, old woman, I would tell her today, if she was listening to me anymore.

The bird's eye was glazed, he had no fight left either. Bright crimson against my palms, once proud and wild, now cradled in the hands of a great natural foe. I understood he was hurting and that I could help, *should* help, by snapping his neck—that death is a release, not a prison. It's not like this would be the first bird I've had to kill.

And yet, still I sat, not able to grant that small mercy. Dry-eyed but undone, beyond easy reckoning. Zero sum, this game we call life, zero sum. So why keep on counting?

But then he blinked. Once, twice, with no pause, as the fire relit itself from within and his beak drew blood without visible effort from my closest finger, hauling me to my feet and back into the yard, arms flung high as he righted himself and flapped up and on, dipping low at first, but battling upward again and again, till he gained the safety of an aspen's middle limbs. One small splash of red in a white-hardened world. From there, after a moment's rest and not one backward glance, he went toward the river.

Badly hurt but flying. Straight into the teeth of the incoming storm.

Leaving me sucking on my finger to stop the blood, knee deep in wet socks and cold snow. And very glad I hadn't done anything more to ease his pain.

My name is Tally Nowata. This much I know.

And not one jot more.

~

There's no code for survival, no number that sums up continued existence, no shorthand for when you get to somebody and they smile or curse or simply say, "Hey ranger, it sure is good to see you." No call sign for how it feels to be searching for a pulse and hear, "Easy, I'm still in here." No symbol for numbers above zero.

In our line of work it's simple: presumed alive until proven otherwise. Life is our default.

Maybe that's part of the problem.

11:00 A.M.

The call came in at four. Laney and I have been slogging ever since. Two-man hasty team, minus the men and the hasty, out to locate a couple of stranded climbers on a rock wall 5000 vertical feet above the valley floor—12,800 feet above sea level, dead of winter. In the front neck of a blizzard, no less.

That's one thing you can count on in the Tetons: when the fates decide to run the table up here, they kick the legs out from under every last chair in the room first. Then they wing it.

And I do this for a *living*.

~

"Seen the end of your own nose lately?" Laney calls, voice thinned by the icy wind. Thirty hours ago, when these climbers set out for a fast day's run up this peak, it was downright balmy up here, shirt-sleeve weather. At dawn, when they realized they couldn't descend on their own and called us, it was chilly. Now it hurts to breathe.

"Nope. You?" We're go for full whiteout here any

second. Me perched on a skinny ledge about the size of a coffin, child-sized, and Lanes twenty feet straight down, just below a sharp overhanging roof.

"Same. Still no folks?"

"Negative. He*llo*! Anybody home?" I shout again, hoarse, hands chapped, working the belay but trying to peer above as well. I might as well be staring into pea soup, the color of old pewter. We're supposed to assess the situation and call in the team, if necessary, but for that we need bodies, at the very least. Still breathing would be nice, though the dead ones are easier to move—don't have to worry about hurting them any worse. Or getting sued. Paul would have a cow if he heard me saying that, always did. He never worked SAR. It looks different from my shoes, I used to tell him. "Yoo-hoo, rangers on deck! Y'all hear me?"

There is no reply. Snow lashes my eyes, I duck deeper into my parka. "You at the crux yet?" The toughest move of this pitch is just below that overhang.

"That's affirmative. Slack," Laney replies, and I play out more of the rope to her. There's a brief lull in the wind as her right foot hits the roof and she torques her body up, then shinnies the sheer face between us like a monkey on a light pole. Tips my stomach on its neck just to watch, but Laney Greer is all savior in motion, no fear. She's what you could call a natural.

If you have a need for pretty concepts like that.

~

Pretty works fine down there in the valley, I believe, where the right pair of boots and one toss of an artfully bleached head of hair will get you dinner and anything else you care to sample at any bar in town any night or day of the week. Pretty's fine for TV, too, maybe, or the movies—nice and easy, mussed exactly just so, not one false eyelash out of place. But pretty's less seductive up here at high altitude. And natural? Flat-out useless.

Lanes'd be more likely to chalk her effortless style up to years on these hills and good shoes, a battered pair of old rock boots that match mine, worthless everywhere else and not normally the choice for winter either—soles too thin, for one thing—but we figured they'd give us the edge we needed to tackle this shortcut. It would've helped if we could've outrun this storm; the lighter boots were supposed to help with that.

Laney's head rises from the pea soup, and I yell, "You could do this barefoot, couldn't you?"

She grins, places both hands on the ledge, and lifts herself onto it, executing a flawless classic mantel, seating herself beside me as if we're on one long sturdy barstool, and clipping into the anchor at my back. "Not quite," she yells over the wind, wiping her nose on her sleeve. "But I'd give a pretty penny to trade traction for comfort about now, wouldn't you?"

The storm bites off the last two words. We flatten our backs against the wall and stick to it. When you are one mile above the ground, there's some serious incentive to *stick*.

~

"Maybe you ought to think about switching shoes," Paul said, a couple years after we met. I'd just come off a particularly gruesome carryout. My team had just bodybagged a young kid, too young to even drive, who no longer had a chest cavity—and thus would never get old enough *to* drive, was all I could think, then or now. Darren Oley, from Cedar Rapids. First time in the mountains. Saved his money for two full summers to get enough together for climbing lessons.

"He mowed lawns, eight bucks apiece," his mother said to me in the stunned, far-off voice of a lost child as the coroner's van left with her only son. Then she gripped my arm, eyes tormented and locked with mine, needing someone, anyone, even a stranger, to hear. "That was *a lot of lawns*."

Paul met me at the front door, arms wide for a hug because the tiny village of Moose is too small to keep secrets, especially about death. Eyes down, head shaking, I ducked under his elbow, shedding my pack and hotfooting it down the hall for a shower.

"Don't you want to talk about it?" he asked, as I stripped and stepped in, craving the shelter of hot liquid and steam.

"Nothing to say."

"It's *me*, hon. Here for *you*, remember?"

His gentle persistence hit like a needle in the neck,

so I yanked the shower door open hard enough it rattled and then glared at him, water dripping off my nose and chin onto the floor. I could *feel*, could see him—why couldn't that be enough? "What do you want to hear? You want the truth? The truth is it's natural selection, thank Darwin and don't ask me, O'Malley—we just toe-tag and bag 'em and toss dibs on who has to tote the heavy end."

Paul swallowed, but held my gaze, and I hated the ragged edge on my voice that sounded like Mrs. Oley. *That was a lot of lawns.* Hated that and the fact that we'd already had this same conversation too many times before.

So I went for the jugular. "And today I lost and had to tote the sucker. Is that what you want to hear?"

"Not exactly. I'm worried. You're so hard about—"

"*Hard?* You ain't *seen* hard yet, bub, not by a *very* long shot."

"I just think—"

"I know what you think, you've told it to me often enough," I fumed, starting to line him out, back him off my space. But then I looked into his eyes and really saw them, the deep brown windows into this man that never showed me anything but kindness because it wasn't in Paul's nature to be otherwise, and I stopped. Took a deep breath. Paul would understand about Darren Oley, he would, if only I could tell him, I knew, but no words would come. I've never had words for what matters.

"It just looks different from my shoes," I finally admitted, feeling woozy and weak, Darren's clammy skin still heavy on my hands, hot water coursing down my spine, his mother's tortured eyes still locked on mine. "Just looks different from my shoes."

"Then maybe you ought to change shoes," he replied quietly, throwing his hands up and backing out of the bathroom. "*After* your shower, though, love. *After*."

~

There is no after when you've loved someone well, that's what I'd like to tell him today.

Love deals the temporal out of every deck in the house, Paul O'Malley. This is the thing no one ever tells you in advance, the thing I knew on instinct after losing my mother so young, and the reason I kept almost everyone at arm's length before you.

The day we met I took one look and decided to take a chance. One chance. Seven years ago and counting. Once you've done that, it's over, you've already hit the big middle of all the afters you'll ever want to see.

So you can never get ready for this kind.

That's what I'd like to tell you today, if you were listening to me anymore.

~

"Better check in, you think?" I shout.

"Ya," Laney agrees in her slow Minnesota drawl, comfortable as a polar bear on an ice floe, handing over the nuts and chocks she cleaned from the route as she came up—protection, we call the hardware, pro for short. I clip each piece into my rack, a heavy sling looped over one shoulder, across my chest, and under the other arm so the gear's hanging close at hand, and focus on getting each one into precisely the right slot—making up for my lack of nerve, as usual, with über-organization—each piece arranged in descending order by type and then size. "See if maybe they called to cancel. Feet propped up at the Stagecoach, whittling the corners off their close shave up here today with a couple shots of Jack," she adds drily, toasting me with an imaginary shot glass and then tearing into a pack of beef jerky.

"Charlie One to base, do you copy?" Before I've even finished the transmission, Laney has downed one chunk of dried beef and is working on another. It never takes her long to get at the food, which is the oddest thing for somebody who barely makes 95 pounds soaking wet and hauling a pack. Paul used to call her El Omnivore.

"Go ahead, Charlie One." The reply is patchy, weather's gigging the towers. Lanes shakes her head and peels open a sack of roasted pecans, eyebrows raised in a question. The circles under her eyes deepen. I hate seeing them, wish I could whisk them away—head her troubles off at the pass so they can't mark her face. Slim chance. Can't even do that for myself. So I put out my hand for pecans even though I can't stand them, and she knows it, but smiles and fills my palm anyhow. She thinks I don't eat enough and takes every opportunity to fix that. When you're broken inside, maybe it helps to fix things.

"We're at the reported ledge, Base, no sign of the subjects."

"Copy no sign. Stand by."

~

The order to rest stills nerves that had started to jangle, the mountain stands strong at our backs. Crunching the salty nuts, I let myself feel the earth for the first time in a long time, like an echo passing through, on delay.

Even a glimpse of this valley used to set my heart right for weeks. Now I can be out here 24/7 and not see a damn thing. Until I'm told to stand by, that is, and stuck on a ledge where my options for keeping busy are limited. Laney rests the back of her helmet on the wall behind us and stares into the white abyss. I lean forward, elbows on knees, and do the same.

Jackson Hole's buried in the storm. No sign now of the ritzy estates slung out across the valley, snugged up to the park boundaries, richest county in the nation, they say, and then cram in another tacky development to prove it. Usually we can see across the flats to the Gros Ventres, eyes tugged beyond the misdeeds of our species to the gentler eastern range, but today the wind howls and rolls off the peaks, spitting sleet in our faces, numbing our cheeks, blanketing everything beneath our feet in pale powder.

I bury my fingers in heavy mittens and sip tepid water laced with electrolytes from a thermos we keep

in the haul bag, eyes on white nothing. Lancy hands
me another wool neck wrap and dons a matching one
herself. Work in this weather is ten percent whatever
you're doing and ninety keeping up with the changes
required in your clothes.

Wes Dawson, the new Windy Point District Ranger
and immediate supervisor for our crew, signs on from
HQ, "What's your twenty, 327?" He breaks out the
call sign in digits the way we're supposed to: three-
two-seven. No shorthand for Wes like the rest of us.
He's so by the book he could've written it.

"The reporting ledge, 300 feet below the summit,
repeat, ledge reporting, but no subjects. No signs, zip.
You sure initial report was for this site? Over."

"That's a 10-4."

"No updates?"

"Come again?"

"You haven't had any updates? Nobody staggered
in and said we got down on our own, sorry for the
bother, let's go grab ourselves a beer? Over."

"That's a negative. Just the initial call, one busted
knee, need assist, will stay put." The wind's whistling
now, it's getting harder to hear. The distress call came
into dispatch from a Lee Hunt this morning. Local
man.

"Climber, skier, all-round decent guy"—Jed said
while we packed—"and good enough to pull off a
winter ascent start to finish, so if he says he could use
a hand, two tops, we'd better give it."

"Think it's a prank?" Laney shouts, tearing another

strip of jerky in half and handing it over. "Been six months since the last, Tal. Maybe we should've waited for visual confirm from the bottom before starting up."

"Then we'd still be down there, frozen solid. Report sounds legit, we roll. What else is there?"

"Climb and get paid for it." Laney grins, both cheeks stuffed and one thumb up, waggling. "Hazard pay to boot, a whole thirty-five cents per hour. Fine by me."

"In *June*. Maybe."

"Here, eat. You're getting grouchy."

"It's time for my nap. Dead cow don't solve sleepy." Laney nods. "Missing baby Bess, are ye? I *knew* it."

Suddenly the radio crackles again; it's Jed this time. "We backtracked the subject's cell this morning and called his home, 327. Left a message. Wife just phoned from Sun Valley. Says they're both skiing, been gone since Sunday. He left his cell phone in the charger on their kitchen counter, you copy?" The static's so bad we can hardly hear, but Laney's head jerks up, helmet smacking the rock. "Do we *copy*? He's kidding, right?"

"You want to run that by us again, 21?" Mobile phones don't dial by themselves yet, do they? Get me a ranger, I'm stuck on a hill—bit of a leap for primitive technology, ask me.

"It's a no-go, 27. Subject's skiing in Idaho. Looks like we've been had. Phone may be stolen, some kid pulling a prank, we'll run it down on this end. You copy?"

"10-4. That's affirmative."

~

For a no-go, we barreled out of our warm toasty beds at 4:02 A.M., got the brief while we packed to leave, and snapped on our skis twenty-one minutes later at the trailhead. Lanes and me, not because we're better than anybody else on the team or more awake at 0400, but because we've both climbed this route several times in the past, twice each in winter. Laney did it just last week, during the warm spell, for money. There are perks in this place for that kind of idiocy.

So do we copy? I believe the hell we do.

~

Wes signs on again, "Charlie One, better bring her down, if you can. Repeat, stand down and return to base, we're clocking eighty to ninety at the pass, over." So it's official: the storm's revving up—as if we didn't know that already—wind's hitting 80 mph in the lulls at the top of the range right now.

Laney keys her mike, too cheery. "That's a big 10-4, Base. We copy, stand by one, will assess. Charlie off. So Tal, we checking into this little hotel here or making a run for it?" She's right. We've got enough gear to tie into this wall and just wait the storm out, if necessary.

"Have to share a room." Back pressed against the wall, I stand to stretch my legs. They're already protesting the few minutes' rest. Appendages are like brains: they do better if you keep them occupied. "The way I figure it, we're good for about three days. Fast as you're downing the food, less than two.

Hours. So no, I don't fancy starving to death at 12,8."
In a blizzard. On a rope. For who the hell knows how
long?

"Grouchy," Laney says, smile gone, finger hovering
over the transmit key. "Go on, make the call."

"Let's run it."

"Now you're talkin'. Hey Base, it's Charlie One on
the horn," Laney calls, while I prep the haul bag.
When I get to the top of the pitch and set the anchor,
she'll send our gear up the line after me.

"Go ahead, 352," Wes replies, his voice fading in
the static.

"We'll head up top and come off the lee, standard
ops, give you a shout if we stumble over anybody else
on the way, ETA something on the long end of 16, no,
make that 1800. Will try for comm checks on the
hour, but it's iffy up here—need be we'll tie in and
hunker down, hitch a ride in the bird anon. So. This is
52, over and way out." And to me, not skipping a
beat, "Want the next lead?"

I nod, bracing myself against the rock, stuffing my
mittens back into the haul pack and lacing its neck
securely, wondering why the heck I ever thought taking up climbing could cure my fear of heights when it
hasn't—not even close—and why I still, sixteen years
after that first bad decision, keep dragging myself up
one damn hill after another anyway. Jed once said,
"It's in your job description, TJ." He was posing on top
of the Grand on one foot, like a Yogi master who's just
lost what's left of his mind. I was trying not to pass

out. "And one day the switch on your fear will click off, kiddo. You'll see."

"Provided I don't live that long," I muttered, not joking. He laughed.

That was back when we still had things to say to each other and most of them were funny. Before Australia, and Paul. Hal and Rosemarie and me coming unglued on Pony Sutton, and then Jed too when he got within missile-launching distance. Come to think of it, Laney's about the only person on the crew that still talks to me these days, which is fine, actually, by me. Less people, less trouble.

As I unclip from the anchor and turn to face the wall, Laney hangs her handset on her harness and rips another stick of jerked beef in two. "Well, Nowata, shall we blow this popsicle stand?" she asks, picking up the line to belay, my cue to get moving.

"I believe so."

"Sticking with the fast shoes?"

"One more pitch. Still clean, no ice."

Laney shrugs. "Works for me."

"Climbing." I nod, unclipping from the anchor and gripping the edges of a narrow crack, one hand well above my head, the other about even with my chest. Flex, grip again, lay into it this time, allow for the wind, Tally, read and bend.

"Climb on," she replies, biting into the tough meat like old men tackle fat cigars, both hands attending the rope before my first foot hits the wall.

There's no one I'd rather trust my life to than

Laney Greer. The girl keeps her priorities straight. She's still eating homemade jerky in a PowerBar world.

11:12 A.M.

Another thing nobody tells you: every time you lace up your boots, the mountain's got you caught in its crosshairs. Sighted and stoked.

But we still live like we're exempt. Till it catches up with us, that is, and throws a tire iron in our spokes. Or something more lethal.

We expect to lose a few. People climb, they hike, they ski, they die; we all know this, and it makes a certain amount of lopsided sense. We also expect— intellectually, at least—to lose rescuers, because you can't do this job without sticking a neck or two (or eight) out on every gig, and this we all know very well.

What we don't know, and can't reckon for—not really, not even in the abstract, no matter how much we try—is the ones we lose.

Like Rosemarie. Seasonal, here three summers in a row, had just decided last May to move in with Lanes permanent, when it happened. Total fluke, whole crew strung out on the Grand, Owen-Spalding route in fine weather, simple long-line descent to the Lower Saddle, where the helo would meet us to hoist out a busted climber. So straightforward it could've been a training session, except for the kid with the sprained ankle, who wasn't all that happy to ride down the mountain strapped into a litter while his girlfriend chugged off under her very own steam, flirting with Hal like she hadn't ever met a good-looking man before. And might not again anytime soon either.

I still don't know what happened, nobody does. Did a four-hour debrief later trying to sort it out, but it's still clear as mud. The one thing we're all sure of is that Rosemarie took a header. Eighty feet down, never made a sound, and when we got to her she was gone. Just like that. No fog, no sleet, no ice or snow, no avalanche. Just off rope and one wrong step. That's about the extent of existence up here.

On one end of a heartbeat you're breathing, on the other you're not.

Zero sum.

Which leaves the rest of us to pick up the pieces of ourselves. Trying to get the whole back into some kind of working order.

Laney went into shock at the hospital and cried for a week, then spent the next few months acting as if it had never happened. Until Hal went down during a body retrieval on Teewinot and broke it wide open again, that is, and Pony eventually decided Lanes was acting too much like me over Paul and told her so. Sutton and I haven't said two words off the job since, but I got in enough that morning to last a lifetime. Said some things I didn't know I actually thought. Even Jed steers clear of me now.

So be it. Good riddance. I'm about sick of folks telling me how to grieve. And when to move on. I'll move the hell on when I get good and ready to and not one bloody second sooner, *do you hear me, Paul O'Malley?* That's something else I'd tell you now, if you were listening.

~

So I climb. Every chance I get. For shows or no-shows, same difference, and if I'm scared out of my skull half the time, so be that too. If the fear ever leaves, I'll already be deep six, and it won't matter much then.

Ten feet above the ledge now, I press left into the wind, one foot on a dime-sized nub, the other smeared against a bowl-shaped protuberance a good two feet the other direction and up about ten inches. Left hand working the thinning crack, right reaching for a distant hold. If we can just cover the next hundred feet, we'll be in the clear. All of a sudden the wind dies completely and I sway hard left and then right, one skinny inch from coming off and landing on Laney's head.

"Watch that next bit, Tally-ho," she warns, as I swallow my stomach and crawl on. "It gets hairy, and there's no place to put any pro for a good forty feet." If anybody would know about that, it's her. She did this route just last Monday, guided some guy from Europe—Switzerland, I think—has his eye on a New Year's ascent of the Grand Teton.

"That's a 10-4. Did you really get a thousand dollars for last week?" I puff, talking to keep from thinking. A steely fog hangs over the valley, wind suddenly gone as if it never was. Can't see it, but the ground feels miles away. Our voices pierce the emptiness, and I'm grateful for the sound. The smallest things serve as anchors up here for me. "Ten whole Ben Franklins?"

"Ya." Laney chuckles softly. "I feel like a lawyer. Or a thug."

"Insane's more like. How do you people find each other?"

"Want ads. Seriously, though, some people got more money than sense. So he wants to pay my rent for a climb I'd do for free, who'm I to spit in his grits?" she replies, quoting Pony, which everybody does on occasion. Texans are imminently quotable. Hard to live with, but they can talk. "He wasn't half bad on the rock either, covered some big walls in Europe, Pakistan. Jock with a brain. Easiest grand I ever pulled, that's for sure."

"Which you promptly gave away, Knucklehead." For three months straight, she's been nest-egging a cash reward for a poacher we're after in the park. It's at five grand, last count. I hate to think about the state of her bank account.

Laney laughs. I like the sound of that.

"Keep it up, you'll be in the poorhouse, Greer."

"Already there, no *be* about it."

We're quiet for several minutes, me sweating through the moves. Ice off a deceptively gentle breeze for the moment, mountain shrouded close, unsparing. No sign whatsoever of any climbers, so it was a prank. I'm feeling something less than charitable.

"We oughtta find these little boys and wring their skinny necks!"

"Or string 'em up by a rope. Got plenty if you locate the necks," Laney shouts. "Hey, Tal, you never did answer my question about Bess. Miss her?"

Of course, I feel like yelling. Why does everybody keep asking me that? How could I not miss my daughter? Barely two and away from home for the first time without her mom, off to the National Finals Rodeo in Vegas with my brother Dix and his family yesterday morning. It's just for five days, but it feels like 200. "Yep."

"Break's gotta be nice, though, right?"

"Well yes, since you keep bringing it up." I'm wore to a nub lately. Not being too good a mom. "Are you cold? I'm cold. Ready for a dip in a nice hot tub."

"You should ask somebody out," Laney calls, outrageous now just because she can be. I'm at least 35 feet above her, closing in on an offset flake. "Date. Have dinner and sex once a week with somebody. Like Wes."

"Drop it or I'll let go and fall on your head," I shout, full to the gills with people trying to fix me up. As if dressing up and eating out fixes anything at all worth fixing.

Laney laughs and mutters something sarcastic about my mood, and I pretend not to hear. Then the first rock hits my helmet and I duck into the wall shouting "Rock!" from habit to warn Lanes, and the next one slams into my neck and knocks me loose, and all of a sudden it's not for pretend anymore.

This wasn't supposed to be about dying.

The words swirl soft in my mind as I struggle to stay conscious. I have said them before, once only, in a place I still fight to forget. Stood on hot sand in the red Tanami Desert of central Australia, stranded and scared and skinning a songbird for food, staring at that ocean of dry yellow spinifex and tall termite mounds, knowing I had to cross it on foot, alone, but not why, because I didn't know about Paul yet, hadn't found him, couldn't know, and these words slipped out. *This wasn't supposed to be about dying.*

I have never said them here. Never on land I know better than my own skin. This is my safe place, the one chunk of ground that never turns on me no matter how hard it crunches other folks.

But it has betrayed me now, kicked the legs clean off my chair. Pull up, Nowata. Control the swing. Rope's over an edge, bound to be cut. 11-99, people. Ranger needs some assistance.

~

I am hanging not quite flat on my back in mid-air, bleeding and numb, very high off the ground, we were after the climbers, no-shows, two of them. Me above Laney forty feet, means I'm under her now, under that jagged roof. Five thousand feet up, no, 5200, three to go. One fraying rope between me and lights out.

So that's it. The dimensions of betrayal.

If I fall from here, the impact will drive my jaw teeth through the top of my skull and scatter the rest of me over a good-sized section of federal real estate. I know because I've bodybagged other climbers who've done it. That's my job, search and rescue. I'm a park ranger, not a statistic. They pay me to work betrayal back inside its box. Then sit on the lid.

That's what Hal said, the last search we worked together. Those exact words. "They pay folks like me to sit on the lid." And he smiled when he said it, like always. But then he stepped onto that snowfield and spun away and down and never said anything again.

Light falls on the desert behind Paul's shattered skull, and Foy, the man who killed him, laughs easy as though it was a game, and someone shouts, "Rose's down—she is *down!*" Ruby smiles over her campfire at me, and I yearn for the peace of her red sandy land, but feel only Foy's neck snapping beneath my boot, once, twice, three times, and then four, only it's not him but Bess, just last week, pounding her fork on the table, mad because I served peas and not corn, and she didn't stop at four. Or twenty.

Eyes closed, Nowata, get a grip. The fall inside your head is the one that kills you first.

11:36 A.M.

"Lanes, better call out the crew," I call, trying for cheerful but heaving instead, left hand feeling for the large crack in my helmet, right arm too busted to move. Both my knees took hits, and one of my eyes is bleeding itself shut. We may have to double-line me and hold on here till we can get some help.

"Laney?"

No answer. But there's no give in the line either, so she's got me tied off. Good.

"Hey, Greer, you still with me?"

No response.

Something's wrong. Did the rocks get her too? There were three altogether, I think. Big, the size of small children. Where the hell did they come from? This route's supposed to be pretty clean. And it's winter too, wrong season for rockfall. So do we have stranded climbers up here after all? Steal a phone from somebody's kitchen counter, climb and get stuck, make a call, then get unstuck enough to move on and knock something loose?

"R352, I could use a comm check."

No reply. The wind's coming up again, maybe she can't hear.

Fine, I'll make the call myself. Won't Pony have a field day with this one—Nowata needs rescuing?

But as I fumble for my handset, a sick feeling starts near my knees. Empty chest harness. Radio's gone, mike too. Must not've had the closure snapped; when I dove, it all headed south. Bad sign. Blood drips onto my sleeve and freezes. Worse sign, sort of puts the radio into perspective. Somebody laughs. Must be me, though I can't imagine why, since this isn't remotely funny. Just like a Nowata. To laugh when you ought to be crying.

The wind ebbs, so I yell, "Laney Greer, talk to me!"

Again, nothing. She's down, has to be. Worse shape than me or she'd be talking. Sleet blasts my face, eyes tight, I fumble for the rope. It's beginning to ice up. I *have to get back to that ledge.*

But the wall is several feet away and blurry, like fog, and the section we crossed less than an hour ago's well out of reach. In the dive I swung long to the right of the route, directly under this sharp overhang, and to get back on I could use body parts that aren't as banged up as mine. Eyeballs that would focus, for starters. Fingers that—

Dry it up, Knucklehead. Wall's over there, whining don't outwit geology. Never did.

Laney's down. Means you move up. Stat.

11:39 A.M.

Stomach in throat, dragging myself to a sitting position at the end of the line, I talk myself off the edge, too busted to drop-kick myself past the fear. There is just not enough substance between me and the ground right now. Have to sidle this one, facts up front like a shield.

Fact: we have gear for ascending a rope. Jumars or, failing that, old standby prusiks. Either one grips a line and holds fast till released. I keep both on my rack—

always in exactly the same spot. People make fun of me, call me "anal-retentive" and "control freak." Even Paul thought I was "a little too thorough for healthy, hon."

"That's all right," I'd tell him. "I'd rather be thorough than dead." You got some pithy observation now, O'Malley?

What are you *doing*, Taliesin? *Up*.

Okay. I'm at least set for gear. And when I make it back to the ledge and our haul bag, we'll be fine. Tie in, hunker down for a few hours. First and finest rule for survival: stay put till the cavalry arrives.

But as I feel for the ascenders with my left hand, helmet against the taut rope to hold me upright, I go very still inside. Glance at my rack to confirm and go stiller. Pull the rack into place and check closer. No jumars, no prusiks. I rifle through my gear, nerves in a bundle, again and again. No use. The ascenders aren't out of place. They're not here.

At all.

How is that possible? They were here last night, I'm sure of it, I check this rack every single evening before I go to bed, never fail. I need those jumars. The rope's over that jagged edge, bound to be fraying or worse. Without—

The heck with the rope getting sliced, no choice. I throw myself at the wall, starting to pendulum, feet and one hand out. Everything hurts.

Three tries and four skinned knuckles later, I finally manage to stick, just barely, and yell, more for me than her maybe, "On my way, Lanes. ETA fifteen minutes.

Tops. And when I arrive, you'd better have a damn good reason for this silent treatment, Knucklehead."

Nothing but cold wind replies.

~

And then I hear it. A dull, muffled thud just above.

And see, flying past, one arm's reach away.

A body. In freefall.

"*No,*" I mean to shout, but bile leaps in my throat, someone whimpers, can't be her, too far away, can't be me, don't turn to watch. *Cannot move.* Lose the line it's over, don't move, don't even breathe, and into those blank seconds of silent time bending, I hear her hit the wall below with those sick, swishing thuds, once, twice, each fainter, and then I am alone.

11:41 A.M.

There's a quiet place inside death for those of us who stay behind. Empty. Quiet empty, a looming absence of light.

No words. No sound. No thought.

No escape and no return.

No way to put our pieces back together. The ones that could have helped us do that are gone.

~

I am frozen in place.

Not Laney too, that's all I can think. Clinging to the wall, fingers cramping, legs stiff, loosen up, Tally, or you're down. *Not her.* Hold steady, upright, nose exactly over your toes—lean too far in, you're gone. Too far out, same deal. Vertical, hold the line. Treat this like a boulder problem, pretend it's near the ground.

The wind is still, no sound.

You can't just hang here, Taliesin. It can't end this way. Bess in Austra—no, *Vegas. Dix has Bess in Las Vegas, Laney just fell. That's not possible. She was supposed to ride down with me to pick Bess up. We were leaving tomorrow, road trip.* I feel dizzy. The taste of salt tears closes like a hand on my throat, I clutch the rock, shaking. Trying to remember how to breathe.

~

"Road trip!" Laney belted out the day I asked her at work, and then went along the hall singing, tapping on each door she passed to keep the beat and doing that little 1-2 shuffle step she does when she's happy. Wes raised his eyebrows and said, "Do we not let her out often enough?"

You can't take Laney too, I scream, eyes shut, not wanting to see any of this. She lights candles for us on our birthdays, mine and Bess's, even Paul's. Still. Every year, never fails. At dusk one slender taper in her front window, a tiny flame flickering toward our house. After she and Rose got Ducket—

No. That dog's crazy about his mom, he's the only thing that's kept her sane all these months—*what will happen to him now?* Taliesin, stop it this instant! *You have to move, or you're coming off.*

I try to reach for the next hold, but my fingers stay

clamped to thin shards of granite like leeches to skin, except my muscles are giving way underneath, tired of the job, tired of me. Freezing air closes, hold on, don't pass out.

Suddenly something hits my helmet with a soft thud, and I flinch, instinctively pressing against the wall.

The rope. It's the rope this time, the one she had me tied in with. Falling silent from above into the gray abyss below, where she just went.

Slowly it comes clear. I'm off rope.

Totally. Five up and off rope.

Nothing holds me now but two feet and four fingers, the ground pulls and claws at my skin, the shaking starts somewhere deep inside, giant shuddering waves of bone to gristle, I feel my fingers coming loose, ripping free in slow motion. Knees burning, I fight the hold. Won't turn loose. Will *not*. The rope dangles from my waist, the end that tied me to Laney just minutes ago now lost in the gray void between us.

Feet shaky but planted, I ram my right hand into a jagged crevice and draw up the line with my left. Why, I'm not sure. There's a low buzz at the base of my neck. Something's not right with all this, is all I can think.

The place where the rope spanned the roof's still intact. Frayed, like I thought, but nowhere near apart. I keep pulling. The pain in my neck deepens, I knew it, *knew* something was off. The end comes into sight, and I stop and just stare at it. Swaying gently.

Somebody cut me loose. Had to. Ropes don't slit themselves.

Eyes closed, I rest my helmet on the rock. The muscles in my legs seize, shutting down. I understand more now. Somebody else is on that ledge.

Somebody who wants me dead.

11:49 A.M.

A child cries, for me? From where? No images cascade, the cold fog does not relent. No sound but that call, beyond language or thought. I should follow but cannot. Laney—

Somebody hit Lanes, and now they're trying for me.

I have to move, but there's nowhere to go. Muscles, stones against bone. Skin taut, no give. One arm busted, no use. Any slip, I'm airborne. And when I clear the edge of this roof—*if* I do—it's sheer wall to the ledge. From below I don't stand a chance.

Do we have climbers up here, then? Snapped and striking out?

Makes no sense. Cold gets to people, even phone thieves, but not *that* much. So who wants me dead?

And *why?* There's a ragged break in my mind I can't stand to hear. Why doesn't matter, Tally. At all. Never did, but especially not now.

Suddenly another thud sounds from above, pressing home the point, our haul bag this time, all the extra gear and food and clothes we brought with us plunging down, narrowly missing my right shoulder, rolling end over slow end through the keening air.

My winter boots are in that bag.

That's it. Whoever's on the ledge has this round. The moment I pull over this roof, I'm the target. No contest. Easy as shooting salt fish in a dry barrel.

If, by some crazy chance, I do make it to the ledge, the odds are still all wrong. Whoever's up there won't even have to work hard with me coming from below. So up's out.

But I can't go down either. Downclimbing's lethal under good conditions, especially unroped, but in these—

So that's it, then.

I'm not getting out of this one alive.

11:53 A.M.

When that thought settles, I clutch the rock so hard my fingers ache, lean back, and scream. No words. Just fury that ends in a sob when I feel her body falling again and again, air presses toward me, nowhere to go. I couldn't have reached her if I'd tried, I'm confused, my feet hurt, head pounds. The crux is just ahead—I can't make that move with one arm. Ruby calls to me from the Tanami, *"Pirli!"*

Ruby called me Pirli, the rock. The desert wind echoes my name, and I listen, beyond here, this bitter cold, to a blistering land of red sand gone wet and chilly in the rains, our only warmth a small campfire in the door of a cave, tended by the old Aborigine woman who rescued us at the end. If it hadn't been for Ruby and the white dingo, we'd have died, Jo and me. Paul's daughter. His first, and the only one he ever knew. The men who killed him left Josie for dead at the Land Rover. If it hadn't been for that child, I'd have lain down by her father and never opened my eyes on the world again. The sand would've claimed us both, how I wanted that then. But Jo lived, so I had to, and Ruby saved us both at the end. She looks at me now, no words, only calm eyes from dark shadows, but I know and feel the steel of my grandmothers gathering in my spine.

This isn't the first time somebody has tried to kill me and failed. Not near.

Yanta! Ruby shouts. *Go!*

11:59 A.M.

I thought I was dreaming, but I'm here now, touching her face, feeling for a pulse, it's not a dream.

Whoever fell, it wasn't her. Not Laney. Heart racing in my throat, I whisper it again and again. She's slumped over, still tied in to the anchor. Cut bad in two places, stabbed. *Up here.* Then left for dead. But by *who?* There's no one but us. No one. Just a scrape on the edge, one bloody footprint and two partials, large soles, size twelves at least, maybe thirteens. Stepped through the pool of her blood, started back up the wall. Has to be a man, feet that large. No way a woman could do this, right? Knock loose those stones from above?

I could. Pony could. Lanes could too, in a pinch and mad enough at the swinging end of the kick.

But she'd have to be tall to leave these tracks. Real tall, taller than Pony even, but takes to mountains a lot better than Sutton, who doesn't and makes no bones about it. None of this matters, Tally, move on, you're off point. Probably men. No, one—one set of prints, for sure. So one fell, one headed up?

Then where is he now? And *why the hell would he do something like this to us?* The storm's hitting its stride, snow pouring, can't see more than six feet any direction, he could be right above us and I wouldn't have a blooming clue. I need my good boots, our wall slings, a way to get her patched up and inside a bivy bag for cover. Need a radio, some help—

"Lanes, please hold on," I whisper, hoping he'll think we're dead if there's no sound, and use the knife blade from Paul's old Leatherman to rip a section of my jacket out for bandages. Nothing else for it. He took her radio, tossed off the haul pack, I'll have to stabilize her the best I can and go for help. Leave all the clothes I can spare, and then some—parka, turtleneck, wind slacks, bundle her to hold in her body warmth and break the wind, cover every last inch of skin—she's down, needs the edge my clothes will give her. This is insane, *stay put, Taliesin.*

If I do, it's over. The crew won't go to red on us for

at least six hours—no earthly reason to string the whole team out till 1800, Laney said so herself and she's as good on a wall in a storm as anybody living. It'll take at least six or eight more for them to get here. I can cut all that in half if I can just get off this hill. I'm in good shape, first defense against hypothermia. I know the tricks, know the mental game. And I'm mad as hell—that oughtta make some heat.

Survival: 95% brains, 5% circumstances.

Kick it up a notch, Tally, bring it home.

~

December 14. What is *with* this day?

Exactly three years ago I was about to die from sunstroke in a desert ten thousand miles from home. One year later, in a car accident. The year after that, with Bess in ICU. And today I'm here.

Let it go, Nowata. Move on. The past is a wound that won't heal, let it go and work the now. This is all you have, all you'll ever have. Remember Ruby? It has to be enough. The day will suffice for itself.

~

Laney's as stable as she's getting. Both wounds bound, feet out of those shoes and bundled the best I can get them, hands, head and body too. No skin exposed.

The best way down is up the summit and off the top, just like we planned—*only* way down now, with just one short piece of rope. I don't like leaving her here so helpless with the man who did it on the loose. But he's long gone. Has to be. Probably halfway to the peak by now, thinking we're both dead and no threat, meaning to beat the storm. Did he plan this before the distress call ever came into HQ? *Why?* Somebody we arrested? Insulted? How? What on earth could we've done that would call for this? Lanes especially.

Swathed in my clothes, she looks so frail, so small, like a leggier version of Bess with less hair, slipping peacefully into a blue cocoon. I make a tent for her head with my parka hood and snug her into the space blanket she had tucked into her pocket—never leaves home without it—then tie her in once more for good measure. I'm stalling now, it is clear, can't afford this. Whisper to her, Tally. Cheerful, in case she can hear. "Gone for help, Knucklehead. Back in five."

Laney does not move. I tear my eyes away, meaning to leave, but they land on the tie-off she did for me at the anchor after the fall, and I'm struck still again by the precision of it: double knot on the line, perfectly executed, so she could free up to come after me, if necessary. Working the gig right to the last bloody second, that's our Laney Greer. Minutes ago she was chiding me about my mood, stuffing that damn jerky in like it was penny candy, now she's— leave it, Tally. *Move.*

What next?

I need my arm back in the socket for this climb.

Shoulder toward the mountain, I brace for the impact, hoping I hit it right the first time, feeling with my left fingers where the separated bone is and trying to judge where it has to strike the wall to go back into place. Chunks of sleet sting my skin.

Breathe deep. It's just me and this rock.

And whoever's above.

12:47 P.M.

Three hundred feet from Lanes to the summit, two from me. I've covered that first hairy forty, and the sixty above, by the skin of my teeth, no better, two hundred to go, all trouble in these shoes. Have ice tools, but I really need my crampons and heavier boots to do this well. And a good right arm so I can hang my weight on it every other move. No chance. It took three tries to slam in my shoulder, lost it on the second, thing won't be worth a plug nickel for two weeks, best I'm getting out of it now is ballast. But ballast counts up here.

Silk long johns and ploypro no match for this storm. Busted body, none for the mountain. Legs shaking, hurts to breathe. I'm in the middle of a free solo at 12,9, on a route so tough I wouldn't flash it head-on if it was lying flat on the ground in full summer sun and me with two belays, a top rope, and real sticky shoes. Laney would've been leading this next section, for sure. I know when I'm out of my league.

And when I'm whipped.

Which isn't now. Not by a long shot.

No sign of the man. None. Not a scrape, not a

smudge. Mind's fuzzy when I try to call back the muddy details of his prints. It's so cold, my brain's freezing in its ruts—95% of me gone to slush in a pan. Can't think straight. Have to. I've got to get help for Laney and go pick up Bess and Audra in Vegas. Hate that town. Sin City, they call it, but even their sins lack conviction. No fire, no life, all tinsel, pretend.

"Gonna sin, do it up good," I always tell Dix. "Work it like old Johnny Nowata did. Murder your wife in front of your kids—win a *Get Out of Jail Free!* card from a wily old Okie judge who cheats on his wife and his taxes." My brother hates it when I talk that way. He's always hoped our dad would come around eventually. Change. *Reform.* "You mean stop trying to kill us all?" I laugh at him. Dix is soft, gets religion periodically and mixes it with hope and a democracy he still believes in.

But I guess that beats the Jack Daniel's he used to fall back on.

I'm too hard on him. Keep too sharp an eye out for him tripping again. It's not fair, he's been sober almost six years, and Lord knows he had good reasons to not be with baby Chance like he is. I ought to be more help to Dix and Shelby than I am. Thought once about offering to keep Chance for a week, let them get away by themselves, but took one look at him banging his head against the sofa that night and froze all my intentions. Bess is a snit, a handful, but I don't know what I would do if she was autistic and me pregnant with my second child like Shel is. Or without Aud.

The world is a cold, angry place for people like us, yes, but not near so bad as it could be. At least Bess and I've got Audra. Makes everything more doable. Remember that, Tally.

Remember the points in your favor. A babysitter from London who takes better care of your daughter than you do some days. And says a week in Las Vegas sounds "too right, eh, like a paid holiday?" I need to remember to thank Aud again when they get home. Maybe figure out a way to send her on a real vacation. She's certainly due one.

There. Normal helps.

1:32 P.M.

Missed the route, it's icing over. Had to downclimb and go around. If I cliff out, we're done for. Shaking so bad my bones hurt, hard to stick to the holds. Tools clumsy in my hands, tried to get an ice screw in and dropped it, can't afford to lose any more. Head gone dull inside. Wind down, snow heavy like a curtain.

Can't see two feet, lashes freezing to eyelids, scrub free, freeze again. Maybe a hundred more to go.

No sign of the man. But a raven looped through twice, beady eye checking out my progress—or maybe he didn't, maybe it was that other time, can't remember—I turned away anyhow, for good measure. The last thing I need today is more birds.

10-24, Base, 10-24. Constant monitoring required. Would God they could hear me.

2:18 P.M.

Off route again. Worse this time. Mind searching for clues, been up this before, lots, but nothing looks familiar. Laney can't die.

I'm shivering so bad, can't think straight, first stage hypothermia, window's closing Tally-ho, *get a grip or you're high-fiving the reaper, Lanes too, and then who keeps Bess safe from here on in? Dix won't be able to stand up to John Nowata alone.*

The thought of my father out of prison, not for killing my mom because they only gave him three years for that, but for stabbing a district judge's son in a bar brawl the week he got out . . . which means he's up for parole next month for the first time and he found God a while back so the board's liable to be swayed . . . which means he'll be on the loose again, so Dix and I—

My chest closes, and I gasp, out of air. Nose to granite, vision way too clear now, thin veins in the rock stand out in relief. No belay, Tally, you can't afford this, *I cannot leave my daughter alone in this world. Like mine left me.*

Slowly, like a set of freeze frames hung on a melting wall, my right foot slips off the rounded nub I've been standing on, and I'm falling again, sliding gently into the arms of the roaring wind.

~

I know not to think on a mountain. Instinct is useful up here. Thinking isn't. Thinking's a luxury, fine for the pretty little horizontal world when you've got both feet flat on it. But thinking on a vertical wall will get you dead quicker than anything else. You know that, Taliesin.

Flatline.

Or it's zero sum for sure.

2:29 P.M.

The toe of my shoe caught a fist-sized protrusion a few minutes ago, and I tore the skin off a knuckle grasping for a secondary hold in a rough-edged chimney that was too big to be much help. Arrested the fall with the adze end of my ice axe, barely. Then just held on, frozen, for a few seconds. Finally managed to get onto my feet and stuff my left arm into the crevice, elbow and palm pressed firm against opposing sides, enough to take my weight. Now I just breathe and hang from my left arm, eyes closed. Need a rest, just a few seconds here and I'll go on.

My thoughts are stiff like hoarfrost but insistent. Sleet thrums through dark clouds. Should be stinging my skin, but it's not. The stings come from inside me now.

Bess at the table last week, screaming at the top of her lungs. O'Malley genes, that. Exactly like Josie at two. Paul used to tell me how she was, and I saw for myself later—and now again, with Bess. Slapping her plate to the floor, peas everywhere, gravy on me. Arm swinging, I missed my daughter at the very last second and pounded my fist on the table instead. So hard my own plate skidded off and joined hers. Bess thought that was funny, traded her howls for a belly laugh. Nowata genes, those.

But when she went to sleep, I sat at the table with my head in my hands and wept.

I don't believe I ever saw my mother shed a tear. So what does this say about me?

~

I have lost perspective, Paul. A little food on the floor cuts me off at the knees. We used to laugh about things like that, do you remember?

It's this day. Gets worse every year, didn't think it could, tried to head it off at the pass this time. Sent Bess to rodeo, signed up for on-call, praying not to remember so the dream wouldn't return, and now— all that's gone down—I'm still trapped out there far from you, burning up, feet on hot sand, deep red, smothering sand, rising like swells on an ocean. Spines in my feet, in my heart. You promised forever, then left.

Where did you go, and why can't I feel you any-more?

"When you get to the end of your rope," Grandmother Nowata used to say, "tie a knot in it and hang on."

But what do you do when your rope's been cut? Sliced clean through, no anchor, no chance to steer for home, much less tie a knot? What then? You are the woman who gave John Nowata to the world. Why the hell should I listen to you?

The snow settles gently on my skin and sticks. No longer hot enough inside to melt it off, but I'm warmer now, I think. Elbow and palm fuse with the rock, holding me firm as long as my mind wills it and doesn't sleep. The cold circles soft and soothing; just two minutes more, and I'll go on, it's not even three yet. I still have your things where you left them, O'Malley, isn't that silly? Lost some friends over that along the way. Pony and Jed high among them. They took offense at your shoes waiting patient by the door all this time, your sweater hung limp over your chair, journals silent on the desk. Ashes in a tall urn on a shelf beside a small piece of rubbed mulga Ruby gave me for luck.

And Grandmother Haney's feather.

I know you won't come back, won't ever walk through that door, but if you did, I wouldn't be surprised. You wouldn't even need to buy clothes, I tell myself sometimes, and we could dump the ashes in the compost bin. Grow better basil next year. Pick up right where we left off, with Bess in the big middle. With you to help I could maybe figure her out, we could teach her to grow strong and not mean. With you she would laugh more, rest easy, I just know it.

We all did. It is so real I can taste you sometimes, the salt on your skin when we slept, the droplets of sweat on your neck when we danced, the slow-wending smell of the only time in my whole life I was ever safe.

I let myself feel you now and sink into your arms, warm again, it'd be warm for always if you just came home.

Then it flickers within and burns outward, the white-hot flame, steady and true. The peak is over there somewhere, but I can't see it. With wide-open eyes I can barely see my own arm. I see only this small white flame, consuming me, inside out. 10-22 the 10-24. The only way to cancel constant monitor. Any other wording brings the whole army to your side in travel time, less the corners they cut on the way.

So 10-22 my 10-24. There's no more need for backup here. It's all moot now.

~

I am tired, Paul O'Malley. Tired of the struggle. Tired of trying to survive it all—this land of the free, home of the brave that sucks the hearts of my people dry and feeds their souls to demons. Tired of losing you and having to keep on breathing. Fighting to get Josie out of the Tanami alive, one hair shy of sane, only seldom to see her again. Sitting at Ruby's fire all those months, trying to heal and face becoming a mom without you, and finally being one here, at home but alone, haunted by nightmares of strangers, yet still piecing myself back together again, despite the hole blown through my middle. And raising a child who deserves way better than me.

But sometimes you can't tell it by the obnoxious way she acts. So there, I've said it.

Thought it out loud. Nobody wants the truth anymore, Paulson, not even me. I hide from what I don't want to be true, sidestep the hard facts, trying to smooth off their corners maybe. Trying to fix it all, like Laney, fix it *so it just doesn't hurt anymore*.

Don't argue with me. You're not in my shoes, never were. I'm tired of beating my head against this wall we call living, O'Malley. Sick and tired. You left, remember? Means you don't get a vote. *I* get the vote here, bub, nobody else.

So tally up, Tally-ho. Lay the numbers once without weighting one side or the other with a truckload of hope or hard work.

Laney's not going to make it, no matter what I do.

Dix'll play his own hand when our father gets out of prison and either keep it together or wind up soshed and guttered.

Jo's home in New Orleans with her mom, growing up, don't see much of her anymore but she's safe, that's what counts.

You're gone.

And Bess?

Bess.

Miss Snit. She's the grandest thing I ever laid eyes on, Paul, but I'm failing, failing her every damn day, doing all I can think of but it's still not enough, never is, she hates me sometimes, I think, only Audra can get her to cooperate, so I know the end for us can't be good, and now I'm stuck on a mountain and it's not cold anymore but I cannot move. Nothing works. Can't even blink. Feel empty inside, no strength. I should be fighting, I know, fighting to get off, but too numb. Someone is sobbing, horrible cries close by, can't be me, I don't cry anymore—not over you. Too damn fed up to cry. I understand now my mother's last breaths. He beat her to death with his fists and his boots and left her on that kitchen floor, spilling blood, she had no more to give. I was ten, too little to stop him. Scared and angry. At least partly at her.

But now I understand.

Ruby's eyes are kind on me. No judgment, she lets me choose my path.

~

I have heard my people talk of standing outside the body to watch as death begins its final stalking. I thought they had big imaginations.

But now I stand still and aloof beside Ruby and look down at myself, bleeding, worn out, too cold to shiver, a paper-thin shell huddled on the side of a mountain so far from anyone that looks like home. That is how Rosemarie looked when we got to her. And Hal, Darren, everybody we ever tried to save but didn't, Laney when I left the ledge. Mama when the blood stopped.

I know what I'm seeing, but feel no fear. The brief time of raging has gone silent within, burned itself out. I am calm.

Maybe it's enough, this one span of effort. Maybe that I tried is enough.

And then all of a sudden, I smile. Unafraid. Hey, O'Malley, Jed was right: I'm no longer afraid of heights. I can fly right off from here this instant, somebody flipped the switch, not one backward glance, like the raven, loop the loop, look at me! Flexing my forearm, I prepare to release, aiming for Paul's arms, warmed by his gentle eyes. He'll catch me.

Always has.

~

But from his arms, I feel the prick on my finger, it's that bird again, that damn red bird. Drawing blood.

Mine.

And then it flies strong to the tree in our yard, and I understand.

I cannot fly.

I must climb.

3:32 P.M.

The contours of the cold fold above, and beyond, and a body outside my own slogs through snow waist-high, plowing down the side of a mountain whose name I've forgot. The only name I remember now is a baby called Bess, with red curls and green eyes, who's calling for me, not angry anymore but sad, so sad and afraid, so I lean toward her cries and stay with my skin.

I am getting help for Laney.

The redbird woke me up near the peak, I was almost asleep, but I climbed then. Hard. Came off the top on short rope, broke loose a load of snow on that chute just above, managed to stay clear, just barely. Breaking trail ever since. Dropping into the trees now. I'll follow along the base and cut to the trail soon. A man stabbed her, up there on the ledge, then cut my rope. Wanted us dead, he did. But we are stubborn, so far.

My vision blurs and clears, up ahead I see someone approaching. Fast. Is that him? Tall enough to fit those feet, it *is* him, has to be, who else would—

Move fast, Tally, go another way, can't get help if I'm stabbed, *run, Pirli, now!* The snow opens up, deep at my feet, a yawing to frozen mud far beneath, can't stop, can't jump it—I sink, fast, roll onto my back. Leg bent beneath, funny angle, can't move. Try to reach for Paul's knife, fingers too numb, won't work.

All I can do now is wait.

11-99, somebody, please, 11-99. Ranger needs assistance.

"I *knew it*. JT said you were fine, not to worry, to give y'all more time, but I just *knew* something was wrong! What the hell happened to you and why the cat hair didn't you call in?" Pony Sutton, worked up. Normal.

Over me. And that's normal too, these days. I might've been better off with the man.

Unclipping her snowshoes and leaping easily down into the hole by my knees, Pony begins to assess my injuries. "Jeez, you're a block of frickin' ice—where's your damn clothes, Knothead?"

I can't speak, shaking too bad.

"Never mind," she says, plowing into her pack and dragging out an extra jacket. "Put this on."

I'm registering what she's saying and trying to get my arms to comply, but they're like a couple slabs of stone. "No, it's not your color and yes, it'll hang down to your knees. That happens to short people. What the hell tangled with you? And where's Greer?"

I nod toward the mountain, croak something nobody else in the world could understand. Pony throws me a set of handwarmers and is on the radio before I get two words out.

"Go ahead, 346. Base over," Darla Cleary responds from dispatch.

"Need an open line, D. Timmons, Dawson, the chief, whoever you got. Don't intend to say this but once."

"We're here, Sutton, all ears. Go," Jed says, the

noise from the adjoining room almost drowning him out. "Quiet!" someone shouts.

"Listen up, people. Charlie One's in trouble. I got Nowata at the foot of the descent, Greer's down, still on top. Need a full, happy crew ready to rock and roll at my location stat. Double litters, gear for high-angle long-line with issues. Y'all copy?"

"Affirmative, 346. ETA, five and travel time." You could hear a pin drop behind Jed's voice now. I believe they copied.

I reach for the mike, how I'll talk I don't know but they can't come in here blind. "V perp, 352 severe injuries, knife, one or two assail—"

When I stumble over the word, Pony takes over, white as a sheet, and tells the crew to come in careful, but come the hell on in. Violent perp or perps. Ranger down, needs assistance. She says it in words, not code. We're way outside normal here now.

The second she's finished, I reach for the mike again, but Pony clips it to her chest harness, shakes her head, ripping my boots off one at a time and stuffing my feet up inside her shirt, flat against her stomach. Naked skin to my unfeeling soles, she says, "There's *more?*"

I nod. "Call Bess. In Vegas. With Dix. Get them to call Dix's hotel, number's on my desk."

"Jesus, mother of Christ, can you forget that child for two seconds for once? You act like she's fused to your fuckin' hip!"

I shake my head, pain shoots through, can't fight

with her now, let it go. She's right anyway. Bess is fine, probably laughing her head off at the clowns just this second. They are her favorite part. Or maybe she's keeping Audra busy at the stalls, begging for a pony.

But then why do I still hear her crying for me? Calling "MomMommy" twice like she does it, never just once, so close she could almost be here but I know she's not. "Please, Pony."

"Okay, fine. Base, this is 346, come in please."

Polite, now that the crisis is underway, Pony rangers me. Long arms at work, stomach still reheating my feet, she throws up a wind tarp to one side, fires a small stove, pours warm spicy beef broth from a light thermos down my throat—"it's the longhorn version of Greer's jerky, hell of a lot easier to digest," she told me once, years ago—and starts rubbing some feeling back into my legs and arms. Rough and silent except for one question, "You get a look at him?"

When I shake my head no, she frowns and pokes an extra pair of her socks up under one arm, close enough to my feet I should be able to feel them but don't. The heat of the stove breaks through, a sliver of warmth cracking the dull sheath about me, and I lean back to rest inside the jacket. Pony and I haven't spoken two words to each other off the job in nine months. Haven't said many more on it either. Got nothing to say to each other now, except the few things you ask anytime you're saving somebody's life.

"This workin'?" she finally asks. "Or do we need to

cuddle up?" The best treatment for full-blown hypothermia in the field is to get naked and lie close together in a sleeping bag.

"No. Comin' round."

Pony eyes me, decides I'm telling the truth, and goes back to rubbing my feet. A few minutes later she bundles them into the warmed socks and a pair of her camp boots—huge on me, but cozy inside, lined with thick fur. Cinched down tight with a couple slings around the ankles, they feel good. I can feel my mind slipping back into synch, circling the edges of what's going on again. Wiggle your toes, Tally, flex your feet, get the blood moving. Hold up your end of this bargain.

Pony's silent, intent solely on warming me. She takes one hand at a time and rubs it into feeling, then tucks it inside wool mittens. Drags out a spare set of sweats and windpants—not a one of us ever sets a foot out our doors unprepared. Pony even brought a rope, 9mm, not what we normally climb on, but it is a good weight for rescue. She had to've been worried about us to bring that.

Sure can't tell it otherwise.

"I don't know what you were thinkin', Knothead, but you ran this one right off into the ditch. About two hairs shy of iced and diced, ask me. Where the *hell* did you leave your clothes?"

I angle my head toward the mountain. Pony curses softly and says, "On Greer? That is just exactly the sort of nutty-assed thing you'd do, here I keep thinkin' you'll grow a brain one of these days, but no, son of a—"

She's right again. Leaving my clothes didn't help. It'll be at least two hours before the team can get here. Twice that to the ledge, even from this side and moving fast. Laney will never make it. Darla calls and says there's no answer at Dix's room, and no messages from him or Audra for me have come in, but she'll keep trying, no urgency in her voice or Pony's, no reason for there to be. Bess is fine, everybody knows it but me. I'm being ridiculous thinking I hear her, of course she's calling me, like always. Mad as a hornet at something I've done. Or not done. Or not done fast enough. I close my eyes, and the white flame builds again.

Pony slaps my leg and says, "Where the hell do you think you're goin'?" When I shrug and don't answer, she curses softly, then lifts the tarp and nods toward the mountain, staring at me the whole time with hard eyes. Says, "How bad off're you?"

"Not bad."

"That head wound superficial?"

"Yep."

"Pain, scale of five?"

"Four-two."

"Can you climb?"

I look at Pony. Best tracker I ever saw, but hates climbing. Worse than me. Like a hound hates bees. If we're going after Laney ourselves, though, we both have to climb—and one of us has to lead.

That would be me.

Dousing the stove, I slip one end of the tarp free, motioning her to unhook the other one, and reach for my boots. Tuck them inside my borrowed duds. Need them to be warm when we get back to that wall.

"Let's do it."

4:50 P.M.

Everything you think you know about someone else becomes irrelevant when you need to know it. Not before, not after, precisely when. We fly blind, us humans, every last one, into the teeth of the daily storm, knowing not one whit of what's coming. The open question is not how we keep doing it—leaping off the porch and spreading our wings—but *why*.

Pony plows ahead on skis, breaking trail. We're going up the side this time, can't risk the front. Not enough gear, for one thing, or enough strength. Or time.

On that last, though, we're hauling A. Wouldn't have thought I could've moved this fast on borrowed snowshoes a few hours ago. Then Pony shows up and I'm sprinting, feet warm in camp boots lashed down like a pair of moccasins. That's a SAR team's secret, even for an ailing one like ours, our ace in the hole. Let two of us get strung together, and we can cut our-selves a swath. Big-time. Right down the skinny middle of all the impossibles you care to throw our direction. So there.

The storm folds about like a soft blanket, no wind now, just deep, heavy snow. Nothing hurts on me. The dry taste of old steel in my mouth means the adrenaline's kicked in, backslapped the pain off my deck. I'll pay for it later, I know, but for now I feel fine. The tip of my nose is cold, too, which is a good sign.

But I'm finally warm enough to get in the clear over Bess. The more I think about it, the more sure I am Bess is fine. Audra would kill anybody who tried to lay a finger on that child and, unlike me, she has built-in radar for Bess's tendencies to hie off at the drop of a hat. Or anything else.

~

"It's like those two are hooked at the hip," Laney said one day last July.

We were floating the upper end of the Snake, and had pulled off for a picnic lunch. Bess and Audra were poking about in the long grass with Ducket, Laney's Newfoundland. Dogs aren't normally allowed in the park, but Duck's rated for air-scenting and water rescue, so he travels everywhere with his mom, wearing his little orange vest so visitors won't complain that we're breaking the rules. Lanes and I were unpacking the meal and, as usual, even through her grief, she was noticing things about my life I'd just as soon not've. Hooked at the hip, though, is a good way to put Bess and Aud's connection.

Pony's wrong about Bess being fused to mine, but wherever my daughter is, this much I know: Audra's got a grip on her collar. Has had since the day she walked in the front door and I hired her. Bess was six weeks old; I had to go back to work. Aud was our savior, still is. So I can rest easy about that. It must've been the hypothermia ramping up the part of my brain that's kin to my superstitious brother a while ago. Got trouble enough for two lifetimes on your hand, head goes trolling for more. Gets a damn *feeling*. Punctuates it with sound. Squalling baby you hear plenty often in the real world.

~

"Any idea who we're up against?" Pony calls back over her shoulder, saying "idea" like *hidey* minus the *H* and picking the conversation up as though there was no break.

"None."

"Pissed off anybody lately?"

"No more'n usual."

"What about that eco dude?"

"Eco-Jim?" For about three months this summer, Windy Point got a letter a week from a guy who called himself "The Eco Tramp." Long rants about climbers and skiers and tourists defiling the land, rangers on the take who deserve to be fried. He'd sounded fierce and specific, which gave us all the willies, but turned out to be a wizened senior citizen with serious health problems and a bad attitude based on good reasons. Excellent ones, actually. "He's harmless."

"Psycho."

"That too, same as you and me and everybody else I ever met." My voice comes out rough and ragged, yielding to my need to hear it. "But no, I don't think it was him. Not his MO, for starters. He axed our signs and took out a road grader—nothing sentient. Plus, he's too old, too out of shape, has emphysema."

"He does?"

"Yep."

"How d'you know that?"

"Went to visit him in the jail a couple times."

Pony shakes her head. I get on her nerves. Always did, but it's worse now.

"He doesn't mean any real harm, you know. Has some good points. I even agree with some of them."

She grunts, "You would. He out yet?"

"Week ago Friday."

We're closing in on the bottom end of a long narrow couloir, a small chute shaped like a skillet, except stood on its nose, that leads to the short vertical pitch below the summit. "You kicked this off?" Pony asks, pausing briefly to peer at our end of the mini avalanche I made on my way down. Since it's been so warm lately, we knew it would go without much urging, which is why Lanes and I opted for the face even though coming onto that ledge from the top, this approach, would've been lots easier, safer. Less work, too—except for that one pitch—but not if the new snow became our tombs before we cleared the couloir. I have only vague memories of knocking it loose from above and trying to stay clear as it slid a while ago, then plunging my way down one side.

"Yep."

"Good thinking. Reckon you still have a brain in tow after all. From the looks of that left eye, I was thinking it might've leaked out." Now that's Sutton for you. Calls what she sees. I've missed her. Not that I want to go back down that trail again, no way. We've split out there for good. But at least we can still do the work.

Time to trade skis and snowshoes for boots. We'll rope up too, use a moving belay. Too steep from here on not to. "You'll have to use my crampons—those camp boots're warm, but no tread. I've got my Scarpas in here."

"Thanks," I say, gruffer than I intend. Pony goes still, but doesn't say anything, doesn't look up, just tosses over her crampons and kneels to help me strap them on. "You saved my life down there."

She shrugs, reaching for the plastic boots she'll change into. They're great for kicking steps into the snow, which she'll have to do for us now. "I mean it, Pony. Thank you."

"Thought you were the one with the death wish lately. All set to check out on us, drop of any hat."

I stiffen, try to hold onto the original point—gratitude, expressing it, don't get sidetracked, that all's none of her business—but Pony doesn't stop. Feet settled, she stands, throwing a bowline with one hand on her end of the rope, and says, "Besides. You die, who the hell's left to piss me off?"

I can't think of one thing to say. My mind feels muddled in the face of her clarity. Never had this problem before. Pony saves me the trouble.

"Save your gratitude, Nowata. Not worth one hill of refried beans to you or me. Let's just work the gig like we're paid to and call it square."

~

Friendships never end square. There's no way to right a listing boat when the sidewall's been torpedoed.

There always was a rough edge between Pony and me, ever since the day I stormed into her house and poured a pot of water on her head to get her out of the bed. Years ago. She was so young then, too young to know that the married man who'd just dumped her had done her the favor of a lifetime, so she'd gone into a dark place inside herself—and that damn bedroom—for weeks. Did the job just fine, but spent every other waking minute on that futon. So I intervened. Jed was appalled. Paul too, years later, when Pony narrated the incident. It has grown some in her mind over time.

After that, though, until I returned from Australia anyway, we were thick, she and I. Like a pair of mismatched twins. A tall one and a runt. With issues, yes, but true, solid. That all changed three years ago, and got much worse when Travis Schaeffer showed up and moved in with her last winter. Bottom line, long before I ever let loose over her telling Lanes to "grow up and move the hell on, Greer—Rosie's the one that's dead, not you," Pony Sutton and I were history. All that's left now is for one, or both, of us to leave these mountains.

So far, though, we're stubborn. Run each day like we're strangers, proving to ourselves just how much we never needed the other, bound and determined not to tuck tail and leave. Liable to both still be here when these mountains have washed to the sea, waiting each other out.

Maybe then we can finally call it square.

5:50 P.M.

Hugging the left edge of the couloir, we continue, linked to each other by one rope and one ice axe between us. Pony's kicking steps into the slope, and since she's got more strength and no woolly right arm to interfere with self-arrest, she's got the ice axe, too. On the steepest sections she works a boot-axe belay for me; on these gentler runs, we both move simultaneously. More risky: if I lose my footing, she'll have to get belly down and dig in with the working end of that axe or we'll both be toast. That's what happened to Hal, except he wasn't tied in. And he never went for self-arrest.

None of us could believe that. Even Jed shouted, "Use your damn axe, Robson!" But by then Hal was too far gone and in a full spin. He hit the rocks so hard some of his teeth came out, and the man who'd paid his way through engineering school by modeling and then quit engineering to become one of the best climbers any of us ever met was finished and, when we caught up, "not near so pretty anymore," as Pony put it, darkly, on the way down.

We usually have a whole passel of snitty comments for body retrievals—can't do this job without them—but that was the only one made that day. Maybe we were too tired. The arrogance it takes to try to cheat death and lose, then carry the reminder all the way home, requires a heap of energy, and we had none to spare.

Or maybe Hal broke something important inside us. Showing off like he'd done so many times before, only this time he missed the catch and died for his trouble.

I don't know anymore.

Never did. Just now getting around to admitting it, though. More fool me.

~

And now we're back to the base of the summit pitch, which means we have to climb. Fifty feet laid out several degrees past vertical near the top. Bottom twenty slick as glass and near as smooth. Need my own gear. Good boots, crampons. Not stuff borrowed and rigged to fit.

My bones start to ache, pulling down off the high, and I set my teeth on the bit like a horse hitting the home stretch. *We will not fail you, Laney Greer.*

Pony doesn't ask, "Can you do this?" There's no need. I wouldn't tell her if I knew, which I don't. We'll both find out soon enough.

As I rig up, borrowed headlamp strapped to my helmet and focused on the first few feet of the rock, trying to lay out the sequence in my mind and have my left arm take the hard moves, not that there appear to be any others, she says, almost nonchalantly, "What about Laney's poacher?"

"Still no face." Lanes hasn't just been nest-egging the reward; she's actually had the lead investigator spot on the poaching we've had in the park the last few months. One yearling elk early in the spring, a wolf this summer, another this fall, and last week a small moose. Same person, and just one, we're pretty sure, but that's as far as we've got. Until today. We were stepping into our skis at the trailhead when Laney made her big announcement. "Told me this morning she had herself a plan to nab him, though. Sounded pretty sure."

"*She* had the plan? What about you? I thought you were the tracker on the deal."

Pony's ticked that Laney hasn't called on her to help. It's been me every time. Well Sutton, I feel like saying, Lanes and I don't snatch each other's throats out by the gills every two words. Makes for a slightly better working situation. Besides. You were way too busy with Travis when it started to bother coming down to help, remember? What's a poaching case or two in the face of one's *true love?* Pony reads the anger in me, and I try to pull back but don't get it done in time. "Think 'cause you're Injun you're special, don't you? Got some line on the land us crackers don't have?"

That's enough. "On belay?" I ask, reaching for the nearest chink with one ice tool, steel on my tongue.

"Belay on."

"Climbing."

"Go."

I don't even get a foot up before Pony adds, "My point was maybe the poacher's in it. This thing with Lanes."

I stop to consider that, then shake my head. "Doubt it."

"Heard the reward's topped five g's now." Yes, thanks to Laney Greer, I think, but don't say. Nobody else knows that. "Maybe y'all got him on the run, figures he needs to back you off."

"May be. But I don't think so."

"Why not? Just being your usual old hardheaded self?"

"The poacher's not good for it, Pony. He's got a bum leg, for one thing. It's all he can do to manage snowshoes on the level."

Pony whistles in disbelief, and then stares hard at me. "Are you tellin' me you're half Injun and can't track a man with a bum leg on the flat in a county that's 98% hills?"

"Read it however you see it, Sutton. That's your specialty."

She laughs, but not like it's funny. "I thought you said you were climbing, Knothead."

Shaking my head, I start up, not even bothering to repeat the verbal cue ("climbing") that I've never—not once in sixteen years—failed to use before setting foot on a route. Call me Indian. Say I can't track. I'll show you—

Next thing I know, I'm twenty feet up the wall, and Pony calls. "Texas got you that far, now didn't it?" And then she laughs. Thinks she's so funny. I really need to just move from here. Pull Lanes off this wall, help her find that damn crippled poacher and get her money back in her pocket, where it belongs, and then move. To Tucson. Or Timbuktu. Anywhere in God's green hell but Pony Sutton's home state.

Or the Tanami.

7:01 P.M.

We're on top when the radio sputters with word that Jed's team has made it to the trailhead.

Vince Miller, sheriff and archenemy of Rangers Greer and Nowata, is helping organize a sweep at the base for the body that fell. Jed must've called him in after Pony passed along word that someone took a header a while ago. The crew can't possibly know what to think. Every transmission Pony's made in the last two hours is outside normal ops. Dead and downed at the base, ranger stabbed and down up top, me in mostly borrowed clothes and needing them to bring my spare pack along.

"Why'd they have to bring Vince in on this?" I mutter.

"It's called concurrent jurisdiction," Pony says. "Better thank the stars he's not ruling this roost we're perched on. Yet."

I stand with my back to the abyss, ready for the first rappel of two long ones that'll take us to Lanes. "Descending."

"Go."

Vince radios Jed on the local channel. "Who's on top?"

"Got 346, 327, and 352, fucker," Pony says loudly, to me. "Just do your damn job and leave us the fuck be, would ya?"

"I dare you to say that on air," I reply.

Jed echoes our call signs for Vince and saves Pony the trouble.

~

Vince Miller. He's not mean, just a little too patriarchal and worried about staying friendly with the jet set. That's where Lanes and I crossed up with him first. We can deal with the patriarchy: every woman born since men became God has had issues with that, which gives women an incentive to deal, I believe. But the rich and famous, well, that's another whole different ball game. We arrested one of the jetters one night five years ago for running down a moose in his Jeep on the way home from a party on Jackson Lake, and Vince let him go three hours later—at two A.M.—without prepping any charges or even setting bail.

"I know the boy's mother," he said, and Laney snapped, "I'll bet you do."

Vince took offense. At us knowing about his string of affairs, I guess, and going to the trouble of listing a couple names in that conversation to make our points. And mentioning that a sheriff who goes in for facial peels and teeth bleaching has what Laney called "issues we don't even aim to solve—all we're interested in is our collar." Things haven't been right since. And when the poaching started—whew.

Vince has been on us like a duck on a june bug all year.

Laney's unfazed. She's been threatened by environmentalists, dude ranchers, snowmobilers, politicians, and other common lunatics since taking the case. I'm in the crosshairs by default. She's there by job description: Lead Investigator. Calls me out when they find another kill site, and together we've rattled a few people's barn gates trying to break this one open. Vince is fed up with us, thinks we cross the line too far and too often, keeps saying, "This isn't the frontier, ladies. The frontier's closed. Read your history." It never goes down very well, but he keeps saying it anyway.

"This *isn't* the frontier, my foot! How can you trust somebody who can't bring himself to say 'ain't' when

it's called for?" Laney stormed just last week as she
sailed out of his office, empty-handed one more time.
It would help if Vince would work with—instead of
actively against—us. "Am I right or am I right?"

"Damn straight," I agreed, and resisted restating
the obvious. Man's had two nose jobs in the last three
years—can't expect too much from him on a few
dead animals.

Pony's down the line after me and clipping into the
anchor. One more pitch.

Laney Greer, hang the hell on.

7:45 P.M.

I slip down the rope in the night, sitting the rappel
easy, feet out toward the wall for balance. Sliding
toward the bald run that nearly killed me today, rela-
tively secure, in control of the line and the speed, the
angle, and myself. And a good deal more of the situation than earlier.

No eleven codes now, no need. I've got backup.

And I pity the idiot who'd take a swing at Pony
Sutton with a knife, even up here. Wind up beheaded
and dismembered. For a start. Her people're not that
keen on subtle. And they never give warnings. This is
something she's rather proud of, scares me sometimes.

But then this spring, when it came time to defend
herself from Travis Schaeffer, she wouldn't raise a fin-

ger for herself. Gave me holy hell for trying to intervene. So I don't understand her take on violence. I've
seen her beat grown men into the ground down at
the Rancher for making a drunken pass at me, but
when Travis came at her with that knife, she didn't do
one blessed thing. Not one.

Except refuse to press charges when it was over
and get mad at me when I did. Go figure.

Drop it, Tally. That all's done for. There's no fixing
it, now or ever. Stay with the night, get Lanes home
and well.

The storm spent itself two hours ago, left us subzero
temps and three feet of new snow, but no wind. The sky
above Jackson glows to the south, and the change alone
scrubs the corners off my ungenerous side. Who's to
say, if I was rich, I might not pine after a house snugged
up to the prettiest peaks in the northern hemisphere,
too? As it is, I do the poor man's version: National Park
Service. NPS, where they value my life at 35 cents more
per hour under hazardous conditions. Rescues, wildland fires, all helo jaunts. Getting shot at, too, I'd imagine, though no one's specifically mentioned it yet.

"Well, don't that just make us feel special?" Pony
said eight years ago, when Jed informed us of the
raise—actually a little more than thirty-five cents, but
somebody called it that in the meeting and it stuck for
good—and just the thought makes me chuckle.
Which kills my head, so I quit.

"You'd do it for free," he countered. "And you too,
TJ, so shut up."

TJ. First thing Pony did when she met Jed and me was administer nicknames. TJ for me. JT for him. Said, "Where I'm from, you're not real till you have at least one good nickname, and I ain't about to work next to nobody with guns on their hips and the badges to use 'em without they're real. So get used to it." We did. Me especially, I guess, because mine ties me to my mom. Taliesin Joy. Jed doesn't have that kind of incentive. The Timmons line is normal. No fathers in prison for putting mothers in the grave.

The last nine months, though, Pony hasn't called me anything but Knothead or Nowata. And when Jed gets on her nerves now, she lets him know it too, with "Jethro." Laney is still Lanes or LG. Despite everything, Sutton hasn't turned on her. I think it's the difference in height.

Or maybe it's just Laney Greer. Girl doesn't make enemies. Never has. Never will.

Almost there now. If I have anything to say about it, she will live to carry that straight on.

Passing the point I fell from earlier, I get ready to brake. This is it, Knucklehead. Cavalry's arrived. You're on your way home.

And then I come to the ledge, and the thin beam of my borrowed headlamp plays across it, hopeful, and the line begins to slip from my suddenly nerveless fingers as I crumple to my knees on the empty, bloodstained rock.

Pony starts yelling from ten feet above. "Get the fuck up, Nowata—I thought you said you were okay!"

And then she freezes when she realizes I'm alone, and what that means.

Laney's gone. Somehow after I left her, she got loose and fell.

Seconds later, Pony drops down the line in total silence, feet landing solid, one hand pressed on the rock. "This the ledge? *The* ledge?"

I nod.

"You sure?"

"Of course I'm sure!"

"Look at me," Pony says, shining her headlamp in my eyes.

"Tie in before you fall off," I snap. "And quit poking that damn light in my face."

Pony kneels, hands shaking, and hooks into the anchor I set so long ago, hours ago, back when the weather was for shit and so was the gig, but Lanes and I were *just fine*.

"I said *look at me*, TJ. *Now."*

So I do, helmet resting against the wall, and Pony moves the light. It doubles and wavers. Something's bad wrong with my head. Don't need her jabbing a flashlight down my eyeballs to tell me that.

"You said you were okay, Knothead, except for the pain, but you're not—are you?"

"Been better," I admit.

"Jesus," she says, white around the mouth, yanking her helmet off and running one hand through her hair.

"Wouldn't call on him, if I was you. We ain't what you'd call buds—"

"Son of a— I have to tell Jethro. He'll fuckin' kill me for lettin' you come back up here—"

"No."

"Have to." Fingers poised on transmit.

"Pony, I said no. Please."

She stops. Takes her hand away from the radio.

"I can get us down. So leave me out of it. Just tell him—you have to tell him—"

"321, this is 46 on top, go to secure channel stat."

It's not secure. You can't secure all these channels, but Pony's pulling off the main track. *She has to tell Jed they need to look for Laney's body at the base. What code is there for that?*

~

I huddle against the anchor as Pony talks, her voice far off and dull, and try to think back to what went wrong, how she could've gotten loose. Did she wake up and break free? Surely not. I had her tied in with three separate 'biners. No way she could've unclipped all three.

No way.

But the only thing that is Laney on this ledge right now is her blood. Pony focuses her light on it, as if to collect evidence, and then suddenly slumps away and back. Sits down hard and leans against the wall. Like Lanes and me this afternoon. An eternity passes before she says, "You tied her in?"

I nod.

"You're sure?"

I nod again.

"Words, TJ. I need it in words."

"I tied her in. Three points. Not possible she could come loose on her own." At that slurred admission, I understand what I've done. Left Lanes up here with a madman. Somehow he was still on this mountain when I left it, maybe up and off route, back over on the other side. Waiting. And she was down, helpless, no way to defend—

Tears sting my eyes, I start heaving, and lose the Texas version of beef jerky over the side.

9:00 P.M.

I can no longer see my watch dial, but Pony says it's 2100. The whole crew works in military time on missions, except for me, that is, in my head. Australia cracked my deadly precision. The 10 codes are second nature, the elevens an inner skin, but everything else I have to translate now.

"Precision's required for both killing and saving lives," Jed told me years ago. I'm not even sure I've wanted to rescue anybody anymore, though I've gone through the motions. There's a numb place within me that's already dead—no hope to walk toward when it is dark all around. So how could I save someone else?

And what might've happened if we'd had people with those skills in the Tanami—on our side? Would Paul still be here, trying to smooth off my rough edges, me stuck in mission mode 24/7? Would we still have pulled this gig tonight? Would I have left Laney?

We are rappelling down the front to meet the crew at the bottom.

They didn't find Laney.

Found a man, near the boulders at the top of the approach, same time as Pony managed to get us set up for single-line rap, and Vince ordered the two of us off the mountain stat.

Pony told him we were on our way, but Vince repeated the order, so she snapped into the radio, "We'll get there when the fuck we get there, bastard, now back the hell off."

I used to help head her around the pass. Stood between her and the fuzz, Park Service or public, you name it. I kept her mouth from getting her nethers in a sling. But it hasn't been my job in a while now, and I sure the heck wouldn't want to tackle it again tonight.

Pony is *pissed*. She's convinced the guy who stabbed Laney waited somewhere above, just off route, and then came back down, picked her up, and solo-roped her and himself down this hill.

"Have to be Superman to do that without backup," I said, not convinced. He'd have had to *carry* Lanes. In the dark. Impossible.

Pony disagreed. "Clear signs several places. Somebody came down during the storm."

"Not seeing well enough to confirm that," I had to admit. My vision'd been coming and going since the ledge.

"See there, I knew you Injuns weren't all you're cracked up to be on spoor."

I said nothing. No point. I actually agree. Indians can't see sign any better than anybody else, but I'm not about to admit that to a redneck with a bad haircut and worse temper. Still got better sense than to think somebody could take Lanes off this hill by himself on one line. No way. Had to have help. How many were there then? Three? Four? And where were they? Why didn't I *see* them? What good is it to be a tracker if you don't notice clues that damn obvious, Nowata?

"You know, Knothead, I could just beat the shit out of you for comin' back up here with whatever the hell's wrong with your head right now."

"Can we *please just leave it?*" I asked, more faint and desperate than I like to sound, or feel.

"Fine. But I'm tellin' you, this dude brought her down, TJ. Left clear drag marks every anchor point, all during and after the storm. Lower we get, clearer they are. He might've still been in the process when we started up."

Pony's already warned the ground crews, but they've reported no signs at the base. A few minutes ago, when Vince called to check on our location again— not because he cares whether we get there in one piece, but because we haven't yet obeyed his order to be there *stat*—Pony answered by ordering him and everybody else to back the hell fifty feet off the approach. "Tape the perimeter and stay out!" She's worried that they're elephant-herding any sign the guy's left.

Can she be right? Why in God's name would he stab Laney way up here, then carry her all the way down? That's insane.

The whole thing's insane, Nowata.

Got *human* written all over it. People are idiots. Plain and simple. When we get this one in the barn, I'm quitting. I'm tired of that too: playing savior to fools. Let the whole damn species go extinct, for all I care. Paul was right. I need to switch shoes.

Maybe buy me a fine pair of high heels, for a change. Bess might like that. She's a prissy little thing. Always has been. Don't know where the hell she gets that. Maybe Audra. She's usually put together fairly well. Takes some pride in it, I think. Certainly not me. I don't give a rip, never have, never will. High heels make my head hurt. *Everything* makes my head hurt right now.

"The way I look at it," Pony says, grimmer than

usual, which is saying something, "is, she's still got to be alive. Left enough blood along the way so far, heart's got to still be beating. If we can just get to the ground, TJ, we can bring this sucker down."

"So let's quit jawing and do it." I don't have enough energy anymore to talk and move at the same time. Got to pick one and stick with it. Leave the rest for a day that starts on a different foot.

Pony takes the lead going down. Rap to a good stopping point, set the next anchor, yank the line for me to follow. It's the closest thing we have to a safety net tonight.

DECEMBER 15

It's long after midnight when I put my unsteady feet on the ground to find everybody's still here, which is odd. I figured some of them would've gone in by now.

Jed's in my face like a flash. "What the hell do you mean, pulling a stunt like this? You're in no condition to be on a rock!" he yells, angrier than I ever remember seeing him, ripping one glove off and reaching out to hold my face steady while he eyes it. Then he slams the glove on his leg and points four fingers at Pony, before swinging back my way. "Answer me!"

I shrug and shake my head. There's no good

answer. Under other circumstances I'd be yelling at myself, but I'm not about to admit that to him.

"Be still! You've concussed. At the least. Maybe worse. Keep your head stationary." Jed is furious, laying out an OSS II kit that'll stabilize my head, neck, and spine.

"They came off the rock here," Pony says, pointing at the wall to my right. "So there should be some tracks under this new snow. Give us a direction of travel at least."

"Help me get her into the SKED," Jed orders Nels and Susan, this year's seasonals. Bet they wish they'd signed on at Death Valley about now.

"I don't need to be dragged, I'll walk if y'all just give me my pack," I say, aiming for cheery. "Dry boots, you know." The weak grin I aim at Jed gets ignored.

"You'll ride. Now. Crawl in or I'll put you in."

"I need to ask her a couple questions first," Vince says. I hadn't noticed him before. So he's still here too? And two of his deputies, Luke and Sam. Everybody looks tired and cold. And fuzzy.

"You can ask your questions after the ER's done with her," Jed snaps, no concern for interagency tact, which is really unusual for him. Most of the time he keeps the peace, mainly because he just doesn't see the sense in scrapping. "Never should've been outside this long. Look at that eye—swollen shut—and that head wound. Sutton, what the *hell* were you thinking to let her do this?"

Pony wheels away from the bottom of the climb to

face Jed. "Give it a rest, JT. We did what needed doing. And now we've gotta pick up this trail. You can yell at TJ and me tomorrow, after we've found Lanes."

"I don't see anything here, Pony," Wes says, peering at the rock with his headlamp on high. Even Wes is here? He's usually back at headquarters.

"It's subtle," she replies. "Just a few scuff marks to the left there."

"I don't see it either," Vince asserts, moving to glance over Wes's shoulder.

Pony steps between, pushing them aside, leaning in, trying to stay clear of whatever tracks the guy made coming off, which is hopeless right now because the ground is torn to bits. Pointing to the wall, she says, "If it was a snake, it would'a bit you, boys."

"She could've made that," Vince counters, nodding toward me. "Or you, for that matter."

"You're right. I could've." Pony's holding her head at that angle she does when she's about to come unglued on somebody. I'd better say something. Quick.

"We were careful to stay off their tracks, Vince, in case we needed them later. That's why we came down over here." I touch the rock near my head with one hand. Talking is making me seasick.

"So you say."

"Just look, doofus, and you'll see for yourself," Pony interjects, leaping well outside the bounds of professional courtesy, but I guess that's all moot after she got around to calling him a bastard on an open channel a while ago. That one'll go into her file, I'll bet anything I own. They probably won't leave out the multiple uses of the F-word either. "Her marks, here. Mine, here. The slasher on Lanes, there. It's not rocket science. Three different shoes, three different patterns, means three different people, one made much earlier."

"While the two of you were out here," Vince says, deliberately. I recognize the ploy. Cops play all ends of a conversation sometimes, trying to trip up their suspects. But why does he suspect Pony and me?

"Look, buster," Pony retorts, "just 'cause you got Travis Schaeffer laid out on a slab over yonder don't mean—"

"Travis? He's—?" How the hell did I miss that? When did they tell Pony? How come she knows and I don't? Did they ID him on the air while I was rappelling? When did we get into the business of ID'ing corpses on the air?

"The one that fell, TJ. Trav," Jed says, fastening the strap over my head.

"Yeah, it was him. Good old Travis. Somebody gut-cut him, too, just before he took the header," Pony adds, not a trace of feeling in her voice. "And this genius thinks we had something to do with it." I feel sick. Travis is the one who fell? Stabbed?

"You do have history," Vince points out, reasonable. "Rough history."

"And we were both out here today—her climbing with Laney, me nosing around because I got worried about 'em," Pony says, a little too soft and reasonable.

"So you play connect the dots with any loose data, that it? Didn't get enough kindergarten in college to suit you?"

"All right, people," Jed interrupts, fastening the lines from the SKED to his waist belt. He's going to ski me out himself. "Let's move. You can chitchat back in town. Nels, you ferry Schaeffer. Let's stay close, though. We don't know for sure what we're dealing with out here."

"I'm parked, need to get a handle on where they headed," Pony replies as Nels clips on his skis and reaches for the lines to the litter that holds Trav's body. I missed that too, before. A full body bag strapped in a few yards away, immobile, like me, waiting for transport, but not breathing.

"No, you're coming with us," Vince says.

"Am I under arrest?" Pony replies, and it's not a question.

"If you need to be, yes."

Wes interrupts, "Go on in with him and answer his questions, Pony. You know he's got to do this, give him a break. The sooner you do, the sooner you can be clear of it. Sue and I'll cordon off this area and see what we can cover till we can pull some more people in. Yellowstone's on standby already."

"Abe and Standish are in Pakistan," Pony interjects, reminding Wes that Yellowstone's best trackers are climbing on the other side of the world. "And you can't see for shit, unless something's changed in the last two minutes."

"But I'm not wanted for questioning either, and you are," Wes replies, gentle but firm. He's a decent man, a bit out of place in this rabble. "When Vince is finished and you've had a few hours' sleep, you can come back."

"I'm not fuckin' tired—don't you morons *get it? Laney is out here somewhere!*"

Jed intervenes, steel in his voice, "We get it, Sutton, but if we play this wrong we lose more than just one, and we can't afford that again, so *pull off,* and that's an order. You're going in for at least four hours, and that's that. There's two foot of new snow on the trail here anyway, not a damn thing to see, you'll just be—"

"Don't tell *me* what's here to not see," Pony interrupts, looking set to argue the point into the ground.

"I said pull off, and *I mean now.*" Nothing in Jed's tone suggests he's ever seen Pony before. This is his biggest strength: He knows when to draw down the cannons. If Pony doesn't agree, he'll fire her. Permanent. I've seen him do it to two other people; she has too. So I say, "It's just for four hours, Pony. By then you'll have some daylight. That track'll be hell till then anyway."

Wes adds, "Four hours. We'll do our best to move on it till you get back."

Pony hesitates and then abruptly yields. The tiredness is starting to show, just a hair. "Fine, I'll go, but if you muck up my trail, you every last one answer to *me*, are we clear?"

"We're clear. Tally, take care. We'll get this thing

sorted out and Laney home," Wes says, trying to help. "Safe and sound, you'll see." He ought to know you don't promise things like that, but he means well, lifting a hand to wave as we set off and nodding to Pony. "Get some sleep."

She shakes her head. Beat. Needs a break. I don't like Vince, but he's in the right on this one. I'd make the same call in his shoes, maybe not for the same reasons. He tells Luke and Sam to stay on scene and joins us.

"Travis is dead?" I ask, a few minutes later. Pony's on one side of the litter, Vince slightly behind. Both on skis, like Jed and Nels. We've done this a hundred times, but I've never been the body. It feels strange, unmoored, schussing through the snow in the dark, arms and head trussed for no movement, flat on my back. Our crew more strung out than ever before, the rifts between us gaping now. One more person we knew dead behind us, without a why. Travis Schaeffer.

"Yep. Good riddance, ask me," Pony snaps, and I say the first thing that drifts into my mind.

"Maybe you shouldn't say that around Vince."

"Aw, fuck Vince Miller. If brains was gunpowder, he wouldn't have enough to blow his nose."

Somewhere in the fuzzy night I think I hear Vince chuckle, but it's been years since he did that, so many years, I must be mistaken now. "I need to call Bess," I say, and then the white sleep comes for me, and I do not resist.

A luminous clock dial glows in the semi-dark; hospitals have something against patients sleeping. Constant interruptions, cheery people barging in to take vitals, blood, or O$_2$ levels, switching lights to high beam—"Hi, how are you? Don't let us keep you awake." Oh no, no problem at all. I always have folks stick me with needles when I sleep. Very restful, actually. You should try it.

This is not a good place for the sick.

I think of Laney in the cold and cannot breathe. Somehow I have to get out of here, have to find her. But the doctors say more tests, very soon. I should resist.

But I can't. My legs are like water.

~

"Resist nothing," Paul once told me.

"That's easy to say," I replied. "But do you actually do it?"

"Oh yes, love," he smiled. "Always."

Is it still so simple for you, then, O'Malley? That you bend with any wind, lean into each storm?

Could you really have lost me in the Tanami and not come undone? Healed and remembered and walked on, not wanting to die even a little bit? Held it together, been a dad and, one day soon, a lover again?

Oh yes, love. Always.

This is a difference between us.

I see more of them today than when you were here.

~

I must find the bottom of my mind and stand on it. Too much is spinning beyond my control. They've said Vince was in the hall, waiting to speak to me, but the shift supervisor sent him down to the cafeteria.

"Waiting for what," I said, and the PA did another neurological test with his fingers. Then asked me who was president. "I'd just as soon you not make me remember that," I replied, intending humor, but he wrote it down as evidence.

When they left, I closed my eyes and saw Paul and me down by the stream, watching the trumpeter swans from the snowbank. Laney is out there somewhere. So maybe I will do what Ruby showed me to do at her camp, and hear the Aborigine women chant the strength back into my legs. And then I will get up and leave this place.

There it is, at last. The bottom of my mind.

8:00 A.M.

I'm trapped in a spin cycle of helpful people and bad ideas. Everyone has a theory about Laney. And me.

Which wouldn't be a problem if they thought it and moved on, but four people have been here since daylight, one to offer support, one to yell, and two more to sew up the details of how I offed Travis and where I stashed Laney's body, and now my head's about to explode. It is amazing how fast the world turns uncivil when you're accused of a crime.

Pony, thank God, didn't come. She's back in the field. Didn't take Wes's orders to sleep very seriously, went through the motions with Vince, then apparently told him to arrest her or step the f——out of her way, so he held open the door and she headed straight back to look for Lanes, working solo and tired, which makes me sicker at the stomach than I already am. Worst-case scenario for a tracker, even a crack one like Pony. Does not bode well for Lanes.

The edges of what happened yesterday and last night are fuzzy, and I'm worried that I've missed something huge.

Something that will mean the difference between life and death for Laney Greer.

9:00 A.M.

I have wracked my brain, looking for anything off-kilter in the last year. Aside from a shouting match on my front doorstep with Travis Schaeffer in March, which ended with me dialing 911 and rousing the whole damn village of Moose in the process, nothing stands out. It's not as if I go around making enemies on purpose.

Even the link with Trav reeks of coincidence, but I can't explain it away.

At the very least, he knew the man who took Laney. But beyond that, I draw a blank.

~

Vince doesn't share that problem, and his questions don't leave much doubt about the general direction of his ideas. He thinks I did Travis and vanished Lanes, period.

Whatever the hell for? I would like to ask, but don't dare. He's been here almost as long as I have. We've had two "chats" already. This is the third.

"So what time did you say you reached the bottom of the route yesterday morning?" *Somewhere around five-thirty, six, dispatch'll have the numbers, you can check with them.* "And why choose to go up the face when the back's more passable?" *Because we were concerned about that chute sliding, especially not being able to assess from below.* "Yet you went up with Pony later?" *I kicked it off from above on my way down.* "You did?" *That's what I said.* "But by then you were pretty much out of it, right?" *Right.* "So do you actually remember starting the avalanche, or do you just assume you did?" *I started it. Anybody that comes off the top like I did would've.* "Ah, so you don't *remember* starting it, you *assume*—well actually, never mind. That's not important right now, we'll come back to it later. What I'm really wondering is why you chose to climb, without any protection, instead of rappel off the front?"

On that one I just look at him. There's no reason the man should know beans about rock rescue, so no reason he should know rappelling is the choice of last resort. Inherently dangerous. Cute for the movies, a good deal less so in the real world, where we have to operate sans stunt doubles and steel-corded cables strung to a ceiling in a room that's climate controlled. But I've already told him *twice* in the last two hours that the man who stabbed Lanes cut my line. "How do you rappel long faces with just forty foot of rope?" I finally ask.

Vince shrugs.

"You don't. That's how," I snap, sounding more like Pony than me. "There's two sections on that route you need 120 for—and even then you have to nail the stop, or you're screwed—and a couple eighties, plus one pendulum. Had no choice. Up was my only option."

"I thought staying put was the best option in these circumstances," Vince says, playing dumber than he actually is, which gives me the distinct feeling he's trying to needle me. It's working.

"On minimal gear, no comm, so no net for at least fourteen hours?" I am edgy, too edgy to be talking to a cop. My brain's not functioning well enough for this, might as well have been taken off at my neck. It's like I'm in pieces, still shivering, even in here. I should just shut up, wait till it all comes together better in my own mind, but no, if I do that, Vince'll never leave. "We had *no chance* with us both staying put. The best thing I could do was give Lanes my clothes and climb like a bat out of torment. Which I did."

"That's hard to believe," he replies, casually almost, but deliberate, fingering the frame of a mirror on the wall and ignoring the fact that a nurse is hovering in the doorway.

"What is?"

"That you made that climb unaided. Free solo, I believe's the term?" When I don't respond, he adds, "Wes said he didn't know you could climb at that level."

Neither did I, SOB, but I'm not about to admit that to you. "Your point."

Vince shrugs. "I don't really have one. This is just an initial interview."

"Good," the nurse says, rolling a wheelchair to the bed and patting my arm. Zee Landimer's a local, knows me from way back before Paul. We all used to dance together at the Cowboy on Thursday nights. She's originally from Alabama and not in the mood to forget it, total pro here but can drink the hardest alcoholic slam under the table downtown and still get up and dance Slap Leather in tall boots without missing a beat. "Because Ms. Nowata's got an appointment with a CT scanner and, believe it or not, Sheriff, it's more expensive than you. You'll have to come back later."

"Oh, I'll wait right here," Vince says, flashing his too-white smile. I could smack him. If Pony could only read my mind, she'd be so proud of me right this second. She approves of violent urges, especially when acted upon. That's one of the primary sticking points between us. Always has been.

Zee shakes her head and hoists me into the chair. "Oh, no sir, that won't work. You may own the jailhouse and every last road in the county, sheriff, but this hall belongs to *me* from six to three this day. So you run on along and have yourself a cup of coffee, some doughnuts, somethin' like that, whatever it is you boys with the badges hanker after, and come back later. We'll be busy with her till at least noon."

One three-hour reprieve.

We're halfway down the corridor when she sniffs and says, "Men in uniform. Can't find their feet half the time, Tally. And we let 'em carry guns."

I chuckle and pay for it with shooting pains that crisscross my skull and shoulders. Oh well, so be it. Worth the price. As Zee wheels me swiftly down the hall, I draw back in the chair and focus on keeping my knees in so if we crash they won't get banged up again.

All this trouble, and it's my kneecaps I'm most concerned about.

~

And Bess.

There's no answer at Dix's hotel room. Or Audra's. But I finally got the harried clerk to take messages for when they return. Maybe they're at breakfast. I have to see if Dix and Shelby can detour on the way home, bring Aud and Bess back, or get them on a plane. From the look in the tech's eyes when she said, "We need to run you through the MRI," I won't be driving a car today. Or tomorrow. Not that I would leave this valley with Laney still gone for anything in this world. There are lots of ways to get a woman and child from Vegas to Moose that don't require my personal attention.

A dull ache spans the base of my neck, and I feel nauseous. The phone rings.

Dix?

Vince.

Zee takes the call and snaps, "I told you *noon*, Miller. That's both hands straight up on the dial. Or a one and a two and two zeroes if you don't have a dial. And at this point, we may be lookin' at somethin' more like three anyway. She's scheduled for an MRI, and there's a line."

Phone tucked on her shoulder, Zee pulls the covers over me with military precision and pats my hands. Still don't have much feeling in them. Or my feet. Though they say I probably won't lose much more than a couple top layers here and there. No digits, which is good. Better than I expected. In light boots I could've lost both feet, ankles down. Hadn't been for Pony showing up when she did, I would've. "No, that's fine, Sheriff. You're just too used to talkin', need to start listenin' more—all right then, apology accepted. We'll see you at three. That's right. You show your nose a split second before that, I'm callin' the law, got it? Good."

Someone knocks on the door, and Zee glares at him. "How can she get back on her feet with y'all draggin' in here all the damn time, Jed Timmons? You never heard of visitin' hours?"

"Ten minutes, Zee," he pleads, well into the room.

"Four."

"Six, and I'll say bye from my car."

"Five, and at five-oh-two I start manual eject— now, are we clear?" Zee says, but she smiles as she leaves, and gives Jed a high five. They dated a couple times, years ago, before he met and married Lisa. Jed dated lots of women back then.

He looks awful today. "Hey, TJ," he mutters, eyes on the floor.

Zee sticks her head back in to interrupt, "And don't go grillin' her—had enough."

Jed nods. Catches my eye. Holds it with his.

All I thought I'd never live to see with this man, I see now.

~

I met him the day I arrived in Wyoming. Sixteen and scared, out on my own and not sure what to make of it. When our state-sanctioned parents died in a car crash that summer, Dix and I headed back to the res at first. Not to stay, I was determined then. Dix wanted to visit with an uncle through the school break, though, and I had a bone to pick with my mother's mother. Then I was heading west; I just didn't know where.

Four days later I wound up here. Sitting at a table in Dornan's, staring at these mountains, listening to the ebb and flow of voices around me, people who had somebody, all of them, it seemed, happy people. Obnoxiously happy, spilling over. Jed was two tables away, having lunch with another ranger and a woman in a tailored suit. Serena, his sister, I found out later, and Jay Kinney, the chief in those days. When our eyes met, Jed nodded at me, and I nodded back, then turned resolutely toward the range, wondering if climbing lessons could cure my fear of heights, slowly hatching a plan to find out.

An hour later I was at the Exum office—"best climbing school in the valley," I'd been told by a bartender with a Ph.D. in analytical philosophy and rippling biceps that'd never seen the insides of a gym—when a patrol vehicle slid noiselessly up beside me. Jed Timmons.

The next day he took me up a training ridge above Jenny Lake, called me a "natural," and promised the fear would subside if I gave it time. Told me I ought to consider a career in the Park Service, said I had an automatic "in" being Indian. I told him we had lots of "ins," and few of them ever worked out very well for us in the long run, near as I could tell. But Jed kept after me till I agreed to try, and spent every day off for two solid months helping me learn to walk rock. Then he insisted that I go away to college.

I thought he was the best person I'd ever met. Still do. We were best friends for years. Not lovers, I didn't want one of those. But a friend was a different matter. I'd never had one. Jed was the first. Then came Pony. Paul. And Lanes.

Rough numbers today. Two gone, one dead, and one missing.

Jed looks at me from far away, blue eyes in dark pain, and says, "What were you *thinking*, TJ? *Light boots?*"

The full extent of my misdeeds is known.

~

"We thought we could save time."

"In *winter?* You *know better.*"

And then he just stands there, staring out the window.

I hate the silences that ensue with this man when I'm called on his rug for something. There've been quite a few of those in the last couple years.

"And you went up the back with that head injury? I wouldn't lead that pitch in summer, perfect weather, *high noon*. What made you think you could do it?"

"Wasn't any think to it. Had no choice. She was up top."

There's a long pause, Jed staring out the window as if he can't bring himself to look at me. "You've been at this too long." It's true. This has gone way beyond a little lost hope. I'm taking crazier chances every day the last few months. Walking a high ridge in a lightning storm. Glissading a snowfield without my ice axe. Dumb, stupid stuff. When you've lost your will to live, you probably shouldn't work this job. Jed's right; you're putting other folks in danger now, Taliesin. Figure it out.

"When this is over, I'll leave."

"I didn't mean that!" Jed objects.

"Well, I did."

When this is over.

And there's the snag.

Jed says Pony's having a devil of a time on the trail, and—aside from one clear set of prints near the base of a tree, at a place where the man clearly paused—we have nothing to go on. He was loath to tell me that much, but I pressed, and now I'm wondering what else he held back.

Swinging my legs over the side of the bed, I hold still a moment, gripping the rails. They did the MRI two hours ago and said the doc would be in to talk to me about it, but he hasn't come. Meantime Pony's out there slogging on no sleep. I feel like a slacker.

Before my feet hit the floor, though, there's a low knock at the door.

Wes enters with one hand raised, spit-shined and not a thread out of place on his uniform, looking as if he slept all night and woke refreshed. "Stay put. I'm just delivering this."

It's a small, lightweight thermos. "Chicken soup, from Jedediah's Original House of Sourdough. I thought it might beat the mush they'd feed you in here. You did say you liked it, right?"

Nodding, I hold the thermos close to my stomach with one hand. Its warmth seeps through the thin cotton of my hospital gown. Tears sting my eyes, not sure why, probably just more of me being tired, so I don't look up. That was months ago, my quip about

Jedediah's soup being the best—not long after Wes got here. He remembered? "Thanks."

"Not a problem. It's the least I can do."

"Is Pony okay out there?"

"I was afraid you'd ask that."

"And?"

"Tough going. Three to four foot of new snow. Deeper drifts in sections, Sue's out with her—"

"Sue?"

"Yes. So Pony's on her own—I know—but at least she's got a pair of eyes at her back. We assume the guy headed for the parking lot, but she won't assume anything. She thinks, well—"

"That he might've dumped Lanes before he got there," I say, completing Wes's sentence when he pauses, hating the flat, dull sound of my own voice. "So it's body recovery then."

Wes nods and looks hard at the floor. The edges of all this aren't clear for anybody but Vince. Everyone else is struggling.

"It doesn't make any sense, does it? This whole thing with Laney and me."

"No, Tally. It doesn't."

"I can't figure it out, why he'd attack her up there, only to—"

"Carry her down? Yes, that has to be a first," Wes agrees and then pauses for several seconds, walks to the window, stares out. Doesn't look at me when he adds, too quiet, "Are you sure you've told us everything?"

I fumble for words. "Yes. All I can remember."

"What about the thing between you and Travis? That was before my time—"

"You should thank whichever God you deal with for that."

Wes turns back toward me, a small grin playing at the corners of his mouth. "I try to cover my bases— pick a different one each day. Jesus, Muhammad, Jehovah, Yahweh, Buddha. Figure some percentage of the time I'm talking to the guy in charge."

"Or girl."

"Or girl. Look, I've got to get back to the park. I'll stop in again this evening. In the meantime, would you please just lie in that bed and cooperate with these people for a few hours?"

"Thanks for the soup," I say, mind made up, but I nod. What Wes Dawson don't know won't kill him.

12:20 P.M.

The taxi weaves its way out of St. John's just as Vince's Landcruiser rolls in. I lean against the seatback, still not quite steady, thinking what Zee will say when she sees him and checks her watch. Nowhere near three yet.

Of course, since I slipped out without her permission, she's liable to corral him to form a posse. Shared history doesn't matter to a nurse. You behave or else, I think. They must take a class in that.

Go harass somebody else, Sheriff. The worst thing I

did yesterday was wear the wrong shoes for a few hours longer than I'd planned to. And climb a little less well than I should have. Neither's a crime. Embarrassing, yes. Criminal, no. And okay, I'm checking out a little early now, but the second we find Laney Greer, I'll come back. Ruby's teachings didn't take quite as well as they might've. If I could've ever stopped doubting at her camp in the Tanami, maybe they'd work. I can still hear the women chanting, but my legs are so wobbly I barely cleared the front door, so I'm well aware I could use some modern meds. When this is all settled, I'll come back for some. At this moment I'm just glad the taxi was where his dispatcher said he'd be.

The driver, a young man, asks, "You live out at Moose?"

When I nod, he continues. "Nice. Me, I just got here. From Ohio. Big change. Out East it's city wall-to-wall, here it's just skiers and you folks. Are you a ranger then?"

"Yes."

"Yeah, I figured."

"How?"

"Oh, I don't know. You're all light and lanky, I guess. Look like you've spent some time in the sun, too, usually. No offense."

"None taken."

"I like crow's-feet on women. Name's Mike, pleased to meet you."

As we thread our way through the ski traffic

north of the square, Mike's voice papering the small heated space around us, I remember Grandmother Haney's greeting from childhood. Always, when we would arrive at her house on the res, she'd walk to the car, pat the hood, and say, "Light and look at your saddle." Even when the gout had her strapped to a chair, she'd nod at our wheels and greet us with that line.

I loved her for that the longest time. Nobody else seemed to know a journey's substance could be gauged by the wear on your transport. Know or care. Bess Haney spent time with the minutiae of life. She knew its curves and hollows, understood the slightest touch down of a bird's foot, or butterfly's. Gathered eagle feathers dropped from the skies and passed them on to Dix and me for our birthdays. Mailed them to us after we were sent to the foster homes. Never any notes, just one feather apiece every year.

I burned all but one of mine the last day I saw her. Stopped my shiny new car by the road outside the boundaries of her world and set fire to those feathers. Done with being Indian, pitied and demeaned hand in hand by even the well-meaning. Part Potawatomi, part Lakota, part gringo, who cares? I was young and *done*. Had my eye on a fresh start from mid-leap. But then, at the very last moment, I snatched the smallest feather up, smudged out the flames on my new clothes, and tossed it in the back seat.

That singed feather is still with me. On the shelf next to Paul's ashes.

But why?

Laney is the only one of my friends who's never said a word about it. Her and Audra. That has slipped neatly past me till now.

The answering machine blinks as I open the door. Sure enough. Dix. Frantic. *I need you to call me now, Tal.*

The second message is from him, too. Slurred.

Bessie's gone. I start dialing. What the heck is he talking about?

Shelby answers the phone in their hotel room. She's been crying. Says, "I'm so sorry, Tally, we—"

"Put him on the phone. Now."

"Tally, he can't talk, he's—"

"I said put my brother on the phone."

"I can't," she finally replies. "He's not here."

"Where the hell is he?"

"In dryout. I had to check him in last night. He lost it when we couldn't find—"

"What do you *mean*, you can't find—*she's gone? Where?* Where the hell does a two-year-old go by herself? And where's Audra?"

"That's just it, Tal, we—"

"You *what?* Dammit, Shelby, I don't have time for this!"

"Tally, please listen to me," she pleads, and I finally draw a deep breath and do, one hand over my mouth so I won't interrupt. "We don't know what happened. Dix didn't mean anything by it. He was just letting Bess have a sip for fun, but Audra saw and got really mad." The hand falls away on its own, and I speak, way too quiet and controlled.

"Shelby, start again from the top. I don't understand." There, that's better. I'm not yelling, not technically. If Audra was with her, Bess is fine. Ease up, Taliesin. "A sip of what?"

"Coors. Well, actually, Coors Light—"

"*What?*"

"It was just for fun. The guys thought it was funny the way she wrinkled up her nose and spit it out. They didn't mean any harm—"

"I let him take her for five days, and he feeds her *beer* on the second? Has he lost his—"

"It wasn't—"

"Never mind. Just tell me where she is."

"We don't know. Dix looked everywhere yesterday afternoon. Audra checked out, and didn't leave a message."

The light on my answering machine blinks steadily. It'll be Aud. Has to be. She called it just as I would've, yanked Bess out of there, I could *strangle* my brother right now, good thing he's a thousand miles away or it'd be all-she-rote for Nowatas. Dropping the phone in its cradle, I click playback.

Sure enough. Audra. "We rented a car and started home, Tally. I'll explain later."

Okay, it's all going to be okay. Bess will be home

very soon. Tomorrow maybe. Audra's got her, didn't wait for a yes from me. Thank God.

Or Jehovah. Who the hell ever.

So now I'll help find Lanes and bring her home. Provided I can get clear of here before Vince Miller shows up.

And then, when this is all over, I'll deal with Dix.

1:00 P.M.

I outfitted an overnight pack even faster than I'd planned, but not by choice. Duress.

In the form of the sheriff of Teton County.

Vince pulled into my driveway as I walked into the kitchen for food, and he was knocking on my front door ten seconds later as I ducked out the back, heading for Laney's. If Rose's old truck still functions, I can possibly clear Moose before Vince sees my tracks. That would be a good thing. At this point, he's liable to arrest me just because he's mad and come up with PC later. In Wyoming probable cause isn't all that hard to come by anyhow.

My key slides into the front lock with a soft click, and Ducket greets me with a bear hug before I've cleared the sill. Ruby's magic must be kicking in or I'd be on the floor by now. Giant paws on my shoulders, head well above mine, Duck licks my face, looking for Bess or a cookie or whatever I'm bearing, which isn't much today but bad news. His food and water bowls are full, so that's good. Darla always looks after him when Laney's in the field.

"Enough, kid," I say. "I need in." And Duck drops obediently to his feet, still excited, but backing off so I can pull myself, pack, and skis through the front door. Drawing it closed, I step into the kitchen and look across the street to the back of my house. Still no sign of Vince. Good.

From his box on the refrigerator, I toss Duck one of his favorite crackers and shush him when he tries to bark me into playing.

He's sniffing at the door, me, my pack. Worried sick. Listening. He knows. Reads it, smells it maybe. Understands somehow that this is different from other times his mom's been gone. Or maybe I'm just needing him to know that without me having to say it.

"It'll be okay, kid, we'll find her, you'll see. You just have to stay, D. Stay here," I tell him, raiding Laney's cupboard for a handful of beef jerky and a couple sacks of dried fruits and salt nuts. She is always better stocked than I am. There's an unnerving regularity to all this. How many times have I let myself in and helped myself to whatever I needed? About as many times as she's done it with me. This is the way we live now, intertwined.

Except today.

All those threads severed last night. All but the ones for memory and faith. Laney is okay. She has to be. I think I would feel it if she were gone, and I don't. Not yet. We Just have to find her and get her to St. J's.

There's still no sign of Vince in my backyard, so I snag Rose's keys from a nail by the garage door and load up. The truck protests but fires and, after a couple false starts, idles well, smoothly. Laney drives it to the post office once a week, from some undefined need she can't name, but that works to my benefit now. When I go to open the garage door, Duck leaps into the front seat.

Dragging him out, I hug him one last time and lead him inside. "Stay. I'll be back soon. It'll all be okay, you'll see."

He stomps one foot but offers no other resistance, big shaggy head peering out at me to the last, pushing the curtains over the picture window aside with his nose, watching me leave.

Minutes later I'm out of Moose and through the park entrance. No Vince. And liable not to be anytime soon, either.

I wave to Ren Lowe in the booth. It pays to be nice to the fee collectors. Sometimes it's the little people who hold all the cards in the game. Seconds ago, after I frowned and said, "Miller talked my ear off all last night and intends to keep at it, I think, but Pony needs a hand out there," Ren shook her head and leaned out of the fee booth to pat my shoulder.

"Nice not to've seen you, then, hon," she said, waving me on, every last one of her fifty years plain in her knowing nod.

Turning the nose of Rose's truck to the north, I pray, in spite of an old vow never to do it again, that we find Laney soon. Alive, with her whole future still intact. My arm throbs and my feet hurt, beneath the outer layer that's numb. The PA said they'd do that, come alive in sections and ache when the skin starts to slough off. Have to avoid infection then, and stay off them. "It would help if you took it easy with this arm for a few days, too."

Right.

Suddenly it hits me: I hung up on Shelby. *Dammit.*

2:00 P.M.

The trick, now that I've made it across the meadow and into the tree cover undetected, with a full pack and belly and the right clothes at last, is to get Pony's attention without Sue seeing. That shouldn't be too hard. I've been watching them for a couple minutes, and Susan Lunn is beat, wore slam out. I somehow doubt she's even seeing the snow anymore, but don't want to advertise that I'm here just the same. Sue's too new to have history with me. No telling which way she'd leap if Vince made her choose.

Using my mini-mag and a carabiner, I tap two quicks and a long, the way Pony always knocks on doors, hoping she's paid as much attention to her quirks as I have, or at least that she's as jumpy as she's been the last few months. There've been a couple times at HQ that somebody came up behind her and she about came out of her skin. Surely she'll hear my signal.

The first attempt doesn't connect. Wind's up. We're in the lee of this wall of storms, supposed to get hammered again in the next few hours. Absolutely *have* to find Lanes before then.

Tap again, one-two-THREE. Pony stops cold, but Susan's facing the same direction, still no help. As soon as they return to the trail, I tap one more time, same sequence. Sue's turned slightly west now, so I step from behind my tree trunk to wave, then line up with it once more.

Pony immediately says, "Okay, Suze, time for a break. Full sun's a real bitch. Why don't you call it a day, head in and grab some shut-eye? I'll finish this line and do the same. We can pick it up again this afternoon."

"What about the guy?"

"What about him?"

"I can't track, Pony. Everybody knows that. I thought they put me here to cover you in case he's still around." Susan's built a lot like Pony, wide shoulders, narrow hips, just not as tall, though that's relative, since Pony's six-three. Sue's six-aught. Thin, thin, freckled face, weatherbeaten already; Mike the cabbie was right about us, she'll have wrinkles on her teeth time she's thirty. Same as Pony and me. "As close in as you're working, he could be on you, no time."

"Yep," Pony says, wiping sweat off her forehead with a kerchief. "But you wouldn't want to lay eyeballs on him tomorrow if he does."

"He is *armed*, Pony."

"Your point?" When Sue doesn't respond, Pony continues, "My take is, he's cleared Dallas. Last night, Lanes in tow. All I'm hoping for here is to nail down some basics. Pick up a set of footprints or something for court, when we fry the sucker."

"You think we will?"

"Yep. Like I told you before, you learn a lot about somebody when you track him, and I can tell you one thing about this boy—he ain't any good at this shit. Had any sense, he'd've left Laney on that damn mountain."

"Why didn't he?"

"Don't know. Crazy or got a conscience, either one's fine by me. Means he'll trip up. Probably already has. Which means we take the field."

"So you're really okay for me to leave for a while?"

"A-okay." Susan looks unconvinced, Pony presses, "So move it."

"Shouldn't we tell Jed or Wes?"

"Tell 'em when you get back. Blame it on me. Say I got bitchy and needed some space, they'll believe you."

Slowly Sue yields, more tired than she probably even knows. I've pulled a few all-nighters in this business, and it sucks you dry. We're losing our weather window here, we need to get moving, *will you just leave, Susan Lunn, before it's totally moot?*

Sue's taking her sweet time.

Pony holds the line, just barely, pretending to track and not seeing one thing, I would bet, until Sue waves from the bend and rounds it.

Then Sutton explodes, my direction. "What the Sam Hill are you doing out here again? They let you out already?"

"More or less. What've you got?"

"You good to go?"

"Yep."

"Anybody else agree on that?"

"Nope." I scan the ground, trying to deflect her gaze, but Pony catches my left arm.

"What about your head?"

"Too hard for permanent damage, they said." I tug my arm away.

"Nailed you there. And that eye?"

"Got me a new one ordered, blue this time. But it won't be in till next week."

Pony shrugs. "Anybody else, I'd send home."

"That's because you have control issues. Now will you tell me what you've got, or what? We're burning daylight."

We set to tracking, Pony on point, me working the flanks. There isn't much here, but she has covered what is.

"Just one. That's it, TJ. Might be more somewhere else, but there's just one guy out here. Big. Long stride—twenty-eight, couple thirties in spots." Pony points to a well of snow around a large tree where the tracks haven't been blown over. Or covered by new snowfall, which is very lucky for us.

She's right. The distance between one footfall and the other is close on thirty inches. Means he's tall. "Six one or two?"

"Yep. And he either ain't the brightest bulb in the package and never had a plan, or he got spooked and tossed it, 'cause he's *carrying* Laney. On snowshoes. Trying to stay clear of the trails, near as I can tell. Aiming in the general direction of the parking lot, but going acres out of his way to get to it. Which tells me he didn't want to be seen."

"Or had trouble navigating in the storm."

"That too. Still wouldn't put him local. There's ten better ways to avoid people and reach that lot quicker. Even in a storm. Been tempted to cross-cut him, but you weren't here to help, and Susan meant well but the girl can't see shit for shinola."

"Want to cross now? Our weather window's closing. I'll take point, you work the parking lot out."

"And what do we use for comm? Your little taps, Caveman Girl? Or park radio, so Vince has an excuse to hog-tie us both? Nope, let's just stick to it tight, tar on a flea's ass. And anyway, our bad boy might show up again."

"I thought you told Susan he'd cleared out."

"Yep. Don't mean I think it. Had to get rid of her and doubted she'd go otherwise. Look here." Pony bends to run her fingers along a low branch. The snow load on it is less than half its neighbors', which means somebody brushed against it in passing. Again, near the base of the tree, there's a partial print. "This is the kind of crap trail he's left us," she says, as I sweep back the loose top layers of the snow three feet behind that track. Sure enough, the icy partial outlines of a snowshoe.

"Okay. So he can climb well enough to do that face and bring her off solo, and he's fairly well outfitted, but he's cat-skunked down here. Reckon he's hurt?"

"No sign. Carrying an extra ninety pounds the whole way, too, got to be strong as an ox."

"Sport climber or mountaineer?" I say, bending to check another dip beneath a tree. Still moving, but he reliably pulls in close to these bigger trees, even though it's much harder work, lots of up and down, breaking trail. "City boy?"

"Works for me."

"And there's no sign of anyone else? Just this bit—does he think he's being pursued? By who? Can't be us. We sure the hell didn't have our act together enough last night for it to be us."

"I know. Can't nail that yet."

"Well, you've nailed a hell of a lot with very little to go on, ask me."

"And who did? Shit, TJ, when did you go all soft and mushy? Will you just cut that polite thank-you-praise crap? Don't fit. Makes me nervous."

"Sorry—"

"*Jeez!*"

I raise my left hand, thumb and little finger up, the other three down. That used to mean truce, back when we were friends. Pony looks at it and nods. "Better." She starts to move on, but then stops.

"He has put her down twice to rest." Careful not to look at me, she pulls off her parka hood and runs a hand through her hair before bending toward where the next track should be. "And she's still bleeding."

~

It's a long while before we speak again.

The trail's shot. Circling, doubling back. You'd almost think it was on purpose, but the pattern's not smart enough for that. What the hell's going on in this man's mind?

"Maybe we should bring Ducket out, let him work—"

"Think he could?"

"I don't know. Without Lanes—"

"Well, that's real helpful," Pony says, irritated, bending slightly, head tilted to scan the snow a few yards away. There's a faint indentation, a subtle dipping. Could mean our guy passed through underneath. "Let's work it through to the lot, see what we come up with, can't risk mucking this up any worse than it already is. Then maybe go get the dog." After a pause, she adds, "You hear anything from Bess yet?"

I point to the next indent. "Looks like she's on her

way home with Audra." Winter tracking's tedious, especially after a storm.

"See there—what did I tell you? So you finally got through."

"To Dix, not Aud. She checked out of the hotel yesterday, though, so she should be home today or tomorrow."

"Had a run-in with your little bro?"

"Something like that."

"He drinking again?"

"Why?"

"What do you mean, why?"

"Why do you ask that? Is he drinking again—like it's just a matter of time. He's been in the clear for five years. Six, come May."

"Yep, and his next warm one's just a heartbeat away, same as my pa. Can't never trust a drunk, TJ, that's what I always say."

~

You cannot trust him when he's drinking, my mother used to tell me.

He doesn't know what he's doing, so it's up to us to pick up the slack, to remember him back to his better self. I didn't want this to be true for my father, didn't believe it, thought he could change if he wanted to bad enough, right up to the day he beat her to death. After that I set my sights on Dix, steely-eyed and steely-tongued, determined my brother wouldn't carry on the family line in that way. He was only eight; I had a chance. Then came the foster homes and the adolescent years, me controlling every drop of liquid that went down his gullet till the day I left for Wyoming. And after that, his time to run with the spirits, crazed and wild, one visit and two phone calls a year from the Black Indian rodeo circuit, until five and a half years ago, when I slapped him upside the head and told him to get out of my house and my life. That very day he quit cold turkey and put himself back together, on his own, *without my help*, and that took guts. So whatever happened this weekend in Vegas, what he's done in the last five years has to count.

You *can* trust a drunk, I want to tell Pony, but don't. Getting them to trust themselves, now *that's* the problem. I deserted Dix once. Not again. Might slap the tar outta him when we cross paths next time for pouring beer down my daughter, but I will not quit.

"R346, come in. This is R302." It's Wes.

"Go ahead, 2," Pony says.

"We've lost track of 327, seems she's left the hospital. Have you had any contact in the last couple hours? Over."

Pony looks at me and raises her eyebrows. "That's a negative, you try her house?"

"Thanks," I say.

Pony's eyes flash fire, and she snaps, "Cut it out, TJ. I mean it." She's right. I *have* gotten overly grateful. When did that happen?

"Copy, will do," Wes responds. "302 out."

"46 out," Pony says, sucking in a deep breath and staring at me. "We're not done yet anyway, not by a long shot. Jed finds you here, hornet hits the porch, you won't be able to say thanks. Me neither."

How in hell did we ever get to this place? Total strangers who still know all the details of each other? My plan when I first came home was that I'd figure things out and get back on my feet one day, maybe after Bess came, and then I could explain all I couldn't say to my friends on returning. It was as if my head was missing, not just nonfunctional, but *gone*. Sliced off clean at the neck, and me with no way to reattach it. The harder I tried, the more lost I got, so when Pony and Jed tried to pull me out of my shell, I just froze. And when they tried again, I fought back, kicked them out of my own private corner of hell. To protect them, I told myself, and it sounded like the truth then.

But now my eyes land on the ugly scar on Pony's neck, and I feel sick—I should've done more than call 911 on Travis, maybe could've stopped that happening. She catches me staring and yanks her turtleneck higher, turns away, fierce. "Save your fucking thanks and your pity, Nowata. I'm full up with both these days."

The radio stutters, live again, looking for me. "R327, if you're in range, respond please. Base over."

Pony shakes her head and moves forward once more. She might as well be a planet away. I click the extra radio I nabbed from Laney's desk to off. They're fishing now. If I don't bite, they don't net me.

Nothing we can plan for has heft beyond now. I had put so much together for myself when I met Paul. Friends, a job, a home the government couldn't take away—only to find it sifting through my fingers lately as water bleeds through paper and then flees with the wind.

The sun is setting in the west somewhere, but you wouldn't know that here. By the time we reach the parking lot, we've been crawling up the belly of a white-leaning sky for at least an hour. Steely quiet between us. Although the south end of the lot's been cordoned off since dawn, we can't raise a trace of the man's tracks from here. Too far gone.

His snowshoes bit into the deep plowed area at this edge, then nothing. The crew used it as a staging ground last night, too, so it's not lacking for tracks in the harder layers below the new snow. They're just not the ones we need.

"What now?" I ask, strictly to break the silence, the bitter chill of night beginning to eat through to my bones. Time to add another layer. We're crouched near the last print we found. Pony's made a tent over it, but there's no definition whatsoever. No way to nail a sole pattern, much less cast it. We're even guessing on size at this point. "Ducket?"

Pony shakes her head. "Might as well try. But Jethro'll have a cow if he finds out. Neither one of us is rated to work that dog."

"So?"

"So he'll pull us both. We're lucky he didn't drag me in a few minutes ago." Jed's been hounding Pony to pull off for two hours. She keeps stalling for time.

"What else can we do?"

"Search Laney's house, maybe. Trav's apartment down in Crater Lake. Get some phone records, see if we can make a connection," Pony says, head in her hands momentarily.

"That's where he was? Crater Lake?"

"Last I heard."

I feel awkward, like I should say something, like I'm sorry, I know you loved him, but Pony's wall is up. If I apologize again, she's liable to hit me. "What kind of connection could he have with Laney? I doubt they ever even spoke—him in maintenance, her in resources. She never mentioned him, that's for sure."

Pony shakes her head and rests her elbows on her knees. She's exhausted. I at least had a few hours enforced rest at the hospital. She's been up a good 36, no breaks.

"Why don't you grab five when we get to her place? I'll run the Duck, you can join us later. You're not any use to Lanes bone-tired."

"Neither are you."

"I caught a few at the hospital."

"And I plan to catch up on my sleep when I die. Not until."

"Oh, good. Fine. *Excellent* plan."

"Give it a rest, TJ."

"When you do, I will. That was my original point."

The faintest of smiles flits across Pony's face as she pulls back her hood and runs all ten fingers through her short, dark hair.

Black, it is, same as my mother's or Ducket's. So black it's blue some days, but not this one. Snowflakes melt when they land on Pony's cheeks, but not on that hair. It's peppery white. "Premature aging?" I would've asked, long ago, but not today. Today I just look at her hair taking the snow and ache deep inside for what's lost. We used to have such a good time, she and I, zinging each other for kicks. Now the quirks that drew us together are spines in our skins, ripping at us every step. It feels uncrossable, this chasm of anger and mistrust.

But at least we're speaking again. That's something.

Pony stands, abruptly, reaching in her pocket for the keys to her old Suburban. "Let's go get that damn dog."

Two steps away, she stops and turns. "Get in the truck. I ain't fixin' to leave you out here all by your lonesome."

"I don't need a sitter."

"Tell that to some other fool, Knothead, one with more time on his hands for your nonsense," she says, snatching up my skis and not even bothering to place them in the ski rack, just tossing them in the back and then swinging the passenger door open. "I said get in the truck."

"Fine." As I crawl in, Pony bangs the door shut, barely missing my foot, and stalks around to the driver's side. "But it's ridiculous, you know. That guy's long gone. And he wasn't after me. Had every chance up there yesterday, yet here I am."

Pony's diesel rumbles, and she switches the heater to high. "We'll see." A ghostly white blankets the land, the road, the truck; the windshield wipers are nearly useless. Snow falls in silvery sheets, whipped into drifts nearing the center line. The plows are out, no doubt, but it always takes them a while to make it up here.

"I don't know how Ducket's nose will work in all this. Liable to freeze."

"You think we've got better options?"

There's a long silence. It's been two years since I rode in this vehicle. Two years and some change. Pony picked me up at the airport when I returned from Australia. I'd forgotten the smell. Tobacco, which she doesn't smoke, and sage, which she does. Keeps bundles of each tucked in the seat pouches, to remind her of home, she always said. The scent is more comforting than I remembered.

"I like your truck."

"A lot of people like my truck. Look," Pony says, sounding tense, tapping her fingers on the wheel, "I haven't wanted to say this. But I don't have a good feeling about this thing."

"You mean Laney?"

"Her. And you. It's a bit too much trouble not to've

been planned." The same thought's been rattling around the edges of my brain all day. True, the guy didn't get me, but he came pretty close. I feel uneasy, would rather've been the only person trying not to think that. More chance of it being plain paranoia that way. The Sub fishtails through a drift—Pony always did drive too fast. My head whirls and aches. The soles of my feet tingle numb. Ruby's magic is starting to fade.

So much for magic, I should've known. "So what're you saying?"

"I'm saying soon's we find Laney, you need to get Bess and lay low for a few days. Not here. Somewhere else. Not till we get a handle on it."

"That's not my way, cowering in a corner somewhere."

"Then change your fuckin' way for a change! Trav was in with a bad crowd, Tally. In deep. Connected."

"So?"

"So let's just say I'm real happy I got out alive." Pony pauses, then adds, in a rush, "Didn't expect to, for a while there, this summer."

"Why the hell didn't you say something?" My skin feels cold. What Travis did to her didn't end when he left the park?

"To *you?* The Ice Queen? Lose the king and don't even blink?" Pony shakes her head. "Oh no, I don't think so."

"That's not fair, and you know it. I blinked plenty—and he was never my King—is *that* why you wouldn't press charges last winter? Because he was *connected?* To *who?*"

"R346, this is 321, status check, over." Jed sounds tired.

"Go ahead, 21."

"What's your twenty?"

"Just left the parking lot we staged out of last night, heading for the barn. Change of clothes, back in fifteen."

"Line of travel yet? Over." Do we know which way Laney was taken? Hardly.

"That's a negative."

"I'm at the south entrance right now, 46. Catch you there, 21 out."

"46 copy and out," Pony says and looks over at me. "He'll lop our ears off, somewhere down near the neck."

"I'm going, I'm going," I say, crawling between the bucket seats to the pile of gear stowed in the back. "But make it snappy, would you? I'm getting too old for this."

"Getting?" Pony mutters, rounding the last bend before the entrance, rolling her window down as she brakes. "Done got, ask me."

"Nobody did. And don't think we're finished on this Trav talk," I call, " 'cause we're not. Plan to fill me in soon as—"

"Keep talking, just keep talking, I never did have all that much use for my skull," Pony drawls, so I shut up and flatten myself on the equipment. Things jab and rub, my sore shoulder hits a crampon, and then the side of a cardboard box and my skis cut into one thigh. The night is dark, lit only by the reflection of the headlights, soft against pelting snow.

"How's it hangin', Jethro?" Pony asks, a little too hearty, as the vehicle bounces to a full stop.

Air from the open window rolls in as he replies, "Fine. You?"

"Can't complain. What's up?"

"What've you got so far?"

"Next to nothing. You come to fire me?"

"Nope."

"Console me?"

"I came to see if you need some company."

"Who you got?"

"Pocatello on standby."

"Keep 'em there." Pony hates working with the guys from Idaho. They're all big-game hunters and deputies, have most of their givens mapped out pretty well. Testosterone-poisoned, Pony says, with her usual tact and, on one occasion at least, has suggested that's sufficient reason to be put down. Compassionate euthanization, she calls it, compassionate to the rest of us. "Who else?"

"Medicine Bow."

In this storm? All flights grounded, most of the roads closed or closing. "Uh-uh. Not near enough to go on. We get something, you can call. Got me a hunch or two to play, I'll just snag another hit of caffeine and be off again."

"I don't like this—"

"Save your spit, Jethro. Like and get's two different hosses. I'll do what I need to do tonight. Period." No one on our crew has ever talked like that to Jed Timmons and still had a job the next morning, Pony—*back off*.

"All right then, fine," Jed says, in a defeated tone I've never heard before. "You do that. Till 2200. Then you come in for the night, understand? That's long enough."

"We'll see. Catch you later—"

"She hasn't contacted you yet?"

"Who?" Pony stops accelerating.

"You know who."

"Oh, you mean TJ? Y'all still lookin' for her? She's not at the hospital?"

"No," Jed says, drawing out the one syllable. Pony's right. He would lop us off at the neck. Jed's as straight an arrow as they come. Even weary, or worried about Lanes or whatever he is tonight, if he knew I was in this truck, he'd pull both our badges in a heartbeat. "She hasn't been there all afternoon. So she hasn't contacted you?"

"Nope."

"You wouldn't lie to me, would you?"

"Well, let's see," Pony says lightly, tapping her fingers on the wheel, two shorts and one long. "Not for money."

Jed sighs.

"Relax, JT. I'm sure she's fine."

"No, she's not fine. Vince's gunning. And not just for her, for you too. The Trav connection's muddied the waters. You need to stay absolutely in the clear on this."

"Hard to stay in the clear when they've painted your coattails, Jethro. But sure, fine, whatever. I'll color in the lines on this page." Pony revs the motor, belying her words.

"And you'll let me know if she calls you?"

"Absolutely. First thing."

They don't say good-bye; we never do around here. That's something I never noticed before. We act as if tomorrow's a given, even when it's been snatched from us for keeps. Is that what saving lives does to you? Cleans it up, flattens it out?

The Sub putters forward, slower now. I wait until Pony's put the blinker on for the residence area, and crawl back up front. Jed's patrol car goes on to HQ.

"Got his doubts."

"Yep," Pony says. "But he'll live. I need me another chug of Folger's. And we've got to give this dog a chance. If it works, JT'll yell at us for a couple days, make a note in our jackets, and get over it. If it don't—"

There's no finish to that, no quip to make it better; we can't joke our way through this. We have to succeed. Or rather, Ducket does.

~

Seconds later, steamy warm, we're pulling into Pony's driveway, two doors down from Laney's. My house sits quiet across the street, two lights on like always when we're out late. They're timered, for convenience, because I hate coming home in the dark. While Pony makes coffee, I wade through snow thigh-deep in her backyard and one neighbor's to Laney's back stoop. She never locks this door. Says it opens on heaven, faced toward the range as it is, so there's no need for security. "Which makes locking your front door sort of weird," I told her once, after a series of small burglaries in the area.

"Oh no, not at all," Laney said, with the kind of off-beat logic she relies on. "That's just smart."

When I step inside, the lights are on, Beethoven's playing, and the sound makes me wince. Laney always leaves lights and music on for Ducket in the evenings when she's out. He likes the Ninth Symphony best. So Darla's keeping the routine, that's good.

"Duck! Hey you!" I call, quietly, but there's no answer. His leash is on the counter, so he has to be here. "Ducket, c'mon, let's go find Mom!"

There is no sound at all.

5:20 P.M.

I pick up the phone and dial Pony.

"Duck's not here."

"Of course he is, did you look?"

"Yes, I looked and he's gone." As the words clear

my throat, I feel a rush of cold air. In a warm house where none should be. "The window, Pony. He's smashed the front window, cleared it."

"Damn dog—that's what you get with animals—headed where?"

"Guess." Ducket's tracks lead unmistakably away, toward my house. He's not waiting for us. He's looking for Mom on his own.

"Shit. On my way." She'll perk the grains in the thermos, always does.

~

Five minutes later, we've just cleared the entrance when I pick up what's left of large dog tracks on the roadside.

"Drove straight past him before," I say, snow in my eyes, left arm tired from hanging the light out the window, knees on the front seat. "Why the hell didn't we see him?"

"Weren't lookin' for a dog. Least I wasn't."

"If we don't intersect him before he gets Laney's scent, we'll be trailing him—"

"Son of a—"

"Road might stop him."

"You hope. Hey! Over there," Pony exclaims and brings the Sub to a fast stop.

Sure enough, it is a dog the shape of a bear, covered in snowflakes, eyes gleaming red against the light. Winded, for no good reason, I turn around and sit in my seat for two seconds. Pony jabs my arm lightly. "Oh nosiree, you don't get to sit. You get the hell out and lasso that dog. He knows you." And then she leans over me and pushes the passenger door open so I can't miss her meaning.

Something about it makes me laugh. "Ducket, come!" I call, and while he decides whether or not to obey, I giggle nonstop, head whirling and spinning. Pony Sutton, tall and fierce and mean as a snake when she needs to be, is afraid of dogs. Even marshmallow weenie dogs like Newfs. Laney would just *love* this. The thought takes the smile and I choke.

Pony opens the back door while I try to cajole Ducket inside. He doesn't want to come. "Have to, Boo," I say, slipping into Bess's nickname for this dog. Those two are *tight;* she likes him even better than Audra. Has to see Ducket every single day at least once. I bet she's harassing Audra all the way home about that. "C'mon, guy. We know for sure they had your mom up here a few miles. We have to go find her, Ducket, let's go."

Slowly he yields and leaps easily into the Sub, unconvinced still, it seems. I crawl in beside him, and Pony grimaces, makes a comment about the stench of wet dog, but drives on.

When we reach the lot, she reaches in for my skis and drops them beside hers on the ground. We both step in as Ducket begins trotting away, so I call, "Where's Mom, D? Go find!" Hoping he knows what to do, because we sure the hell don't. I've seen this done, have even helped Laney work him a few times, but it's beyond me. Suddenly he barrels across the lot, forsaking the ground—and us—entirely.

"This might not've been such a good idea," Pony says, as I hook into my second ski.

But then Ducket skids to a stop, picking up the scent fifteen feet from that last print we marked, it's clear: full stop, nose in the air, tail extended. He doesn't even glance our way, but as soon as we're following, light from our headlamps bobbing along beside, he moves on. Straight to the prints, where, nose barely above the ground, he sniffs cautiously in a wide circle.

For a moment he seems confused, glancing from the track to Pony and me and back again, frame taut, legs planted. "Find Mom," I urge, and with a swing of his head over the print once more, he starts off past us at a trot, only to stop a few yards away. In a slow, careful circle, he smells the ground, close, paws at it, and whines. Pony flicks on her headlamp, and I pull Ducket off so she can look more closely.

"I'll be fuckin' damned. It's her. Look." Pony points to a small faint stain in the snow. Laney's blood.

"So he was parked here, and had to lay her down to get the door open—*yes*." Both our lights are trained on a partial print. "He can do this, Tally. Let him go."

Ducket needs no second offer.

"Find Mom, Duck!" I call and, to Pony, "Right or left?"

We ease into flanking positions behind the trotting dog. Ducket's head is higher than I'd have expected, at least a foot off the ground, but I remember Laney once saying that scents gradually rise in some conditions—maybe snow's one of them, don't know. One thing's for sure, this dog is following his mom right now. Every cell tuned to signals ahead we can't smell, see, or probably even comprehend, though he checks over his shoulder periodically to see if we're keeping up. When we turn from the parking lot onto the main road, headed south, same way we just came from, Pony says, "He's following the car. I've heard some dogs can do that, but—"

"I know. Impossible."

"Should I get the Sub?"

"Sounds good. You can work the front end, monitor for traffic, give me a heads-up if they're coming."

"What happened to your radio?"

"Not mine, nabbed it from Laney's, but it's here. Right here." I pat my chest harness and tighten the straps of my pack once more.

"And is it on? No—course not! What was I thinking? Turn the damn thing on. Monitor your own fuckin' self! What if I can't get to you in time?"

With a quick, exaggerated motion I crank the radio's knob. "There, it's on. You happy?"

"Can it, TJ. I'm half a mind to tell Jed you're out here anyway—he's probably right, you know. About Vince. We need to stay in the clean. They put us together on this thing tonight, we're fucked."

"So what're you saying? You want to turn me in? Fine, go ahead. I don't have time for—"

"Not turning you in. Nobody'd take you, they're not stupid. I'm just saying—"

"Drop it, Sutton. Suit yourself. Catch up and let me know when you decide. I've got work to do."

Pony explodes in a string of expletives, and I leave her standing there. Ducket checks back over his shoulder to make sure someone's coming and, when satisfied I am, keeps moving at a fast trot along the right shoulder. Laney has trained him well; he knows enough for both of us.

"I'll get the Sub and move out in front of you," Pony says, skating alongside me again. The beam from my headlamp bobs up and down, keeping Ducket's hindquarters in view. "Quarter mile, so I don't mess up his nose. You hear me call in for a weather update, you'll know somebody's coming north. Means you'll have to watch your own back, though, got it?"

I nod, but Pony doesn't leave.

"You still want to know about Travis?" she finally asks. We're both huffing some.

"*Now?* Months of silence, Laney in trouble, and you want to *talk?*"

"Forget it." Pony one-eighties her skis.

"Okay, sorry—no—*fine*, then. *Yes*, I want to know. *Now*," I say, from a full stop.

She almost goes on, but stops at last, back to me. I pole up beside her, Ducket holds the trail. Pony finally speaks, so low I can barely hear. "I meant it, TJ. There's not much to tell. Just that he ran with a rough bunch from KC and Tulsa, men that could get things done, he said. I wrote their names down last summer, put it in my safe deposit box in case something happened to me."

"You *what?*" I turn my headlamp straight into her eyes. She looks away. My skin's crawling again. What all did she not tell me?

"All I had was names. But maybe you bent their pens when you got him thrown into jail."

"So this is revenge?"

"Don't know. Seems a little far-fetched—"

"And overdue."

"Yes, but Trav falling off the same rock—"

"Clear as mud. He didn't climb, right?"

"Not that I know of. Not much anyway."

"Then how did he get up there?"

Pony frowns. "We need this other guy, caught and talking."

"No, we need Laney home safe. The men are just a means. I don't give a rip what happens to them as long as we get her back."

"Well, I do," Pony says, darkly.

"Oh, yeah, Sutton, we all know your take on the world. Eye for an eye. Lucky for the rest of us you don't run the joint. Except when it matters, when some thug's comin' at *you* with a knife, then you sull up and freeze. Now would you please go get your truck and run interference up front, huh?"

"Fuck you too, Nowata."

"You wish." That does it. Pony pushes off without another word.

The things we say now.

Not that we didn't say them before, because we did—all the time—but there's a new edge to it now, and neither one of us is kidding.

Soon the Suburban rolls slowly by. Ducket doesn't break stride, neither do I. His coat is blanketed white, he's blending in. I'm sweating from the exertion, my head throbs with each step, but I'm probably blending pretty well, too. What does this mean for his mom and my friend?

Please, somebody's God, at least let her know we are coming.

6:05 P.M.

We'd've been coming a lot faster, it's clear now, if we hadn't pulled Duck off the trail and north to the parking lot in the first place. He had the scent before we ever arrived and was already heading south. That's several miles of extra work from this point.

But Pony's ahead, and I've no way to signal. We didn't think this through well enough. And we're barely clear of the Sub's taillights before my radio crackles. Pony on local.

"R346 to dispatch, over."

There's a long pause, too long. Sometimes our dispatchers get a little caught up in their off-air conversations. Darla alone talks enough for three people.

"Go ahead, 346."

"What's the word on the weather?"

Barely has the transmission ended before I see a set of lights making their way north through the snow. Fast.

"Ducket, *leave!*" I shout, hoping he listens, flicking my headlamp to off. "Come!" And then I dive into the ditch bank on our side of the road. Please work with me, dog, this is important. The sound of a large engine comes closer, it's the plow, gotta be, damn, that's worse than a ranger—the snowplow guys sit up high and scan the roadsides for trouble out of habit, find plenty of it, too, which keeps their radar tuned to high. I crawl over the bank, wriggling half into the deep snow, trying to look like a lump, and lie flat just as the plow comes even with us. And a wet nose hits my face.

"Down!" I whisper, and Duck hits his belly. Without a why. Just lies flat in the snow, head on my chest. We wait. Spattered with fresh road grime.

7:35 P.M.

Six miles behind us now, one more plow, heading south this time, one ranger on its heels heading north, and two more warnings from Pony. She had to get downright creative with that last weather call to base.

But we've managed to make it past the entry station, shuttered and locked up, and are coming up on the PO at Moose. Housing area's on the left, and the VC's just beyond—no visitors hanging about this time of night, but the center's lit up anyway. Ducket is still working, steady on, and Pony falls back beside us and rolls down the window. "What'll we do at the main road?"

"Hell if I know." Ducket pulls a hard right. He's taking the back road to Wilson? It's not even open. People ski that track, but cars don't use it in winter. Is his nose freezing? "Hey, wait up!" I call as Pony crawls out of her truck, leaving it idling, and walks toward me. "You think he's still on it?"

Ducket is waiting, but impatient. He's sure.

"R346, this is 321, over." Jed sounds out of breath, which is unusual.

"This is 46, go ahead."

"What's your twenty?"

"Shit!" Pony hisses. "What do I tell him?"

"Better stick with the truth. Duck, wait!"

"I'm at the turnoff to Wilson, over."

"Stay put till I get there, ETA less than two, 321 over and out."

"*Two?* What the—I copy, 21, 46 out—get the fuck outta here, TJ. I'll try to draw him off your tracks. What the hell do you suppose's up?" Pony asks.

The faint lights of Jed's patrol car appear just ahead, he must've been in the residential area— thank God for this whiteout, or we'd be in his headlights right now. Ducket's scruff in hand, I plow into the deep snow behind us and dig in once more, asking him to sit and then lie down. Click the radio to off, can't afford to have it blare out in the next few minutes.

Jed makes a 180 and pulls up behind the Sub, then crawls out. Pony's talking before his feet hit the ground. Loud. Aggressive.

"You come to harass me some more?"

"Nope, to tell you you're done. Laney's at St. J's." Laney's safe? At the hospital?

"Shit and amen, *yes!* How is she?"

"Two stab wounds, just like Tally said. Critical—they may move her to Salt Lake, but she's hanging in for now."

"How the hell did she—you catch anybody?"

"That's the strange part. Anonymous 911 about an hour ago. Vince responded to a rented condo in Wilson, found her there. No one else."

"Well," Pony says, sagging back against the Sub's grill in relief. I feel like crying. "Good. Now maybe he can start looking for the right bad guys, leave me and TJ in peace."

"You're off the hook."

"About time."

"But Tal's still on, and likely to stay there."

"Fucker. Vince's been gunning for her, and I'm about fed up—"

"Pull in your claws, Sutton. That condo was rented last month."

"Yeah, so?"

"By a couple. Travis Schaeffer and Tally Nowata."

Pony misses the same beat my heart does, but recovers quicker. "Can't be. Somebody got it wrong." The cold is starting to wear through to me again.

"Owner made a copy of their IDs, Pony. Standard practice, he says, since somebody ripped off his TV. I saw them myself. It's Tal." *How is that possible? How could somebody show my license? It's always on me. This doesn't make any sense.*

"That's too neat. Makes no sense. Tally wouldn't rent a Handi-Wipe with Travis. They hated each other. She's the one that got him thrown in jail, remember?"

"It gets worse, Pony."

"Worse?" Now she sounds uncertain, and I start shivering.

"Vince found personal items, hers and his—"

"What kind of personal items?" *No way.*

"Some of Bess's toys, their clothes, pair of Tally's shoes. It looks like they've spent some time there." *No possible way. How are they coming up with that?* "Vince's got his crew doing a full workup. Meantime he's issued an APB, calling it a material witness warrant for now, but between you and me, he thinks Tal's good for both charges." *What?*

"Good for *what?*"

"Stabbing Laney and Travis."

"You have got to be joking. He told you that?"

"Yes."

"And upped an APB?"

"Fifteen minutes ago."

"Then why didn't I hear it on the radio?"

"Vince convinced the chief to keep park comm in the dark, thinks Tal may have a radio with her. So it's on the wire, but we're relaying to on-duty rangers and staff in person."

"Son of a fucking bitch."

"I need to know where she is, Pony."

"You can't possibly believe she'd do this."

"I don't know what to believe. I just know we can't figure it out with her on the run. Whatever she's bit off—she's in over her head. So if you know where she is, or have even a hint of an idea where she might be heading—"

"Already told you I didn't. What're you doing next?"

"Executing a search warrant on her house."

"You *what?* When?"

"Soon as Vince gets here with the paper. And there's more. TJ's scans came back, real trouble. Doc says there's pressure building on her brain, and if they don't get a shunt in ASAP, it could kill her. Might anyway."

That's all I need to hear. In the amount of time it takes to blink twice, I've pulled Ducket along with me and turned my skis into the woods. We'll loop around behind them, break for the houses at the bend.

Pony's gut was right on. I have to get to Bess, take

her away from here till I can figure this out. Surely Audra will be back by the time I get home. The shivering turns into cold fear. Ski, Taliesin. Ducket resists leaving Laney's trail for a heartbeat, but quickly falls into step beside me. Your mom is okay, thank God. It's me we have to worry about now, D.

My head throbs; the pressure's building again. It's a concussion, that's all. I've worked harder with worse in the past. MRI bull teats. Shunt flack, no way. Vince probably told them to say that to sway Pony. Sutton, don't you dare let them con you.

Paul O'Malley, if you exist anywhere anymore, I could use some help down here. Ruby?

Strength pours into my legs as I round the bend for home.

7:54 P.M.

There's a patrol car out front, silent, but the windows are fogged up from inside, so someone's in there, watching my house. But I need to check my machine one more time, see if there's any word from Audra and Bess. Load up some overnight gear, get ready to haul it, be gone before the rest of the fuzz arrives.

At the end of the street, I slip across and weave my way into Laney's from the back, hurrying Ducket inside and down the hall to her office, pulling the door closed, whispering for him to stay. Can't leave him out in the house with that window smashed.

Can't risk taking him with me either, because if he barks or they see him, I'm done.

"You stay," I whisper, rubbing his head. He raises his chin, trusting, wanting that scratched as well. Talk about routine. I used to rub his chin when he was a baby, months before Bess was born, and he's never forgot it. "Your mom's coming home soon, Boo. Be good."

Suddenly, he stiffens, heavy frame blocking the office door.

"Back! Ducket, back," I whisper sternly, the way Laney does, pushing on his chest when he doesn't respond. "Soon," I promise, pulling the door to as he barks loud, almost a growl. Quiet, Knucklehead, you'll give me away. "We'll be back soon."

Skulking across the open street now, cloaked only by the heavy, falling snow, I plunge into the drifts in our backyard. At the stoop I pause to listen—no posse yet—and unclip my bindings. Skis in hand, I push the door open and step inside, kick my boots off on the mat, can't afford to leave wet tracks. The APB's not stretched very wide yet, or they'd have this covered. No sign of Audra or Bess and none that they've been here, but there are two new messages on the machine.

The first is from Miriam, Josie's mom, telling me to call ASAP, pretty much like always. Everything's a crisis to Paul's ex-wife. I fast-forward to the next.

"Tally, it's Aud. We're—"

And that's it.

Maybe she got cut off? Probably was calling to say they were stopping at her cabin, figured I was working since I didn't answer. She takes Bess there sometimes when I'm on call—Bess has her own room, more toys than here. I'll head over now. With any luck, Vince won't have that covered yet either. Probably thinks I'm too smart to come home. Giving me more credit than's due.

Two lights here are on, the living room and front porch. Thank God for those timers, or I'd be working in the dark. I hurry around grabbing gear for a long overnight—no telling when I'll get another chance— and am just heading into the kitchen for some extra MREs when I see it.

Them.

My jumars and prusiks. Laid neatly in the middle of the kitchen table near a small pile of gray dust.

Next to a large padded envelope that I have never seen before. The foil pouch of a Meals Ready to Eat slips from my suddenly nerveless hand.

The envelope's addressed to a *Ms. Nowata*. My knees buckle as I reach for the table, trying to hold on.

8:09 P.M.

Thoughts run, untrained. Must get with this, still the chaos. Those ascenders were supposed to be on my rack during the climb with Laney, but weren't.

They weren't here today when I stopped by from

the hospital either, to change clothes. The table was empty, except for Bess's bib and one candle, like always. Now everything has changed.

But how? Reaching for the package, I step in a puddle and stop, pulling away, close to the wall, staring at the floor. My grandmother's feather, near my foot. And something else. Much worse.

A footprint. Boot, lug sole. Big. Melted snow. Pointed toward the front door. Was it him? All the way in *here*?

Hyper-alert, I crouch and step into the entry. Nothing.

No one. And then peer down the hall. The wet prints go out the side door, through the garage. No time, Tally. Move. Pick the damn thing up, let's go— isn't that a car pulling into the drive? I reach for the package again, but the contents spill onto the table and floor. I feel sick. Photos, large format, black and white, close-ups to near field, Bess in the bathtub, Bess and Audra at the zoo, Bess and me napping on the couch. Bess everywhere, both birthday parties, with Laney and Ducket sledding, with Audra swimming. Laney and me and Rosemarie climbing, Bess and Duck flat-out on the floor, her between his massive paws. Me sleeping, curled up with one of Paul's shirts in our bed. Skiing, on backcountry patrol. Talking to Wes during a wildland fire this summer. Bess making snow angels on Thanksgiving, *this* Thanksgiving, in our backyard. Bess and Chance throwing snowballs at Dix three days ago. Me naked, in the shower. Bess naked, in the tub.

Confused, terrified, I rifle through them. Scads of 4x5 photos, each one neatly dated and time-stamped on the back. Snippets of our life for months; who could've gotten this close for this long? Only one is in color, and not of us.

Foy.

Dead on red sand, his head still turned at a funny angle. Earl J. Foy.

The man who killed Paul.

I left him lying face down in that desert, gathered his weapons, his knife and his gun, and slipped away into the night. I never saw him like this.

Only one person could've.

Rayburn Smythe. Foy's boss, the man who gave the order to kill Paul, and us. Jo and me. But—

Why spread dirt on the table—*NO!* I know before I wheel to face the shelf what it is, what they've done. Someone knocks at the door, but I can't move. Paul's urn is gone, only a small pile of gray dust holds its place. The same as here on the table. You sorry—

Scoop it up, Tally, careful. Get it into something, don't lose any. He asked me to sprinkle his ashes on the ridge above Jenny Lake one time years ago when dying was about as possible as the sun falling out of the sky, we thought, so I promised then and meant it. I just haven't been able to do it yet, and now he's gone. Somebody has him. Somebody connected to the man who killed him.

Rayburn Smythe.

Unstrung, shaking so hard my shoulders hurt, I

sweep the ashes into a small baggie and put it in an inside pocket, next to Ruby's piece of polished mulga—for luck, she said, did she know this was coming?—then reach for the smaller package. Newspaper wrapping, tied with string.

Whatever's here, you can deal with it, Tally. You've been through worse before. Get it out in the open, reach Audra and have her and Bess steer clear till it's done, Pony was righter than she knew. Vince calls from outside, "Tally, if you're in there, you need to come out with your hands up." Stay quiet, I get three warnings before they blow through, it's okay—

But then the wrapping falls away from the package, and my skin crawls, the shaking stops, a low moan escapes, there is no way to plan for something like this, I was wrong. It is not okay.

It will never be okay again.

~

Bess's nightshirt. Folded neatly, it's her favorite, the one she asks for every night, the one with the tiny yellow rosebuds she picked out this summer in Saratoga when we went camping on the Medicine Bow, the one she packed for Las Vegas for herself, only it's different now. Covered in a dark muddy substance.

Dried blood. Just like Paul's when I found him. You don't forget that sort of thing, can't. I touch it and draw back burned fingers. The top line of the note pinned to the collar says, *Do as you're told, no more, no less. Tell no one or your daughters die.*" A tiny square of a topo map flutters off the table to the floor. The only identifying mark is a small red *X* near the elevation number at the center. I turn Foy's photo over. It's inscribed:

All best,
R.S.

Time spins again, I close my eyes and hold on. A car door slams, a long way away—have they called me twice or just once? Can't remember.

So it *is* him.

Rayburn Smythe.

I knew one day I'd have to face him. Knew he wouldn't let it go, when he slipped out of the police's trap in Sydney and showed up at the airport the day I left Alice Springs for home. But *here?*

And why take Laney—

He'll pull me out somewhere, away from familiar turf. It's all a big game, I'll need maps, lots of them, and all the gear I can carry. How did he get through Audra? What did he do to her? Is that what happened when she called the last time? He cut her off. I need to phone Dix, warn him. Miriam, Josie.

Tell no one or your daughter dies.

Another vehicle turns into the driveway, the lights sweep the interior of the house and go off, then another. That'll be Jed or Wes, one of the seasonals. Somebody that counts as a person I can't tell. Or afford to run into. Snatching up the envelope, I stuff everything in my pack but Bess's shirt. It goes inside mine, next to naked skin. This child came from within me, Mr. Smythe. We outlasted you once, we'll do it again, I say in my head, the words circling and running back on themselves as I shrink from the sound. I am one heartbeat shy of stark raving mad; my ears ring, muffled.

They bang on the front door, ordering me to come out, hands up, it's Jed this time, I think. Clamber back into my touring boots—the hell with the wet tracks now, a few more on this floor might muddy the waters in my favor—and snatch up the feather. Run down the hall and into my office, hoisting my pack as I go, dragging my skis along behind, I need maps, they're in a drawer right over there, here, good—

Nothing. Whole drawer empty. How the hell am I supposed to find that red *X* without a bigger frame of reference? Move, Tally, they're go for forcible entry by now. From Vince's jail you can't do one damn thing.

Raising the far south window, I unlatch the screen and toss the skis out, crawl through, dropping to my knees in waist-high snow, stepping into my bindings, checking around the corner to be sure I'm still clear. An officer is moving to cover my back door, can't tell who, just a shadowy figure behind the garage, crouching forward, prepping to enter without an invitation. Moving as if I'm a menace. No code I can call. They're after me.

I become part of the night, fading into the snow-angel-pocked drifts that surround where I used to live. The storm cleaned their frames and edges, but the yard is still roughened, not pristine. If Pony's with them, she'll see where I've gone in a few minutes. If not, I have a few more. Either way I've got a head start.

2029

Verging on 8:30 now, this is taking too long. And raveling on me. I got about half what I need, in terms of gear, to be out in this weather. Package threw me off, forgot what I was doing. Still makes me sick.

The images from the photos tumble through my mind as I ski through the houses just beyond Laney's, aiming for the trees behind so I'll have some cover.

Somebody was in close. Real close. Stationary cam maybe, couple places inside. Bathroom, my bedroom, at least. And then all over outside, at Laney's, Audra's, on the river and in town, following the three of us, it's clear. For at least the last year, maybe more. Why didn't I notice? How could I miss that somebody was taking photos of us *in the bath?*

My skis bite into the crunchy roadside snow and bend; this short run of trees isn't a good place to hide, but I don't have a choice. I need maps. Have an office at work slam full, the VC's got stacks for sale, but I can't exactly walk up in there and grab an armful. Headquarters is lit up like a strip mall, everybody on overtime, my account. There are more cops than neighbors in the housing area now, both streets crawling with jackets. My best bet is Laney's. She's on this outside loop. I can come in from the back. Have to get in and out fast, hope the noise doesn't startle Ducket so he barks and they hear. Still snowing; that helps.

Skis off in the trees at the edge of her backyard, not bothering to shed my pack, I crawl up to her door and push it open, whispering, "Duck, it's me, Tal," but the house is dark, no lights, no sound, no music. And no big furry dog to say hello. In the ten minutes since I was here, did Darla come get Ducket for his walk? But why would she turn off the lights? Maybe took him home for the night? No, you nit, the window's smashed so you shut him in the office, remember?

With the maps.

Probably flicked the lights off on the way out, not thinking, Knucklehead, that's real helpful. So now you have to navigate in the dark.

I hurry down the hall, hands feeling the way— same layout as mine, same Mission 66 floor plan, thank God and the NPS lack of imagination—and into Laney's office. It's neater than mine, which is usually a good teasing point but now's just plain good. Can't risk a light, even my headlamp's too much, so I'll have to feel for her maps. Below the bookshelves. Plastic file boxes. She's got two I know, maybe three. Have to clean them out, sort through later. *Laney.* She's in hospital, unconscious, Jed said. Does Rayburn know that? What can I—

The room feels too warm and muggy—I'm sweating—so I pull off my knit cap and whisper, "Duck!" Kneeling and reaching for the map boxes—why isn't he meeting me with a hug—but then I feel something hairy and heavy on the floor.

"Hey D." I run my hands through his fur, but he's too still, soaking wet, something's wrong, I leap up and away, banging my left elbow on the desk, pack's so heavy it nearly pulls me over backward. *Ducket, is that you?* No sound, no panting, no drool, can't be him. I need a light, two seconds tops. Flipping the red lens onto my headlamp, I cup it in my hands and switch it on.

Let me out of here, I have to get out, I cannot breathe.

Gagging and crying, light off, I crash down the hall for the back door.

2035

Head tucked against the snow, I dive for the break in the trees behind Laney's house. Sobbing out of control.

Ducket. Shot just like Paul, no face left, then his throat cut ear to ear, son of a fucking bitch why'd you have to do *that?* He wouldn't have been trying to bite anybody, too friendly, not till they crossed the line anyway, tried to take Laney's things maybe? Her maps. Both boxes empty.

Duck dead on the floor, bled out right there, his huge gentle head mangled and still, pulled back at that sick angle, they'll never get that rug clean, it's like the puppy Mama found one summer. My father killed it a week later, one swing of a board, no thought, no regret, said, "Let that be a lesson for those savages you're raising," looking straight through Dix and me as if we weren't there. It was a lesson all right. Haven't said boo to a dog since then.

Didn't intend ever to do different. Until the white dingo in the Tanami and then coming home and Laney had this little black bear of a pup so I spent more time with Ducket than with everybody I know combined until Bess was born. And now he's—

I should've taken him with me. Should never have left him alone.

Oh, no—that bark! Almost a growl. He never barked like that before. I was moving too fast to think anything about it then, but how could I miss it? Someone was already in the office when I pushed him back inside. *"Back, Ducket!"* Into the path of a killer. I did that.

Move, Tally. Need maps. Have to hit my office at work, that's all there is to it.

But not now.

Now I need to find my skis and get someplace to wait and pray Pony doesn't pick up my tracks; she's wavering on this, not sure which way to jump. Probably has her doubts about me too, at this point, but surely she won't turn me in. *First Laney and now Ducket. And what about Bess? Audra? No. I will not come to pieces now. Pony. Go back to her. Find the skis and think about Pony.* She has to know I didn't do what Vince thinks. We've had our problems, but she has to know I couldn't do that.

Maybe tonight she'll give me a break. The rest of them'll eventually quit and go home, and then I can slip through to HQ. Meantime I have to find a spot where I can lay out this package and search it for clues. *Do as you're told, no more, no less.*

My skis are gone.

The place I had them stuck in the snow is empty. A deep plunging trail that I didn't make turns back toward the houses. It's him. Headed straight into the arms of the law.

All right then, go ahead on. I've got your six. And every law enforcement officer in Teton County's on your nose.

2049

Chest hurting—and not from exertion—I throw myself forward, only to reach the main road a few seconds too late. A small four-wheel-drive, foreign, I think, pulls away east. Where's the damn stop cop? I feel like screaming toward the residence area behind me. You're running a hunt and don't have this road shut down? *There he goes! The man that did it all. But you, you're digging through my stuff. All of you, like you've got good sense.* Tears blur my vision, I'm losing it. What now? Where do I go now? *Ducket's blood is freezing on my leg, my palm, I can't stand the feel of it. I should never have left him.* For a moment I yield to the cold and don't pull up.

Eyes closed, I see Ducket working the trail just ahead, determined to find Laney, turning toward Wilson without hesitation, but waiting for me when I called. Can it be that was just minutes ago? Head in my hands, I crouch low, unable to move a muscle. They've done it again, Rayburn's people, just like they did with Paul. Ripped everything away, down to the quick. Laney calls, "I can't see two feet in front of my face." The nightmare rides hard, not stopping with Paul now but a small girl calling not for me, for her dad, my foot on Foy's neck, once, twice, three times . . . it's starting all over again.

2059

The small bundle of Bess's shirt wakes me up, drags me forward. I put everything out of my mind but getting some distance between me and my house. Staying to cover when possible, though it's snowing so thick they'd be hard-pressed to see me, I turn, without conscious thought, toward the tiny Chapel of Transfiguration, navigating by feel and memory. Holding on by a thread from the past.

Last time I set foot in this chapel, Paul was with me.

We were checking on using it for our wedding. Eight hundred dollars for two hours' use, they wanted, the capitalist Episcopalians who run the place. More, if you needed a minister or organist.

"Society's roped and gagged marriage," I complained to Paul, bitterly disappointed, staring through the stained glass window behind the small podium, suddenly suffocating and needing to be outside. Always wanting, this was me in my life before him. Always longing to belong to someone, some place not fancy or fine, just safe. The old wooden building—which had charmed me for years, so plain, so sturdy, so unpretentious—felt dank and empty of grace.

Paul swung me up into his arms and carried me outside. Moments later, all four of our feet back on earth, he grinned that lopsided grin that never failed to cheer me up. "We don't need the paper, Tal. I'm here for life, hon, and you know it. I do."

"Then I do too." And that was it.

Our commitment. Other than to tease each other about the whole idea of socially sanctioned unions, we never mentioned marriage again, and I never set foot in the chapel either. Had plans to die that way. Despised the rich hypocrites who lorded it over the place and people like me who couldn't afford to be part of its community. Talk about usury.

So I'm uneasy about going in here, but it's a roof and a floor, and that's what I need. My mind is spinning, won't touch bottom. I've lost my grip somehow. Pattering on in my head about money and churches when my whole world's come unglued. What has a church got to do with one damn thing now?

It's due to me that Laney's down, and Ducket gone, Bess in the hands of a madman, Audra I don't know where. How do you begin to answer those charges, God or no? The warm smell of Ducket's blood hangs close, I cup a handful of snow on one cheek, eye throbbing and me grateful for it. Pain keeps you centered when a hole's just been blown through your middle.

I reach for the heavy wooden door in the dark.

2115

The nerves in my face burn like a brand, hot and cold, no relief. Doesn't matter. I have the photos spread out on the rough floor of the chapel, headlamp on, still red, and am crouching over them, looking for something, anything, when I hear it.

One footfall.

Then another, crunching through the snow cover. Just outside the only door.

I should've known. Pony saw my tracks, turned me in, they're here to pick me up, should've known I couldn't trust her.

Flicking my light off, wheeling to the back wall, I pause. I'll have to take them one by one, that's all there is to it, collect my stuff and clear out, if I can, go from there, where or how I don't know.

And then the door swings open, a dark figure steps in, and I coil and leap, hit with both feet, tumbling, but controlled. The person goes down in a heap, grunts, "Hey!" Stays down. It's a man. Is it Rayburn? Someone working for him? The one from the ledge? Same as the one in the vehicle or different? How many more are there?

Careful, Nowata, he's bound to be armed. Brief check of the shoveled path outside; empty. Not Park Service, no backup. Then it's just me and him. What now?

Pulling the door closed, poised to strike again, I switch on my light. The man cowers against a pew, back to me, hands in the clear. No sign of a weapon. Something about him seems familiar. Grabbing his arm, I ram it behind his back, forcing him to his feet and against the wall.

"It's me, Tally," he pants, struggling for breath. Eco-Jim.

"What the *hell* are you doing out here, and where's my daughter?" I never should've befriended this old fool. Psycho, like Pony said. Should've known better. Now he's fixated on us or something. But what's the connection with Rayburn? And what on earth has he done with Bess?

"I mean it," I say, grinding the words through my teeth, pressing my left arm into his Adam's apple. "If you don't tell me where she is, I'll finish you off right here."

"Your kid?" Eyes wide and uneven, trying to shake

his head—can't, if he moves, he stops breathing. "Haven't seen her," he manages to cough.

I slap his face with my sore right hand, hard enough to bang his head into the wall, then pin it there, fingers clutching his hair. Too numb to feel. "Don't you dare lie to me!" I yell, throat raw, tightening my choke hold; his skin is clammy, makes me ill.

He slumps, moans, "I swear!" A flash of Foy in the desert rips through like lightning—my boot on his neck, once, twice, that awful cracking sound. Ease up, Tally, back off. Even if he's involved, he's not the brains. You can't blow through this on macho. They have Bess. *Back off. Now.*

I release my grip slightly; Jim nearly collapses in a coughing spasm, eyes scared.

"What about Rayburn? How're you connected to him?"

"Don't know any Rayburn."

"Australian. Big man, tall, blond. Walks with a limp I gave him. So where is he?"

"I have never seen such a man, swear. I just came out here, to pray for you."

"Whatever the hell for?"

"It sounded as if you needed it."

"Sounded where? We're radio blackout."

"It's all over the local channels, has been, last half hour. They're looking for you, say you're armed. Dangerous." So I'm a fugitive, first order. Vince has kicked things up another notch, brought the public in on it. So much for his worries I've got ears.

What the hell do I do now?

"I drove to your place first, Tally, but they were thick over there, so I came here. I do that, sometimes. They meant well, whoever built this church, don't you think?" he says, weakly, tentatively, the coughing fit finally easing.

Rougher than necessary, I drop my arms from Jim's neck and shove him into the nearest corner. He struggles to breathe, wheezing, no way he could've brought Laney off that mountain, he's not right for this. Bad fit. Wrong feet. Too short. I'm missing something. "Keep your hands out where I can see them."

"Somebody has your daughter?" he asks, staring transfixed at the photos scattered on the floor. He's never seen them before, I'd stake my life on it. No glimmer of anything at first, then a creeping comprehension, something akin to horror. "Who would do that?"

"And shut the hell up so I can think!"

2122

Minutes later, still no closer to knowing what my instructions are—there's nothing on any of these photos but time and date stamps—I finally come to the tiny piece of topo with the red *X*. On the back are some numbers I missed before. Neatly printed: 16.12 1500.

Date and time, has to be. Date backward like the Aussies do it, military time, December 16, 3 P.M.

Clearly I'm supposed to be at this *X* tomorrow, 1500. But where the hell is the *X?* Only a few contour lines and one elevation show, 8276, it could be anywhere in the Rockies.

"Tally."

"Shut the hell up."

"Somebody's coming."

Hurrying to the nearest window, I see lights weaving their way across the open meadow behind the chapel. Jim's right. Three lights, in a point-and-flank pattern. Pony found my trail, and she didn't dawdle, probably agrees with Jed that I'll be safer in custody. They'll be here in a matter of minutes. Two maybe, three tops. Swiftly I scoop up the photos, stuffing them into the package—have to go quick, but where? Shouldering my pack, I flick open the blade of Paul's knife and grab Jim's arm, steer him along in front of me. "Move," I hiss in his ear. "Yell or alert them, you're dead, got it?"

He nods and stumbles forward, onto his knees in the snow-covered path. "Get the hell up!" I whisper, dragging him back to his feet, struggling to hold onto my footing. Damn it, why did he have to show up here? This was hard enough before. I thought all eco-warriors were atheists, but no, I get one who *prays.*

"I am not your enemy, Tally," he murmurs quietly as I push him down the long path. The lights are bobbing steadily this way, moving at a good clip; tracking on snow's like following a double yellow line down the middle of black asphalt unless your perp's got a big lead, which I don't. And if they've communicated direction of travel to base, Vince will have a squad car waiting for us at the road, too. "I'm not. I'm your friend."

"Shut up," I hiss. I'm sick of people right now, just tired of the whole damn species. The sound of Bess's cries fill my ears; I can't stand this, just *can't*. She was calling for me yesterday—has he had her since then?

"My truck's over there, in the pullout. I'll give you a ride." No cops, not yet.

"No way. I'll drive—where are the keys?"

"What will you do about the roadblock?"

He's right. They'll have the park entrance sewed up tight by now for sure. This can't be happening, none of this! How am I supposed to get to Bess from jail? Rayburn means what he says. I *cannot* be arrested. Not now. "I came through, Tally, just before. Told them I was coming to pray. I can get us out, if you'll trust me."

Torn, I see the lights of a vehicle headed our way from the north, and finally agree. It's not as if I can be picky about my options. But when Jim opens the back window to the camper on his pickup and tells me to crawl under a stack of well-worn blankets, towels, and old newspapers, I almost back out. "I don't need a ride, I just need a map and some skis."

"I have maps at my place. Skis too. Let me help."

"And why the hell would you want to do that?"

"You were kind to me when nobody else was."

Something about his sincerity clicks. I believe him. Have to, I'm desperate.

But what if I'm wrong, and he's working with Rayburn?

Then so be it. I'll just get to the SOB that much sooner. "Fine. Let's go." I throw my pack under the pile of laundry and recyclables and crawl in after it.

"Good," Jim says, scattering stacks of newspapers over my legs, tossing an old blanket toward my head. This is insane. What if I'm wrong, and he turns me in to Vince's crew? Or my own? What then? I can't do this, have to get out, take my chances afoot.

Too late. The motor growls, the gears grind and take. We get underway only seconds before the southbound vehicle comes along behind. I hold my breath, sure we'll be stopped, but we aren't. Whoever it is stays behind, pacing us to the park entrance. Cradling my head in my hands, trying to ease the throbbing, I hunch under the heap of cold refuse as we roll toward the checkpoint at the main gate. All thoughts of Bess have stopped, frozen in their tracks. If I think of her, I cannot function. Rayburn wants revenge. He is not the type of man to take it subtle or swift, or by proxy. Could've done that any time in the last three years, but didn't. He's waited till now. Bess is a tool to him, the same as Jo when he had her trapped at his camp in the Tanami.

Josie.

The message from Miriam on the machine. Call ASAP, she said. Eyes tight, I try to see the lettering on the note in the package again, paying more attention this time. *Daughters*, it said, I'm almost certain. Not just *daughter,* the way I've been thinking it. *Tell no one or your daughters die.*

He has them both. That would be his way.

The truck comes to a slow stop, refrozen snow crunching beneath the tires. I can see flashing red lights just outside. Carefully I ease the edges of the blanket down; all light recedes. Fingers stroking Ruby's tiny piece of mulga, I wait, flat on my back, no recourse but the man at the wheel. Bess's nightshirt weighs cold and heavy on my stomach, Paul's ashes lie still and silent in my pocket, negating the weight of my feather.

My situation—no, *our* situation—is entirely in the hands of a near stranger that I helped throw into the county jail five months ago.

God help us all.

~

Zero sum. Makes scorekeeping a cinch; points, and prayers for each one, moot. If you bring your girls home and they live to breathe on to a death of their choosing, you've won.

There is no *if not.*

2208

The kettle starts to whistle, and I flinch. Jim reaches for it from his green naugahyde captain's chair. He's making tea. Insisted.

I'm perched on the edge of a matching seat roughly

the age of Wyoming, surrounded by piles of magazines, newspapers, and books as high as my head. Thick blankets are stapled onto the windows, two cats are piled up on each end of an army cot, a small compost bucket sits in one corner. The stove's next to the other chair, the bathroom behind a curtain that appears never to have been drawn.

I don't know what I was expecting, but Eco-Jim lives in a hovel, the worst I've ever seen, and that's saying something. Jail might've been a step up.

That aside, he did rescue me, slipped me out of the noose the park had strung, and brought me here. Now he's making tea, and in spite of everything, it smells good.

"You can relax, Tally. There's no reason for anyone to look here. Make yourself comfortable," he says, stirring a dollop of honey into a cracked cup and handing it to me. I lean back, dislodging a stack of newspapers as high as my head. Now there isn't one clear pathway through this room. Bushed, I sip the tea, cradling the cup in both hands. It warms me through, except for the nightshirt's patch of skin. I'm not sure that can be warmed. Or should be. Even the thought of what it means causes me to shake so badly I can hardly hold the cup still. Jim flips the switch of his oxygen machine on.

"Sorry about the noise," he says, hooking the breathing tubes over his ears and into his nostrils. The places under his eye where I hit him at the chapel are red and inflamed. They look painful.

"I thought you were him."

"The man who took your kid?"

"No, yes. I really don't know." I don't have enough of this figured out to explain it to anybody, but suddenly I hear myself doing just that. The whole thing, too, Rayburn and Foy, Paul, Jo, and Ruby, the white, Lanes and Travis, the package and Duck, Audra with Bess and out of contact, probably dead by now because he'd have had to kill her to take my baby away, she loved her that much. "But he'll keep Bess alive, I think. Bess and Jo. At least until he's no more use for them." What is wrong with me? I never do this, never tell people my life story. Even Paul didn't know the big points. Those have always been mine.

"So you'll do whatever he says," Jim observes.

"Yes. But that's just the thing, he left me an inch of topo map with an X on it and a date and time to be there. Tomorrow 1500." There's an edge of insanity in my voice. I try to swallow it down. "That's three P.M."

"I know—I did time in 'Nam. May I see it, the scrap?"

Hesitant, and not sure why, I fumble for an answer.

"Look around you, Tally. This is my life. This is all I do," he says, motioning toward the walls, which I missed before. The room is papered with topo maps. Wyoming, Montana, Idaho, Colorado. All the maps I own and many, many more. "Well, this and write the occasional letter to the Feds and wish evil on a few large machines." He smiles. It was that smile, on the witness stand, that made up my mind to stop in and see him at the jail. He has the face of a young boy who hasn't yet learned the world's a bitch and then you die. Reminds me of Dix.

Before Jim's finished speaking, I'm crawling over the piles of books and papers, scanning the nearest wall. "I have to find that spot, narrow it down." Where would Rayburn have started from? No clue. Maybe he wants to take me out on my home turf, like I did him, which means here, Yellowstone or Targhee. Or maybe not. Maybe he intends to draw me away from anything familiar, increase the disorientation, confusion, somewhere north, or south perhaps? Toward Vegas. Where Bess is. Or was. "Damn it, this'll take forever, *and I don't have forever,*" I shout, hoarse, furious, tears welling up.

The room is quiet for a few seconds, then Jim says, "Without meaning to brag, I probably know these maps better than anyone. As I said, this is what I do. Try to help save the planet with my pen. Study the land from indoors, since I can't be out in it anymore."

"Fine, good. Here," I say, gruffer than I mean to be, sliding through the piles toward my pack. "Elevation 8276, that's all I've got."

Jim takes the tiny piece of paper and looks closely at it.

"8276," he says, getting up, unhooking his breathing tubes and draping them over the machine. "Excellent."

"It is?"

"Oh, yes, I remember that one, Geoff and I used to camp on a side hill nearby. It's in the Jed Smith."

"Wilderness Area. Good. Means we'll all be on foot."

"I wouldn't count on that, from what you've said of this Smythe. Somehow I get the impression he might think the 'no motorized vehicles' doesn't apply to him. There," he says, pointing at the wall a few feet from his chair. Sure enough, the contour lines match exactly. Relief courses through; I feel weak and dizzy and lean over to rest my hands on my knees. "It's up west of South Bitch Creek. You can go in over Jackass Pass or maybe drop off the back of Moose Basin, I don't know. We were never there in winter."

"Moose'll work, I can ski. I owe you one. No, make that several."

Jim is removing thumbtacks from the map's edges, hands trembling, worse now than when he was in jail. "Oh no, Tally, it's not about owe. Here, take this, you'll need it more than me."

"Thanks."

"I somehow doubt this will be the end of your trail, either. So you'd better take these others, too. Quads for Yellowstone, Targhee, Bridger."

Folding each map carefully, I lay it inside my pack.

"Now, what else do you need?" he asks, throwing open the door on an old standup cupboard. In it are stacks of gear, all vintage, but most never used. Mylar space blanket. Packets of ERG—it's been years since I had electrolyte replacers in powder form—tins of ski wax, skins, a very long pair of waxable skis. Alpine camo gear, full set. "I'll never use any of this again, so take whatever you're missing."

Within minutes, I'm packed and ready to go. Jim offers me a ride north to Lizard Creek. From there I can cross the top of Jackson Lake and head up the trail. Rayburn was clearly counting on it taking me longer to find 8276. He allotted too much time for travel. Good, I can arrive early, maybe pick up some info.

"But first you have to sleep, Tally."

"Can't."

"Yes, you can. And must. There's no telling what you'll meet out there. You can't start it tired."

Is this a trick? Did he lure me in here and befriend me just to call Rayburn when I doze off? Or Vince?

He reads my glance around the room. "I don't have a telephone. And if I'd been going to rat you out, I could've done it back at the park."

That, at least, is true enough. When the young ranger at the stop asked him to open the back door of the camper shell where I was hiding, Jim did, covering with a light jibe, "Only garbage and recyclables in here. Have to be a fool to crawl into that." The shell closed immediately, and we were released seconds later. So if he'd been going to say something, that was the time to've done it. Still—

"Those kids are depending on you being at your best. How can you do that on no sleep?"

Well, if it's a trick, it's a damn good one. He's right.

And decent. Didn't have to stick his neck out for me like this, especially after I nearly strangled it for him at the chapel. I cannot afford to let Rayburn make me suspicious of everybody. That's what my father did to us, stalking Dix and me before he went to prison. Busted up our first two foster homes and nearly burned down the third. Artis and Elaine were stubborn, though, rebuilt and added on at the same time, started adoption proceedings, and did their best to keep us safe. But John Nowata stayed in touch just enough to make us distrust everyone. For years. That's what it does to you, being hunted like a wild animal. You get feelers that scan for danger like bat sonar, and they read friends as close as strangers.

But if that's the case, what's happened to mine over the last few months? Missed everything. Cost my girls—I do need a nap. I'm tripping all over myself right now, and sleep would help. "Two hours then, not one second more."

"Take the cot. I never sleep before midnight anyway, most nights not before two or three. I'll wake you in two hours, on the dot."

Nodding my thanks, abruptly exhausted, I crawl in with the cats. They leave, miffed. Good, more room for me. I expect it will take an hour to even doze, this is a waste, I should be on the trail. What if 8276 is a red herring? Worse yet, what if they keep the entrance sewed up and we can't get through again?

Jim picks a magazine off the stack closest to his chair and opens it. Has he really read all these? No wonder he's upset about the state of the world. If I kept up with the news this well, I would be too.

Seconds later, one hand in my pocket, a dull thudding at the base of my neck and feet, I feel the darkness closing, Bess calling, "MomMommy, see Bess?"

~

From a murky well far away, I hear loud raps on the door, and start up only to bump into Jim, who is motioning me to be quiet and take my pack. Pushing me toward what looks like a broom closet; I can't possibly fit in there. The knocks come again, this time followed by an order. "Open up, it's the sheriff!"

Then another, "C'mon, Mr. Kemp, we know you're home."

Pony Sutton.

Jim starts to close the door on me, and I push it open on instinct, can't bear small spaces, haven't been able to since I was little, please no, God, not this.

But he's right, and I know it; they'll find me anyway if they search, but for sure if I'm not out of sight.

As the closet closes, light falls except for one long sliver that seeps in around the frame. I stand stiff and unbending. Afraid to even breathe. Think about something else, Tally, close your eyes; it isn't a closet, it's the side of a mountain, there is a wide valley beyond, you just must be very still. Remember the word pictures Dix used to build all those hours we were locked in the basement in Muskogee? Large sky land and one spirit tree, a woman standing tall with arms wide, us at her skirts, the wind in our hair.

"No one can get us here, Tally," he would whisper. Arm linked with my brother's, I fought suffocation and listened with ears buzzing for clues to what we would find when the door opened again, if it did. Whatever it was, I vowed to fix it, make it better.

So many fears ever since. Each on its own very small, almost nothing. "It's as if your whole life becomes a closet sometimes, love," Paul once said. "As if everything for you is a countermove to fear."

I did not answer. I had no words. Paul saw inside the tough shell I kept intact for everyone else. I didn't give him many details to go on, but he saw me anyway, knew my nightmares weren't limited to the dark but came into my days. My best response, always, was to keep plunging in and plowing through. One foot in front of the other. No matter what. Scared of heights? Climbing lessons and a job that forced me to climb. Scared of small spaces? For two years after arriving here, I crawled into a closet once a week, trying to drive back my demons. It never worked, but at least I tried. Is this becoming a litany for me?

The air feels close and heavy. Thinking cannot push it back. I close my eyes and try not to break.

"MomMommy," she calls, faint now. Almost a whisper. I shake and sob, arms empty.

Jim opens the door and greets Vince and Pony, and I turn my mind to them, wrenching it from my daughter.

Unfailingly polite, Jim is. Except in his letters.

Vince and Pony step inside, someone knocks over

a stack of magazines, and Pony apologizes but doesn't sound sorry. I peer through the sliver but can't see her. My vision's limited to one corner of the cot.

Where my neck wrap lies in full view.

Damn it. Vince might miss that—doesn't know me or my clothes—but Pony won't. Head down, I close my eyes again, tears pour down my cheeks. Why am I crying so constantly now? The blackness strangles. To come this far—

Breathe.

"You were at the chapel tonight?" Vince asks.

"Yes, I was."

"Why?"

"Praying. I do it often, Sheriff."

"Did you see anyone?" Pony interrupts, rough.

"No."

"Are you sure?"

"Yes."

There's a silence before she adds, "You know Tally Nowata, I believe."

"Yes."

"Have you seen her tonight?"

"No."

"Talked to her on the phone?"

"I don't have one, so no."

"You don't have a telephone," Pony says, disbelieving, and Vince continues, "When's the last time you saw her?"

"Tally?"

"Yes, Tally Nowata."

"You had an unclear antecedent there, Sheriff. I just wanted to be sure. I don't know when I last saw Ms. Nowata—several weeks ago perhaps?"

The conversation ebbs and flows, their questions and his short, polite half-truths. Or outright lies. Eyes still closed, I link hands with Bess and Jo, and Audra. Wherever you are, I will be there soon, I promise.

Making a vow I'm unlikely to keep—8276 seems a lifetime away. Cannot check my watch, have no idea of the time, but I can go nowhere until Vince and Pony leave.

If they do so without taking me along. Breathe, Tally. Laney is in the hospital, and that is a good thing. Focus on the good, like Dix always says.

"Show me some, and I will," I usually quip. How hard have I made it for my brother with all my tough love?

"She has a head injury!" Pony exclaims, and I wince. Her betrayal hurts. Even motivated by worry, there's no excuse for it. In her shoes I'd let me die with my damn head wound before turning me over to Vince. Pony's not right these days. Hasn't been the same since she met Travis.

If ever there was a time for prayer, this is it. I should do it, should just say, Ruby, let the women help me now, put blinders on Pony Sutton. I could say that, ask for it outright and mean it. Ruby and Dix think you can ask for things like that, and they happen.

But I can't. Will not.

The one thing I still have left is my mind. Without it, I may never reach Bess and Jo. Prayer is for people who believe in their dreams.

That is not me.

Not now, not ever again.

DECEMBER 16

There is a soft, blind whirring in my ears that drowns their questions and prodding. I bend into myself and remember.

"I do not believe in magic," I told Ruby one evening by the campfire, after the other women had sung themselves out. Even the neighboring dingo band had gone silent. Ruby and I were the only ones still up.

"I'm sorry, Jajana," I said, calling her "Grandmother," when she didn't reply. "I mean no disrespect to your teachings. My brother Dix believes.

Maybe you should have him for a student instead. I am too broken to heal." Ruby just stared into the fire, silent.

"And too angry—or tired, take your pick—to beg for a miracle."

At that Ruby took my hands in hers and squeezed them. Then, without saying anything, she stood and walked to her sleeping place.

I curled up by the fire and cried myself to sleep, eyes so dry they stung.

The next morning she touched me on the shoulder and smiled. "You need not beg. Only ask."

But the night was still close about me, so I shook my head. "Not me."

Since then I've made jokes of it to myself. Called down the magic. Laughed when things went the way they were going to go all along. But now, with Bess gone and in danger, I can't afford to joke. Or lose myself in a spirit world unconnected to now.

And yet I almost did just that. Thousands of miles and many months away from Ruby Piljara and the women who sing the world into being every night, and I almost asked for help.

For these moments I have forgotten now. That I am suffocating, hiding, buried in a closet, a woman whose lover has been lost, a woman with blood on her hands and a shadow of chosen evil on her soul. A mother whose child has been taken.

This is what dreams do to you, Dixon. I will *not* dream or pray. No one is listening to me anymore.

My neck wrap was still on the cot when Pony and Vince left and Jim finally opened the door to the closet with a new plan for me to go to the top of the lake on snowmobile instead—less chance of being seen, he thought. I staggered out, sweating and weak.

And pursued by my ghosts. Not people, words; points the rest of the world makes when your back's pressed against a wall and you're searching for a way to keep yourself together: Whatever doesn't kill you makes you strong. All things work together for good. If you survive it, you can help change it.

"Which lets a whole hell of a lot of folks off the hook," I once told Paul. "Kinda handy, ain't it?"

He shrugged and said, "Just bloom where you're planted, hon. I don't think any of us is given anything we can't handle. The hard spots let us exercise our weak muscles."

What nonsense. Only privilege could make a person say something that resoundingly lame, I thought, but didn't say. Truth exposes cracks in our fictions, so we sidestep.

So yes, Pony didn't see my neck wrap, but I still don't believe in magic. It is too elusive. Pony's been up for more than forty hours straight. Why should she see anything? The time I spent at Ruby's camp didn't transform me; I am still the same. Thinking about her and the other women helps me get through things, like that closet. Paul's birthday. The other anniversaries I wish I could forget. Ruby is my friend, and one day I'll go see her, take Bess and Jo so they can know her too. But that's all.

It is what I *do* that counts, then and now. Bess and Jo O'Malley, listen to me. You must not yield. There may be no healing in this world, no rescue, but you must hold on. No matter what he says or does, we *will* survive this.

We have already survived much worse.

0400

I rode in as far as possible and then ditched the machine—out of sight, I hope. My borrowed skis cut a thin trail now, schussing forward in the falling snow, silent, which is the point. There is no danger of avalanche here. That will come in the morning, higher up, when the sun starts to work on these south-facing slopes. I hope to be on the north by then.

It's still twenty-five miles to 8276, a lot of up and down, plenty of ridge work. My pack's heavier than I like it, but there's too much ahead I can't foresee, so I brought everything I could carry that might come in helpful. There's a strong emptiness in me now, skiing toward the unknown, but no longer for Paul. Bess is out here, somewhere. Bess and Josie, Audra. No guarantees I'm even heading the right direction, but when I think of this, I falter, can't breathe, all motion stops.

So I won't think of it.

~

Where does grief go in a crisis? Two days ago I was missing Paul every time I turned around, which was often. Struggling with ordinary places and things, unhooked from the world and myself. Now I still reach for the small bag of his ashes when I stop, to make sure it's there, I guess, but something has changed. Something bigger than me remembering our differences and the way we papered over them to be together.

From the moment Bess's nightshirt fell out of that package, the fierce ache for her father was gone. Still is. As I ski through the night, on a trail I've covered many times, all seasons, I probe for the pain but cannot find it. Paul is dead, I say inside my head, words I could never manage before without coming apart at the seams.

Paul is dead.

Still nothing.

It's as if a switch has turned off, and I'm done. If I had to put it into words, it'd be unnervingly simple. He's gone, and I can't fix that. All that matters now is the living.

And she isn't here anymore.

~

But while she was, when it would've counted, I couldn't make that connection. The instinct was there, of course, biological tie primal. Every time Bess stubbed her toe, mine hurt. For each baby sneeze, my nose itched. When she went down with that asthma attack with Audra last year and wound up in ICU, I got a sick stomach all the way up in Yellowstone and started home before I even knew why. So the instinct's true enough. But the affinities I fell down on. Way down.

I smiled at my daughter, yes, but never once looked her direction that I didn't see her father. His mop of curly red hair, his kind brown eyes, the way he ate oatmeal as if it were soup, spooning to the back of the bowl. The first time Bess did that, I almost fainted. When she slapped one hand upside her head in frustration the way he always did, I felt cold chills. And when she pulled one of his shirts off the chair and into her fingerpaints this summer, I nearly had a fit.

"I'll wash it, Tally," Audra offered, not understanding.

Snatching the shirt away, wordless, I hurried from the room in tears. His smell—the ordinary smell of him, not the hateful smell of his death—had faded long ago, years ago, but I had faith that traces remained, somewhere in those threads. Washing would remove him forever. Why the hell couldn't anybody *see* that?

When Jo came into my bedroom later that afternoon, her visit with us almost up, she crawled onto the bed and put her arms around me. Buried her sunlit red curls on my chest. "Tally?" she asked, tentative, and the sound of her voice and touch of her small, strong hands made me cry harder.

So I sat up against the headboard and tried to collect myself, to comfort her maybe or me, let us both know I was all right. Josie curled up in the crook of my arm and said, "Daddy's gone, Tally."

"I know that, Jo."

"It doesn't look like you do."

I nodded, eyes locked on a tiny box on my dresser Paul put there for me years ago. Untouched all this time except once a week, when I dust and set it carefully back into place. Jo was right.

"When are we going to take his ashes out like we promised?"

"Soon."

"That's what you say every year."

She was right about that, too. I kept putting it off, scattering his ashes, and didn't know why. Maybe I really was hoping for compost and better basil when he came home. For about twenty minutes, Jo said nothing at all, just sat holding onto me. "Are you tired, Mommy Two?" she finally asked, resorting to the name she coined on our trek through the Tanami.

When I nodded, she said, "Let me tuck you in for a nap." Moments later, with the covers tucked close about me and Paul's shirt in my arms, Jo started for the door, pausing by my dresser to pick up the box. Holding it in her hands, she turned toward me, then shook her head. Replacing the box, she walked on.

At the door, though, she stopped again, wheeled,

and marched back to the bed, planting hands on her hips, and there was a fire in her eyes like the old Josephine. The one who yelled at least as much as Bess when things didn't go to suit her, which was often. "That ranger we met today? Mr. Wes?"

"Yes?"

"He likes you."

"Well, yes, I guess he does. He's my boss. Sort of has to. It's in his job de—"

"No, Tally, like a boyfriend."

"Oh, no, Josie, hon," I said, suddenly sadder. "You've got that all wrong. We just work together."

"Nuh-uh. I can see what I can see. He *likes* you, Tally, I'm tellin' you straight." She had that look she always gets when she's sure she's right and the adults involved are stupid. Which is way too much of the time, ask me.

"So what? I don't like him."

Jo just stared at me, waiting. We both knew what I was going to say. I said it anyway. Some things need to be said to not be forgotten.

"I like your dad."

In a voice made old by early loss, Josephine O'Malley looked at me a long, quiet time and finally said, gently, "But Daddy's dead, Tally. You can't like him that way anymore."

~

If only it had been that simple then, we might all have gone to the rodeo together this week. Jo wanted to come—I said we couldn't. Lied and hid from the truth.

One fact accepted, and a whole host of proper behaviors flow from it. It was the fact I stumbled over again and again. Didn't matter that I'd seen his body, smelled its decay, watched Foy drag the swollen, bloated carcass of the man I loved around in the sand behind his truck days after the kill, shouting like a hunter displaying a trophy. Didn't matter that I'd fought to keep Paul's daughter alive, doing things— evil things—that had nothing to do with her survival or mine. Didn't matter either that I've done the same with his youngest daughter, and failed.

What matters is that I couldn't accept that one fact.

Only last night, when I learned our girls were gone, did it finally sink in. Too late now, I fear, but cannot let myself feel. "As long as you're breathing, there's hope, Taliesin," my mother used to say.

These are the words of a woman who died still believing.

That her daughter would outlast her history.

That she would find a way to make peace with her pain, and not visit it onto the world.

That, in the final analysis, zero sum's a sorry way to keep score, because once you've set foot here, you never really leave. Those you love tether your soul to theirs for always. You cannot count, code, or reckon with that; cannot dream or pray it away. You can only live forward, not behind.

Daylight breaks full as I work my way toward the ridge, skis strapped to my pack because the snow's blown clear of these cliffs. The storm's an echo gone east to the plains. I've had spells of raw confusion, breaking down, not quite remembering where I am, but then I'm suddenly very clear. Clearer than ever, mind racing along at a blistering pace, senses so alert they sting. Makes me think the confusion is a dream maybe. I really am fine, with the accomplishments to prove it. They lied about the MRI to trick Pony, and it worked.

I was on skins most of the night, not my own but Jim's, much older, but they still functioned. The nylon wraps the bottom of the ski and glides on a forward stroke, then catches when the ski starts to slip backward, which is great for moving upward until you hit too steep an angle. Had to switch to crampons and ice axe for a short section near dawn, and go a mile out of my way to avoid one slope that felt as if it didn't need the sun's coaxing to slide, but still, all things considered, conditions are decent. No more storm, Laney Greer. Are you well enough to know that yet?

I feel better knowing you are safe. It's clear skies and the feel of an inversion now, the temp's been rising steadily as I climb; probably 20 degrees warmer up here than down on the flats. I've already shed two layers. Moved Paul's ashes inside Bess's nightshirt, tucked the mulga and feather in my pants pocket, gritted my teeth, sucked down some cherry-flavored ERG in hot chocolate, and kept going. At this pace I should arrive several hours early. Don't know what I'll do then, but at least I'll be there.

I've tried to figure out Rayburn's plan, but keep drawing blanks. He wants to make me pay, that's clear, and he knows enough about how I think to use the girls as bait. I wonder if Travis really was working for him. If so, how did they hook up? Trav's connections? What is it that brings people together to do such harm?

~

Nice try, Tally.

Hiving *them* off from *you*, as if there is some great difference between.

You know better.

~

I have shut my mind to this thing for months—it was making me crazy: I had to. But now I am open again. They called what I did to Earl Foy self-defense in Australia, which is how I wanted to see it then, too, and no one challenged it. No family came to the morgue either; it was as if he mattered to no one. I wanted to feel good about that, but couldn't. Over and over I relived the moment of his death, my boot on his neck in that dark desert night, kicking once, twice, three times, and then four. The sound of his life receding beneath my foot. The raw rage that drove me later, taking Jo and running day after day to survive.

A few months after I got home, my waking nightmare became a constant dream of him dying and a child calling for her daddy. Unanswerable, her cries.

But not for lack of trying. On the first anniversary of his death, with a new baby as incentive to lay my demons to rest, I hired a private investigator in Australia to search for Foy's relatives. Had some notion that if I could just apologize and make amends, it would help. What I'd done could not be fixed, but maybe I could stop the nightmares.

It did not work. The investigator could find no family for Earl Foy, and I didn't have the money to keep searching.

No one alive knows the whole story but me. No one. People here have no clue what I've done, not even Lanes. They all know only that I went to join Paul for his research, planning to stay four months, and came back alone three months past that. Pregnant.

Pony bullied it out of me early on that Paul had been killed in a chance encounter, and she probably told that around because people like Jed got quieter and more odd, so then I dried up. There was nothing more to say. Only Lanes accepted that, and didn't turn away. The rest soon backed off at my walls. This is a tenet of friendship, that you respect each other's boundaries.

It is also the truest kind of lie.

One that etched the first faultline in my life here. Wyoming is no longer home. Who I have become can no longer rest easy in this place.

~

Still, I love the ancient peace of these hills in winter, ice fog bitter blue on my breath, waterfalls trapped in runnels of pale greens and aquas, tree limbs gone heavy with snow. All white, this world is. Even the greens are layered and swaddled in white. And the blue is so true I can never tell where it starts and the snow or I begin. Morality here is a simple matter: breathe till you die, and then die and be done with it.

But the women I come from have never been satisfied with that. "Choose your path wisely, child," Grandmother Haney said once. "It is your only chance to change the world."

Bess Haney. The woman who taught my mother nonviolence. I hated her the longest time after Mama died, hated with the clean bitter flame of childhood, only to learn later that her teachings had got to me too.

They didn't take on first pass, though, or second. Or twenty-eighth. One more test lies ahead: Rayburn. He has my daughters. He means to kill us, I know. Can I stop him?

Who will I be when all this is done?

0600

"Take your risks early, an old sniper once told me," Jim said last night, "and then just hold firm. The people I never had a problem with. It was the animals I couldn't take, even for food."

So he became a vegetarian. Killed for a living in Vietnam, but ate only plants. Had some problems with the ethics of that too, for a while, among other things, he told me when I visited him in the jail. Loved someone he couldn't have for four decades, and that did more damage than the war, he told me last night. Geoff, a local painter who recently died from AIDS. I saw some of his work in a gallery several years ago, but never dreamed our lives would connect.

When I woke from my nap, Jim was sitting there smoking a cigarette. He'd put together a pot of hot chocolate and one of tea, and dragged out two small thermoses to hold them. They were stacked next to a thin flask of whiskey on top of the alpine camo suit.

"The point of the camouflage," Jim said, "outside the obvious one of coloration, is to lump up your shape, make it less human, distinct," and he followed that with a ten-minute primer on evasion and shoot-to-kill patrols. Uneasy now, I'm trying to remember it all.

I would like to believe that I don't have the killing instinct, but my life, my choices to now, don't allow it. The learning time continues, I focus on the mundane, unable to hold fate in abeyance by will alone. Had I that skill, the Tanami would never have been.

Everything reflective I own is gone or out of sight, skis wrapped, poles too, even sunglasses in an inside pocket. There's a light gray fabric screen inside the camo hood I can pull down for sun protection, but that's not my first concern. When I get off this rock I can be covered head to toe, fingers to backbone; even my pack's got its own swatch. While on it, though, I'm in full gray, turtleneck and stretch slacks, moving for stealth, staying off the skyline, working what shadows I can find. Rayburn means to unsettle me, rip my moorings, break me down, and he pretty much succeeded last night. But one thing he can't do is take from me my love of this land, my knowledge of it, my years being out here, all weather, all seasons.

He had me on that in the Tanami, cold. I'd never been in a desert, never wanted to be, never prepped. Paul had enough knowledge for us all, I thought when I went, wrong without a hint of just how bad wrong till it was far too late. But here I'm at the plate, and it may not be home anymore, but it's still my backyard.

Something moves, off-kilter in the left field of my vision, and I turn slowly and scan, breaking off every few feet and doubling back with my good eye to up my perception. Nothing.

And yet not.

Someone's out there, behind me. I wondered how long that would take.

0604

So here I stand, exposed. With a foul-smelling dressing over one eye to boot. Jim got it from a *curandera* he sought out in Mexico when Geoff was dying. It's supposed to reduce swelling.

"I see," I said, thinking. Sure, it'll reduce the swelling—I'll puke my guts out, and there won't be any cells left to swell.

"I doubt it," Jim replied, with a mischievous smile. "But if you use it, you will."

The good that you do, a small handwritten sign taped to the wall near his cot said, *always finds its way home.*

Hmpf. I doubt that.

And yet I'm glad I decided to go see the old psycho in jail, after listening to him in court that day. Eco-Jim Kemp probably saved my life last night. And a few times over the next ones, too, I suspect.

Psycho, my foot. He may be saner than the rest of us put together.

~

The movement from behind is consistent. No clear attempt to conceal, but staying well back and careful when I look, which allows for no definition, no ID.

So be it.

What's in front has to occupy me now.

~

"Remember, Taliesin," my mother used to say, "this one thing you get to choose."

She's right.

How I behave, how I act when faced with the end—that's it, that's all I control. Will Bess have a murderer or a mom in me? One who kills or gives life? One who makes excuses for her meanness or outlasts it?

I've practiced this idea to pieces, run it down in

my head all directions for years: get in trouble, disable, move on, call for help. Let the gods choose the dying. Failed bad in Australia, but won't do that here. Not again. Now I've got warning, I can be prepared.

Rayburn's men'll be armed.

Then I know a few ways to disarm somebody.

But what happens if I can't? What if there are too many? What if—

The thought settles heavy, my sore eye stings, I falter. *What if I fail?*

Well, hell. Then I'll just do the best I can do and let the rough end drag.

Those are my grandmother's words, haven't heard them since the Tanami. Bess Haney told me I would meet Ruby, "a woman with the name of a jewel" who would be my teacher, and I did and she shut up. Not a word, not a phrase in almost three years from her. Yet now, here, they return with the force of a slap on the neck. Comforted, I take a seat on the ridge, fingertips resting against mulga and feather, scanning 360.

Nothing human but me.

~

Ranger Peak and Doane, Eagle's Rest, lie to the southwest. Moran's farther south, and Thor. Rammel straight west, and Red to the north.

Laney's wolves, moose, and elk are out here, somewhere, and that thought cheers me up. Killing and being killed, procreating, weaving themselves into the cycle of the whole. Making life in these mountains. And dipping into a ranger's bank account with no effort at all on their own, too; how savvy is that?

I must remember to tell Lanes she's being outsmarted.

~

I'll traverse along the topline now for a mile or so, slightly below for cover, and then turn down near Moose Mountain. By the time I reach the creek, I'll have only a couple miles to go. Three, if I come in over the top. Josie's with Bess, maybe Audra too. All tough as hickory knots; Rayburn may have more on his hands than he bargained for.

Hang on, girls, I'm coming.

1315

It's a good thing I arrived early. 8276 is a bear of a slope, crusty ice beneath a heavy, unstable snow load, looks like it could go any second. I scoped the peak from the ridge and at several points since, am sitting at the last one, still a good ways off.

There are no signs that anyone's been here recently, except for what appears to be a large round canister hanging from the end of a rope about seventy-five feet below the summit on the south side.

If I set one foot on that hill, the whole thing's liable to go off like a cannon. That canister wasn't hung there this week. Snow has crusted over it and the rope in several places; I'm surprised it's still visible after the storm.

So when was it placed? And how?

More to the point: how long have they been setting this trap?

~

While I lived on oblivious, grieving for a dead man, hunching away from my life, these men were preparing to draw me out for this fatal game. Setting the outside posts, marking the field, drawing up the plays, careful and deliberate. Nothing about this is chance.

They don't intend me or the girls to leave alive.

So, provided I even get a chance to test it, how well does my theory of nonviolence stack up to that little gem?

A blurred image of my father's face that last night holds steady on the snow just ahead, 8276 gone as if it never was. Ruby sits at her fire, winnowing seeds, and Dix at his, making tobacco ties for Sun Dance, bright colors for all the directions, blessing the hard parts of his life. Which includes me. Foy's neck breaks again and again, the snap reverberates in my shoulders and arms; I want to retreat but will not, and I know this.

I am not my mother, or my mother's mother. I have killed once and may kill again. I am too weak to live the one small truth that could save the whole world.

I am like Foy and Rayburn and John J. Nowata.

~

But I am also the mother of a child.

So how does Bess outlast her history if I do these things again? How does she ever escape if I tie her feet?

She doesn't, that's how.

If I fail her here, she might as well be dead. Nothing in the world will save her then, nothing can.

~

Do humans ever outlast our history? I used to wonder about that. Still do, sidestepping down the hill toward the approach for 8276.

Dix and me and our dad. Pony and hers. Even Audra.

Tall, pale waif of a girl she is, Aud. Straight blond hair, deep brown eyes—almost like Paul's on occasion. Eyes far too young to have known so much pain. Not that she ever lets on or complains; she just shows signs of the journey. So I do what I can to make her feel at home—Wyoming's a long way from London—small things. Tried to coax her into the hot springs on our vacation this fall, but she backed away, and wouldn't reconsider even when Bess shouted for her to climb in.

"Bad history," she said, so gaunt and sad that I decided to cheer her up.

"I hear you there. Know all about that."

Audra looked unconvinced. I don't know what got into me, but I was determined to make her see that whatever it was, it'd be okay because it could be worse. So I kept talking. "Take me and Dix, for instance. Got a dad in the pen, not for beating our mother to death with his fists and his boots—oh, no, though he did it, right in front of us kids, too, no less—but for killing the son of a white judge in a bar brawl four years later when he got out. Thirty to life, they gave him for that. Just three for my mom, though. So that's the outside corners of my world, kid. I know about trouble," I said firmly and laughed. This is the way my people take the world on the chin. I could hear it in my voice. Words I'd never said aloud to that point, not even to Paul, pattering out like matter-of-fact bits of chub.

Audra looked at me funny and sat perched on the edge of a lawn chair, frowning when some nearby children splashed her. She'll ride in a raft on smooth water, but won't set foot near a canoe, even in the driveway. And I've noticed the two times we've been out in the raft that she gets much happier when we reach dry land, too, but I never realized it was this deep-set, the fear. Which, I guess, is why I piped up about my father. "Are you serious?"

"Yep, sure am, wish I wasn't," I replied, gliding Bess around in the water. She loves it. Could pass for a duck, or baby seal.

"I had no idea."

"Well, don't feel bad. Nobody does. It's not exactly something you tell. But the pinhead comes up for parole in January, so if I get bitchy between now and then, you know why Or at least part of it." I had enough sense to stop there, not go into the nightmares or Paul and all that.

Audra nodded and stood up, took a couple steps back to avoid getting splashed again. "If it's all the same to you," she said, "I think I'll go to my room for a nap, eh? Catch you later?"

"Bye, you!" Bess yelled.

A bald eagle appears far to the west, distinctive only by the silhouette of its wing pattern and its white head. Paul loved those birds.

Bess wants one as a pet. I wonder how that'd go over with her ecologist dad.

1445

Fifteen minutes to all-out suicide.

My plan is insane. Come onto the top from the most stable flank and rappel down to the canister. But if this hill blows while I'm on it, I'll have fifty tons of snow on my noggin in three beats. This would make any head wound moot, Sutton, just in case you were wondering.

So I'm here, Rayburn Smythe. Will you send someone or just watch from a distance?

No one answers my silent, angry question.

1510

It's ten after three, and no one showed. I'm it.

Rappelling's out, there's crust ice beneath the new snow—I touch that, it blows. Maybe not immediately, but sooner than it'd take me to retrieve the canister and return, that's for sure.

Thought about hauling up the rope, but that's out too. It was placed before the storm, runs from under a sharp overhang about ten yards down, can't even see the line in places on the face, but too much motion might create the very avalanche I'm trying to avoid.

So I've set an anchor and tied in close. That way, if the wall breaks and slides, I shouldn't go along. *Shouldn't* being the operative word here.

Lying flat on my stomach, reaching as far as I can, I begin lowering a hook I rigged out of a 'biner with the gate tied open. Made a little sled for it, out of a plastic bag. That should help it skate over the surface a ways at least. I'm running it on a hank of parachute cord Jim gave me instead of rope, too, less weight. This is crazy. No way it'll work. The slope's not vertical enough.

Then again, maybe it is. The sled whizzes down to the canister, barely missing it. Now comes the hard part. Angling the line into place, getting that hook to connect. Thin cord—I'm used to 9mm at least—I overcorrect several times. Sweat beads on my upper lip, still no sign of anyone—1525, might as well be 3:30—*I need those instructions*. With my luck the next leg's forty miles and the time limit's two hours. That's the sort of thing Rayburn would do, so *come on*.

There. There it is, handle snagged. Easy does it. I start the haul.

For nothing. The harder I pull, the deeper the parachute cord cuts into the snowfield, but the canister does not budge. At all. Maybe it's me, no strength in my arms after the last couple days—the right's a wash for sure—so I reach for my haul pulley, rig it from the anchor, and roll up. Nothing again. No movement. The canister's got to be weighted. Or tied down.

Might've known.

Pulling back, I scan the mountains. Still nothing. That's it, then. I'll have to rap it, take my chances.

Uneasy, I drag out my harness and rig for descent, then drop my ice axe into its sleeve on my thigh and strap on my crampons. If I make it down in one piece, I'll have to have a way back up. Slope's too vertical to go without a line, not vertical enough for ascenders on the return. Go figure.

Worried about everything, I close my pack and clip it into the anchor too. Don't slide, don't slide, don't slide, I say to the mountain, stepping over the edge. Please don't slide. Give me a break. Half an hour tops. Ten down, twenty back. I focus on placing my feet carefully, reading the slope the best I can, right and left, above, below. If it starts to go, I might be able to throw myself out of the path if I catch the break. Miss that, and it'll be all over me, and the farther down I go, the less chance I have. Please don't slide.

Dix once told me the first prayer was all that's needed—"Repetitions don't help, Tally"—like he was in personal contact with the Great Spirit. We were really young then, our mom dead two years and us already gone through a string of three foster homes, so our fundamental attitudes about life were pretty well ingrained. Still are. He never has lost touch with his spiritual side; I've never rubbed noses with mine. Even at Ruby's camp I held back.

Too bad. I could use a little juju for this hill. Planting each foot with great care, I ease downward.

Six feet to go. Please don't slide.

It's not really a prayer, I'm just talking to the mountain, talking myself through.

The face is holding steady, I'm nearly there. Tie off. End of the line. Easy, bend and reach.

Lid in hand, I peer into the canister. It's empty. Nothing here. Nothing written on the inside. No instructions, no small piece of map. *What sort of game are you playing now?*

Suddenly there's a huge boom, loud. Snow spits above and around, another boom, second explosion of white off to the left, sharp splinters stun my face, what the—

Somebody's shooting at me, they'll set off—

The next thing I see is a roaring wall of white.

DECEMBER 17

All I remember is unclipping from the rope on instinct and throwing myself into that thundering wall, arms high, hearing Bess cry out, "Swim, MomMommy, swim!" the way she did at her first lesson. So I swam and blacked out, couldn't see a thing, came to still thrashing, coughing up snow. One leg half buried, couple ribs and one arm cracked up pretty good and the heck kicked out of me everywhere else, but otherwise alive.

It's my left arm this time.

Might know. That puts me pretty near out of commission.

But near's not out. Not by a long shot. A raven whooshed past as the sun went down last night, fast circles, happy ones, looked like he was having fun but clearly checking for today's lunch, too. I moved my right hand. Later, bub. He floated off. What on earth did Paul see in birds?

Been no sign of Rayburn or his crew all night—this slope's too dangerous to travel, I'm sure—but I've no doubt they're watching. Probably from the same spot they fired from. At first I couldn't figure out why they didn't hit me direct, then realized that wasn't their aim. Two or three good-sized rounds into the neck of this hill's all that's needed. You can do that from a long ways off. Elephant gun, steady hands. Should've anticipated that, not thinking straight.

But I am not out of this game yet, Mr. Smythe. Fourteen hours since the slide, and I'm closing in on the summit and my pack, maybe fifty more feet to go, that's a few hundred higher than when I started. Once on top, I'll regroup.

And then I'll find you. Instructions or no.

0600

It took over an hour last night to dig out my leg, and it's still not very happy, might lose the toes, don't know, but until then I'll use it the best I can. Might as well have a stone block nailed to my knee and try to walk—no, climb—on that. Makes the spots of frostbite I had before beside every last point. And my head wound, all you damn people back there in Jackson, is clearly a fiction, or I'd be a vegetable right now. No need for code, I'm still breathing. So there.

My ice axe, by some freak of nature, stayed wrapped to my leg and didn't sever anything in the fall. Most likely because every other body part was flying 180 degrees the opposite direction from all the rest. It's a wonder I'm not broken slam to pieces and entombed in a mountain till spring. Instead I regained my rope a while ago, and picked up the end of the one for the canister soon after. This means I'm tied in, at last, no more sliding down when I can't hold the placement and having to reclimb the section, and I'm almost back to where I started.

With my right arm I drive the axe straight in and hang on, shoulder quit protesting hours ago, no more need, pain's almost irrelevant when one of the main bones of your other arm's aiming to break through the skin. I forced it flat as I could before starting up, biting on my neck wrap to keep from screaming, which didn't work, then bound the break tight as I could around a short length of a tree branch that the mountain had helpfully ripped free while it was playing "Let's see if she's bounce-proof" with me. Passed out over and over. Woke up and started again. Finally got it wrapped.

So much for talking to the mountain. Just about as useless as prayer, seems to me.

"I need to remember to tell you that, too, Dix. You

and Ruby," I say, and giggle. It must be the tiredness, or the cold, the pain, the night just gone. Instead of crying, which I was doing too much of yesterday, I am laughing. Out loud.

Kicking my crampons into the side of this mountain, looking for a placement, missing, trying again, laughing till tears stream down my face at the look on Ruby's face when I sass her back. Tell *me* to pray?

If Rayburn can hear me, he'll know I'm done for. Better quiet, sound carries in these bowls.

No, you know what? No. It's fine, let him think what he pleases—that I'm insane or gut-hooked, too drunk to walk. Come to think of it, that might work in my favor. If he thought I was losing it, he might ease up. Give me an in.

So I throw back my head and guffaw, but my ribs and arms fight me, resist, and I end the laugh with a sob. The taste of old silver's back on my tongue. Pain gone chemical, adrenaline battling to keep me conscious. I never understood how my mother could take all she did and still keep going. Broken bones, busted teeth, eyes glazed over, almost never seen by a doctor, but she would still get herself around and us something to eat. Our ragged clothes, made neat and clean. Our backs rubbed and ears fed with a story or two or eight. She'd smile, too, make weak little jokes. I never understood that. Never knew the metallic taste that is the body's flat refusal to give up. The dark humor that is the mind's.

I know it now.

Fifty feet.

Just fifty.

Don't give out here, kid. You are so close. Please hold on.

~

The voice is unfamiliar.

Almost friendly.

The stern admonitions, the berating tone, the unkind, judging words, Nowata this and Taliesin that, Tally get a grip or some such. Not one word of that since the slide.

All my life I've talked to them—the ones gone, Mama and my grandmothers, Paul. Talk like it matters, touches base with the real. I've argued harder with each of them than anyone alive, shared more with their ghosts than I ever did while they lived, told more of my secrets to the dead than the living. Asked for their help every time I turned around, and aside from the occasional brief snit, usually did it fairly polite, not as a prayer but an outright request.

But I have always spoken to myself the way he did. My father. Callous. Cruel. As if I'd just as soon shoot me as look at me.

~

John Nowata.

I've thought of him more in the last week than in the last ten years put together. With good cause, I suppose.

Dix pulled me aside before they left for Vegas. "He's up for parole in a month. What can we do?"

This is harder for him because he and Shelby still live in Oklahoma, in the same house as when John first went to prison. We inherited it from our foster parents when they died, and Dix moved his family in three years ago. So they're easy to find, which isn't good. And John was tougher on Dix from the start, anyway. Hated him, I think. Was jealous of his own son.

"You can move," I replied, and it wasn't a joke or an exaggeration.

"Don't be ridiculous, Tal, I mean it. We can't move."

"There are some states to be in when a lunatic's on your trail, and yours ain't among 'em. Texas neither. Missouri, you're toast. Get out here. I'll help. You can stay with me till you're settled."

"But the horses—"

"Board 'em."

"And the house."

"Sell it."

"Our stuff—"

"You can board that too. I'm not kidding you, Dix. You need to be gone and not easy to find if they spring him, understand?"

My brother stood staring out my window toward Laney's. Bess was making snow angels while Shelby held Chance and watched, bundled up as if they were in Alaska instead of Moose. When he didn't respond, I pressed. "You know what happened before. You can't—"

"I don't remember very much of all that, sis. It's fuzzy, maybe since always."

"Don't remember? What do you mean—how can you *not remember?*"

Dix shrugged. "Sometimes I think I dreamed some of it. Or saw it in a movie."

"Are you serious?"

He nodded, eyes on the floor.

"Well, anytime you want details, just ask me, bro. I'll fill you in. It's seared on my brain for all time, wish it *was* a dream. Till then, bottom line: our father's mean as they come. You either get the hell out of his way, or you'll answer to me, do you hear what I'm saying to you?"

Dix shook his head, then his whole body, like a dog coming in out of the rain. He does that to relax before he gets on a bull. Then he put one arm around my shoulders and pulled me outside, gently teasing, "Do what I say or I'll whup the tar off your hide, huh?"

"Absolutely. Whatever it takes."

"Dix, are you harassing your sister again?" Shelby asked, laughing.

He grinned at her. "Thought I might win this time."

"Never," his wife said firmly. "Give it up, hon. She's the oldest. We always win."

And then we all threw snowballs at each other for a few minutes before Dix moved Bess's car seat to his truck and I sent him off with one last bit. "Don't drive too fast, and think Wyoming—it's where all the real cowboys live anyhow."

Dix grinned and patted my hand, pulled away, and they waved, Bess and Audra from the back seat. That was four days ago. Two days and a thousand miles later my brother was on his way to detox, and Bess was gone.

But Johnny Nowata's still coming up for parole. That's what they mean by justice in the U.S. of A.

~

History's done with me. Had its way. Something about now loosens, breathes free. If we survive this, John Nowata will never shake us again. There will be no entry to us anymore.

Forty feet to go, each step a built-in rest because my upper body's of little use. Started with the sun, but it's already dipping back. More weather?

Not good.

But I've worked in this climate for years, I can deal with it. And pain is my friend, keeps me awake.

~

Thirty feet. I'm nearing the little overhang they used to secure the rope for the canister. Something's on the line, near the anchor, tucked in behind it. What is that?

0800

Instructions.

No.

One blank sheet of paper, both sides.

1400

I thought I understood Rayburn before, had a line on his MO. Ruthless and cruel, yes, but I believed he would draw me in and exact his revenge with the girls present. Now I see my error. He'll toy with me from a distance until it's time. If I break and don't make it there, he'll just kill them and go home.

Either way, he will have done what he came to do.

And I will die as Paul did, knowing the ones who love me, those who are waiting and depending on me *and needing me to show up*, are just out of reach, beyond saving.

~

The idea alone—that one man could destroy so many and walk away so scot-free—put fire in my feet and drove me forward today.

The first thing I did was offload, dump everything I could do without in one plastic bag at the top of 8276. Extra gear, the package, everything I could possibly leave behind. My pack was too heavy, my injuries too severe and strength fading, to tote forty-five pounds of contingency equipment. It was a good idea yesterday, but yesterday's over, and the event's changed.

Beyond recognition.

Next I bound my left arm tighter with a wrap from my first-aid kit. Had to leave my ribs alone, though, not mobile enough to fix them yet. Then I changed into a dry pair of socks and insulated liners, which cheered me up. Dry socks always improve my mood, but so far my feet are intact, and I'm very glad about that. Lots of bruises, not much feeling, but my sore eye's open again, too, which is something. It burns some and itches now, tears up more than it should, but it's no longer swollen shut. I guess the *curandera* had a line on her meds. Lost my sunglasses in the slide, but wound up with my face little more than scraped in a few places. The flukes of the wild, what makes it through and what doesn't. There's no accounting for those.

Finally prepped, as well as I could be anyway, I forced my arms back into my pack straps, choo-choo breathing like they taught us in Lamaze, set my skis at an angle, and left 8276. Backed way the hell off and am now skiing a perimeter, looking for tracks. No poles, no way to hold them. Sorry technique; Jed would spit nails. Too bad. Mobility's the point. That and a circle around this mountain. They had to shoot from line of sight.

Which means they had to leave sign.

I will find it, and when I do, I will track them no matter how long it takes. This is what I've said to myself all day long. No prayer, just a promise.

~

In a small stand of trees just ahead, across a wide valley from 8276, I see the tumbled snow that I've been expecting. One shooter, stood at the base of that tree to get a clear look at me on that mountain. Stayed several hours. Smokes.

Chews gum.

Not concerned about being followed. At all.

Prints lead down the hill to the doubled skates of a snowmobile. Why didn't I hear that? When did he leave? While I was out?

So do they assume I'm dead?

Good, that gives me an edge. I plow down the hill, renewed, only to stop short. No, it's the worst; if I'm dead, there's no reason for him to keep the girls alive—no. *You can't just assume I'm dead and leave, don't you have to check or something? What kind of sense does that make? I could still be alive!* Ski on, hard, Tally— what else can I do now except try to catch up?

Stop again near the base. Another cylinder, propped up in the snow.

1430

Instructions.

Which I have long since disobeyed.

That wouldn't have been my first choice, or my fiftieth. Rayburn is upping the odds. There's no elevation marker on this piece, and the printed name of the site has been blacked out. Thanks to Eco-Jim, though, I know where it is. The Sullen Slipper mine, about ten miles away. I was supposed to have been there by dawn.

The anger in me feeds a hunger, of times before long denied. Pony in my house, broken and crying, as Travis banged on the door, loud and determined to have her back. When the police led him away in handcuffs, Pony left, more angry with me than with him.

I let her go. Then and later, too. The next time he beat her up, she didn't come to me. Or anyone.

And she never pressed charges either, even when he almost killed her. We'd always had issues before over violence. Pony was all for it no matter the cost; I was all against it the same, for what I felt was good reason. Neither of us would bend. But then we each faced it alone.

This break now defines us, and in it, we have crossed paths: her to my mother's, and me, well, somewhere else. If I had known Travis would come back to Pony's house that night last spring and try to kill her, I would never have called 911. I would've killed him where he stood. This is the truth of my soul.

But she pushed me away—just as I'd pushed her after Paul—and I was mad enough to stay there.

I am confused and angry, Rayburn is in control, the loves of all my life in his hands. My skis glide across the land with no sense of how fragile I feel, leaving one winding trail behind.

~

In the Tanami I left a single set of footprints, paralleled by those of the white dingo. Josie named her Eli Two and hung on, just like me, even after Foy shot her.

Ghost dog, she became then, but so real to us, we could touch her. And did. Gave her food, and she ate it. Kept watch while we slept. No accounting for that, so we didn't try, just accepted it, grateful for the help.

All those long miles, trudging through hot sand, pricked by spinifex till our legs bled at times and then scabbed over and didn't. Walking hours, even days, out of our way, hoping for water and finding the mapped pools briny and dry. But the white kept pace, and at the end, she went for help. Howled outside Ruby's till they came out looking for us.

I keep saying we'll go back to visit, Jo, Bess, and I, to see Ruby and her sons, the others who helped. We can sit around the campfire and laugh and listen and just be. Maybe walk into the desert a ways, toward the white. Maybe she'll come alongside again. I would like Bess to see her, just once, and to know Ruby for always. She is the only grandmother my daughter will really have. Paul's mom is too offended, not so much that we're "ethnic," I think, since I look like my father—dark blond hair and green eyes—but because we're so clearly not of the right class. The O'Malleys haven't even seen Bess. I don't think they want to.

The opening for the mine should be just ahead,

though I don't see it yet. Although the tunnel itself is closed off, there's an overhang and deep left bend that provides some shelter. Pony and I huddled in there through a rainstorm the first summer she was here. It's nearing three, ice fog settles in, the upper edge of the storm's crawling northward. Taking a deep breath, I sidestep, easing myself to the next point of this journey.

1800

And now I have reached it, gone beyond, to a time as white as the sky.

As the storm rages a few feet away, I sit by the light of the fire, quiet and warm for the moment, holding the tiny piece of shaped mulga in one hand—it is so very small, smaller than a penny, but oval, perfectly formed, I never really thought about that before, just enjoyed the feel of the hard wood against my skin. When she saw I liked it, she gave it to me. Probably not for luck the way I took it, but just to have. I was having trouble leaving the desert that day.

I need to go on now, but can't yet. The next leg takes me well off my turf, farther than ever from home. The stakes are neck high. Lose, and they die.

Don't, they still may.

I need a break in this weather, I tell her, dry tears underneath, not wanting to slow her down but needing her help. Careful now not to say her name.

~

The two newspaper clippings lie where Rayburn's people left them. The knife I picked up a moment, just till I recognized it as Foy's—the one I took from him that awful night and gave to her on arrival at her camp; she used it every single day I was there, releasing its hateful energy, it seemed, in a string of practical tasks—and then I dropped it. The blade gleams in the flickering light. He stabbed her with it and did not trouble to clear her blood before bringing it here. How do you get something like that through customs?

With the blade of Paul's knife, I stab one clip, dated December 7, "Unidentified Aborigine Woman Stabbed Near Jangaara," and hold it over the fire. It chars first, deep tar spreading upward, then bursts into flames. Then I lift the other one and do the same, December 10, "Woman Identified by Next of Kin." Japanangka Piljara, her oldest son. He has his mother's smile and her steady gaze.

There's a third piece of paper beneath. Handwritten, same block print as the note pinned to Bess's nightshirt.

> 7.12, *Yank researcher shot to death near spring,*
> *remote Tanami Desert. Cheers, R.S.*

I never knew the day Paul was actually killed. By the time I found him, he was badly decayed. Could I've gotten clinical about it, I'd have guessed he'd been there a week or so when I arrived. December 7, it was, then, for both of them. The words burn holes in my mind. I was still back at camp, waiting for him to return. And ten days ago I was—what was I doing then? As he stabbed her and her blood spilled onto that red weeping sand?

Dreading December 14, that's what I was doing, dreading the third anniversary of the day that I found Paul hanging from his seatbelt. Figuring out a plan to send my daughter to Vegas so I could have what I thought was much-needed time alone. Sidestepping Josie when she called to ask if we could reschedule our visit to New Orleans. Calling in sick to work so I could sleep in, something I never did before Australia, but have made an art of since—fighting back the dreams of Foy and Paul in the empty space of my house. So the actual day that he died I marked once again, my yes, but only by retreating further from my life. When would it ever have ended? Before all this, I mean. Without all this, would I ever have found my feet?

And what now? What if this is it, the end, Bess gone too? And Josie? *What then?*

Closing my eyes to the light, I hold the note over the fire, shutting my mind to the roar of the wind outside or within, to the Polaroid of the girls near my knee. Josie is holding yesterday's valley newspaper, cover page toward me.

So it is official. He has them both.

Raw terror in Jo's eyes—she knows the man she's looking at, and what he's capable of—and concern in Bess's, picking up on her surroundings maybe, for this would be her first go at meanness firsthand. Jo looks defiant, angry—hold that in, kid, don't let him get under your skin, turn your attention to Bess, don't let her draw his rage with one of her fits, keep her occupied and quiet, off his radar, and watch for your chance, watch for me, I am coming. We will work together, just like we did before, to get free.

Setting the knife aside, I grip the lower corner of the photo, eyes locked on theirs, and feed it to the fire, staring firm as the girls melt; their captured fear softens to cringing liquid, then smoke. Fingers trembling, I almost retreat, but refuse—no way will I let them stay trapped here. With one swift move, I lift Foy's knife and bury its tip in a wooden board. Release, watch it shudder. Cold blank fury.

~

I would run, anywhere else, run toward my girls no matter the cost, but must find the strength not to now. We are so close to the edge. He has put us here, deliberate, with the precision of a genius, the resources of a general. And the intent of a sociopath.

Snapping the blade of Paul's small knife closed, I return it to my pocket and stare into the fire. If I had just been able to avoid Rayburn and his men in the desert, what is happening now wouldn't be. People wouldn't be dying on my account. Rayburn would've stayed in Australia and done his worst to someone else.

And there's the rub of it. Would I wish that on anyone?

Someone without a child, maybe? Or children all grown up? But older children don't lose their need for a mom, they just feel it different places. Her sons came and went almost every day, sometimes bringing food to the fire and sitting among the women, laughing easy for a while; sometimes arriving empty-handed and hungry. Their mother was still home base, it seemed. So no, I would not wish this on someone else. It is mine to resolve. Three years ago I walked from our camp to the scene of Paul's death, almost sixty miles, and found Josie nearly dead, surrounded by the tracks of Rayburn's men. What came then wasn't fate, it was choices. Mine and theirs. What's now is the same. I can't fob it off on someone else.

I must set my mind to this thing about me, must turn it to understanding what these patterns tell me of the man I soon will face. And then I will have to crawl out into the night and go toward him.

But for now I will sit quiet, across the fire at her camp, polishing a thin piece of mulga between my right forefinger and thumb, and listening for what I couldn't quite hear before.

~

My people believe it's dangerous to speak the names of our dead, she told me at camp once, when I mentioned Paul.

Somehow it holds the traveling soul to the ground, stalls the journey, endangers those who follow. It can cause trouble for a whole village, she explained, and

Lord knows I'd had enough trouble by then. So while I was there the four months, I tried not to say it, and felt the peace of that, but soon after returning home I slipped back into our ways, speaking his name at will. Paul, Paulson, O'Malley, and bub, every combination between. It seemed to me then that trouble was moot.

But now she's gone, too, and on my account, because she helped protect me from Rayburn. So no names, my *jajana*. The least I can do is not slip up on this one thing. I don't want your thorn-worn feet bound to the ground of this unholy place.

No names. Not ever again. Your name to me now is mist before rain. And the storm's come already, washed us clean.

DECEMBER 18

The wind is excruciating, straight-line and icy. I'm in all layers, not for cover but cold. The fire's long out, I ache to move on, but I wouldn't make fifty paces in this. Winter's claiming its spot on this field.

I've used the down time to resplint my arm on a narrow board I found in the mineshaft, chugging a couple pain pills and the tiny shot of whiskey Jim insisted I bring, and the new splint's long enough to provide stability for my hand, too, which is good—no, make that great. Every time I bumped it yesterday, I nearly passed out, and that gets real old real fast, I still won't be able to afford to run into things, but at least now I can pin my sleeve closed over my fingers to help protect them. That, along with the mitten I slit to wrap them in yesterday, should work. One good point in my favor.

I also sweated through getting my ribs bandaged, dried and switched my outer layers, rearranged my pack, and tried to map out an unmappable future.

Three days, and this will be over.

And beyond?

Pay attention, kid, you're still in the running. Don't up your risks unnecessarily, don't burn and don't break. The crux will come when you reach Bess and Jo. He knows it; you must. Somehow you have to get ahead of his game plan. It's just like tracking a fugitive. Coming from behind's the very worst. You need to be out front or, at the least, moving in from the side on a timetable they don't control. Or predict. If you can just come in under his radar, you might be able to get the girls out without a fight. Charge back home, call for help—if Vince hears their story, he'll go after Rayburn for sure. We can let the law sort this out, put him in jail long enough that maybe I could get Bess grown. We could move.

Like Dix needs to now.

Something about that rankles. Why do we have to do the moving? The avoiding. Living on the run as if we've done something wrong.

It's not about right or wrong, Tally. Fair is not the point, my mother used to say. You're here, you're breathing, that's as fair as it gets. Everything else is gravy.

But if you turn mean to make your way smoother, or harm another for any reason, then you fail your own spirit, and you will turn ragged and broken inside. And then—

She never finished that sentence. But she left it unfinished a hundred times the ten years I knew her. My mother was trying to shape fine gold from inside the stove. The world is quick to tell me she's wrong, eye for an eye, tooth for a tooth, one wrong cancels another wrong out, same as in the days of Hammurabi. As a species we haven't grown a lick since then.

Except for people like Joy Nowata. She grew. From a small child with big dreams to a young woman with the guts to carry them forward even after they'd been nipped to the nub. I saw echoes of her in my mother's mother, too—Bess Haney. And in the woman with the name of a jewel. They all knew the same hard path, and had the kinder heart for it. Would you really wish for something better than these three women had?

~

Hell, yes, have and will. I'm no saint. Not even trying to be.

Neither were they.

What I wish for now is the courage to do what I know is right, to do that thing no matter the cost or how scared I am. That's what I wish for.

In the big scheme of things. But right at this exact

moment, I wish only that Bess and Jo could come home.

Finally, a break in the wind. Unbearably still. I step outside, walking like I'm ninety, and read it, wouldn't exactly call this clear, there's no stars, no moon, believe I'll take my chances. Maybe it's the whiskey, but I feel as ready to go as I ever will.

No wonder Dix drinks.

~

In the throes of a storm, the past falls away. Hours go by, no good landmarks, navigating by feel and by nerves. Twice I stop for shelter, once in the well of a tree, later in a snow trench scooped out—barely— with just one hand. I've built much nicer ones before. And I've been warmer in worse blizzards.

But in those cases I was either teaching or training or working, and had a point to make—to myself, to everybody. SAR services are for them, I always thought, the ubiquitous *them*. Other people. People like me are providers, the ones who sit on the lid. Be damned if I'll switch places without a ruckus.

Well, so much for that. Arrogance hightails it in on the petticoats of expertise. Truth is, not a one of us doesn't need saving sometimes, and to pretend otherwise is just dumb. So *there*. How about that for a life lesson, TJ?

The minutes bleed into day into night, day again. Half the time I think I'm lost, the rest I'm sure of it. Breaking trail, falling in up to my chin in places, miss-

ing the best line through because I just can't *see*.
Reduced to counting steps. I need some help with this
weather, I say to the sky. Need some help. Track down
my grandmothers there and y'all send down some
sunshine. Give Rayburn a coma while you're at it,
too, just till I can pull the girls out and make it home.
Now *that* would be of some use.

Bess's cries stop me in my tracks. Where? Where
are they coming from? Eyes shut, I listen, but there's
no voice. It's only the ice in the tree limbs above, the
cries a projection of a much thinner sound, nature
feeding a mother's desperate desire for contact.

"How could he *do* this to us?" I scream aloud,
undeterred by the fact that he could be listening. The
hell with peace and justice—I could strangle him, no
should, *will*, by God. Anger rides high, the heat makes
my left arm ache, good, go on, heal, blood flow is a
good thing, I'd like to see some of yours flow, you
sorry son of a—

Desperation will not help you here, Tally. The more
desperate you are, the quicker the girls slip away.
Rayburn, what he has done, who's helping him—all
beside the point. That's what these women are trying
to teach you. It's all beside the point. Totally. Say it,
say it, *say it* until you can know it again for the truth.

The only thing you control out here is yourself.
Don't be the weapon that ends your daughter's life.
Back off. Think smart. Move careful. Don't thrash.
Don't emote. Save the fury for a psychologist's couch

one day. Pay somebody to give a damn about what all's happened to you. But dry it up out here now. Dry it up and keep moving. Thirty miles down, twenty-nine to go.

The exact distance I walked from Paul's base camp to his Land Rover.

Rayburn has done his homework.

DECEMBER 19

The night passed slowly, and a good deal darker than I thought it needed to be, not that anybody's consulting me on such things, clearly, or they'd be a heck of a lot different than they've been. Blowing hard one second, viciously clear the next. Wind chill might as well be fifty below without any wind, though I'm sure it's not. More like minus thirty, I'd guess.

In one lee I thought I heard the howl of a wolf, and then several. Predators loose in the night. Like my father, Rayburn, and the man he hired who hurt Laney. To be an effective predator, you must be empty inside. Can't go in thinking or feeling, or they'll cut you sure.

"May cut you anyway, but leave the brain and the guts outside the door," I once heard my father tell a stranger.

The first time I laid eyes on Rayburn in the Tanami, we were well out of reach, no danger, and yet I saw it in him from that distance, in just the way he moved. Simple movements. Reaching for a glass, picking up a book. He hadn't got Josie yet, then, but I saw my father in him.

The emptiness that leaves them full for attack. Passion only for the kill, the closing in, total control for one split second. Everything else, irrelevant.

~

Maybe two hours ago, still a ways from the next point, it started again.

Someone following along, well behind. Thirty to forty yards.

Not intending to be seen.

Why hide? Why go to so much trouble?

You have the girls and Paul, me on a line like a bass, Laney and Ducket both cut and left for dead and only one of them pulled through that, and still you feint and weave, conceal? Why not just come out in the open, trail me in full sight? It's not like I could do anything. Yes, I'm late. You shot the mountain off onto my head. Keep doing that sort of thing, I'll keep being late.

Raising a fist in the air, I turn, finally, and yell. "Show yourself!"

All is still, no echo, no sound but the wind in the tops of the lodgepoles. Maybe I'm seeing things, losing it. Maybe my mind's compensating now for all the signs I've missed the last two years—inventing some whole cloth to make me feel better about being such a nitwit.

But as soon as I move on, the heavily clad figure reappears. Leisurely following me, not hiding now and staying well back, making no attempt to catch up.

Okay, fine. It's a free country, last I checked.

~

The trees groan under the weight of the snow, like Bess does when she has to put away her toys. Swaying against each other, except she leans on the furniture, one hand holding on, the other drooped in defeat at her side. Howling to make a point that this business of having to clean up after one's self is grossly unfair. "You're here, you're breathing, that's as fair as it gets," I always say, and she just takes it all up one more notch.

She's consistent about it, too. Has howled every day for the past three weeks, despite the fact that she picked the toys up every day for the three weeks before that and had fun doing it. Stubborn kid. Noisy. A lot like Jo when I met her. When Bess has worn herself out with protest, she slides down onto the floor and leans her head against her dad's favorite chair. Eventually—it can take from ten minutes to two hours—she gives up and drags the toys to their box. And carries the grudge till the next time she wakes, refusing a story if it's bedtime, refusing a back rub if it's just a nap.

To Bess everything's personal, and you cut off your own nose to spite your face fairly often. Heaven help us, I told Audra just last week in the middle of one of these tantrums. Aud was seeing the toy snit for the first time in all its glory. Bess usually saves that kind of behavior for me. "So what do we do now, eh?" she finally asked.

"Wait till it's over and ask heaven to help us when she's a teen," I said. Bess heard me and yelled louder.

If we get there, that is, to heaven. That's what I should be asking for today. Heaven help us get to her teens. And don't let her do something in the meantime to make him angry. Maybe that's the point of prayer: not to bring on the aid of the spirits, but to focus and fine-tune us. Okay. I can buy that. So yes. Please. Don't let her make him angry. That one bears repeating.

A limb gives under the snow and comes crashing down, leaving the trunk above with a new, open wound. My breath makes a fog just ahead, warmer air dissipating quickly in the cold. I pass a small frozen waterfall twice as high as Paul was tall. It's a miniature of Fairy Falls, in Yellowstone. I've never been there in summer, but we used to go every winter. Rent a cabin near the lodge and ski all day, from high in the hills back to the valley, weaving among bubbling hot pools and geysers, bison and elk, a few moose. I sat near Old Faithful for hours one time piecing all the connections together in my mind, from the rust-colored lichens in the warm pools to the huge mammals nuzzling the snow aside for the grasses. Each piece a part of a whole we did not create. Cannot create.

"That, it seems to me," Paul said on our last ski trip, "is the truest measure of our infinite smallness. All our efforts, our know-how, our pride in our know-how and all we have made, and still we cannot make something live. We lack the spark."

"Maybe. Or maybe we *are* the spark, did you ever think of that? Maybe this is what Dix seeks from the spirits," I said, not joking for once about my brother's passion for other realms.

I can't remember now what Paul said to that.

~

The person who's following has started closing the gap, not by much, just a couple dozen feet. No other attempts to make contact, just trailing along behind like a bloodhound gamboling a cold trail, held back by an owner who doesn't want to waste the dog's nose. Working for Rayburn, has to be. Can't be anyone from home; nobody but Pony has the skills to track me, and even she'd need a clue where I left from. Besides it can't be her because Pony would never hang back. She'd ski up and whup the snot out of me, drag me home in a bag. She doesn't believe in stretching things out. So it has to be someone from Rayburn's crew.

But why this way? And why now? Am I getting close to their base? There've been no signs. Other than crossing one snowmobile trail once, single machine, I've seen no signs of humans out here. So why send one to drub along behind me now?

Whatever. I could melt my brain on the whys. My feet and legs ache and shake, the weight of my busted arm throbs fire all directions. Back, neck, and chest. Every breath a stinging reminder of what all's wrong with me now, each inhale, new knives. I'm exhausted, have to keep focused, find new tools to push me forward. Soon he'll draw me in, that's for sure. I just need to be ready.

The route now wends back up toward the ridge. How many times have I done this already? I've about had my fill of this ridgeline.

But it's doing the job he needs done, Tally. It is wearing you down. Body and mind. Spirit.

For an empty man, Rayburn sure understands spirit.

So you want to follow me, do you? Muck about in the snow all the damn day?

Fine, then, follow on.

1100

All right, that's it. Had enough. I don't have to take this.

Summoning all my strength into one quick burst, I plunge down and around a bend in the half-light of the forest—you want to dink with me, bring it on.

Unclipping the parachute cord from my harness, I slipknot one end over a low-hanging branch and take the other one with me until I have a cross branch to loop it over. Then I continue with the end, skiing forward; come on in. Near the end of the line I tuck and half roll onto my right side, easing out of my pack, trying to protect my sore arm, then crouching immobile, mimicking a possum I once saw play dead. Come and get me now, if you dare. Had enough of your big-game-hunter crap.

It doesn't take long. The person rounds the bend in high gear, making straight for my trap. Fast. Somebody else been out here too long, I see, not firing on all burners either. Well, good for me.

~

She saw the trap, but not until one snowshoe had covered it and the second was driving in. Anybody else would've hit the ground and stayed there, for a few seconds at least. This woman landed in a dead roll and wound up on her feet again, legs tangled in my line but upright. Staring at me. No more possum.

Dropping the end of the parachute cord, I stand and ski toward her, stopping a few feet away. Small and wiry, face worn hard as this land, silver hair in a long, heavy braid, she's got to be local, old as no telling, doubt she'd remember herself but if she hasn't seen a century of history, she has to be working on it. And still to hit and roll like that? Could she be on with Rayburn? Another local connection, harder bit than Travis this time?

No, he'd never risk teaming up with someone this tough. He looks for people who are wounded in some way, with a weak spot he can sink a hook into.

Then who the hell is she?

"You're that ranger," she says, while I'm still figuring out what to say. "Wanted, I heard in town last night." So she lives in town. Then why is she here?

"And you are?"

"Not wanted. Did you know you're on the news?" she asks, shrewd eyes locked on my left arm.

"That's enough about me."

"I doubt it. It appears I can say what I please, you're in no position to argue."

"I'm tougher than I look," I reply, annoyed with myself for sounding like a juvenile to a high school counselor.

"And I'm younger. What kind of name is Nowata anyway?"

"Potawatomi. Now will you please tell me who you are?"

"Of course, since you ask so nicely. Adele Youngblood, Nez Perce and Choctaw, dash of the English both sides, not claimed by either and quite happy about it. So who's after you besides the law, Potawatomi?"

Only one thing she says really sticks. "Choctaw? How'd you get to be half Choctaw all the way out here?"

"Roads run both directions, haven't you heard? My people're movers, can't quite get that hunter-gatherer business laid to rest. Even the pen the feds put up out here to buy us off, hem us in, won't hold the Youngbloods. I've got kin in sixteen states."

What am I supposed to say to that?

"Not a one of 'em fit to claim." Her eyes gleam, like she's having fun.

"Look, I don't mean to be rude, but I really don't have time for this. Why are you following me?"

Adele shrugs. "You're in my backyard, meddling. Poking around. Why wouldn't I be following you—now *that's* the question you should be asking."

"Look, Miss Youngblood—"

"Adele. Who said I was a Miss? I've had my share—"

"Adele. Fine, I'm sure you have. But I'm on public land, on my own business, so I'd appreciate it if you'd just go back to yours and leave me be."

"You didn't come up in a woman's shadow, did you?"

"What?"

"With a mother around."

"I don't see how that's—"

"Oh, but it is. My business. How you got out here in my backyard making deals with the devil, yes, that's my business, too, I believe."

"Well, it's nothing to do with my mother. Or you. So I'll be on my way now," I say, bending over to reach for the parachute cord. One-handed anything is tough. "You just go back wherever it is you're from, and we won't have any more trouble."

"Oh, I've got no truck with trouble. Weren't for it,

my life wouldn't be half so entertaining." Adele has bent to remove the cord from her legs. Now she loops it, deftly, one end all the way to the other, retracing my tracks, snowshoes cutting into and over the ski trails. Fastening the loops together with an electrician's knot, she tosses the hank back to me.

"Thanks," I mutter, clipping it into my pack strap.

"Some days I even pray for trouble, just so I can have a little fun."

"You should be careful what you pray for," I reply, darkly, careful not to look at her. "Now go on, go home."

"Ah, but I *am* home, Potawatomi. I am. It's *you* that's lost."

Shaking my head, I turn to leave, reaching for my pack and struggling back into it.

"Sure you don't need any help?" Adele asks.

Eyes ahead, I ski away, as quickly as I can. Please just leave, old lady, before your curiosity gets you shot by the same crew that's trying to break me.

1400

Only now, when it's far too late to do anything about it, do I realize I should've asked if Adele's seen any men poking about her backyard. Standard ops for SAR tracking, Tally—to query people in the field— what were you thinking?

I don't know. Not much. Everything is a blur right

now. Can't hear Bess, but I can smell her at times, the soft sour smell of her sweat. And I thought I felt her once, fingers on my face, but when I reached for her, she wasn't there. It would help to have no senses at all today.

There've been no more signs of anyone. I'm far beyond the mapped point, making a wide circle as instructed. As punishment for being late, I have further to go this leg.

This was the first site that showed signs of recent traffic. The first two were laid over a week ago. This one, today. Not that long before I arrived either, judging by the footprints. They used a snowmobile, the same one whose tracks I crossed over earlier, to get within a few yards—so much for wilderness regulations—then someone waded through the snow waist-deep to tie the canister to a tree. Rayburn's sending me back to 8276, two "checkpoints" between. The day is wearing long, my face is cracked, chapped, lips hot. I'm so tired it aches to breathe. Breathe anyway.

I've tried to get ahead of them in my mind, Rayburn's people. Picked up half a bootprint at the tree, mostly worthless. Don't know how many they are, or anything else about them, for that matter. They're staying well back, that's one thing, so they're a good bit more disciplined than Foy was. No barging ahead. No target practice at the natives, human or animal. No threats. Have seen no sign of any breaks in the ranks either, like we did in the

Tanami. I wonder if all these people are local, or just some? How did Rayburn find them? It's not like you can just advertise, Criminals Wanted ASAP. Prior connection? Fluke? Some loose, last-round conversation bellied up to a bar in town? The Rancher? Cowboy? But how?

And where does Adele fit in? If she's not working for him, why was she so keen on what I'm up to? Sandwiched in between a set of storms just like I've been, back of beyond, miles from the nearest town. Following me like a damn animal, nose to the wind for the scent. She looked like somebody I should know. Have I seen her before?

No memory. But how could she be in town last night long enough to know I'm wanted and all the way back out here this soon? She's in good shape for a senior, but not that good.

Not possible. Not on snowshoes. So my gut's wrong, she's in it with him. Has to be. Knows I'm wanted, but not from in town. From out here.

How could you look in my daughter's eyes and then call me Potawatomi that way, almost like a nickname? How could you know what he is doing to us and just follow along, mildly curious? Or maybe you did it yourself. Did you do it, old woman? Get in close enough to Audra she'd drop her guard? Steal Bess away? Or Josie—are you the one that took her? Why would you do these things to a stranger?

It's the same question I couldn't speak in the Tanami. Same haunting lines. Same grim no answer.

2300

Nearing midnight. I've made it back to 8276. This time they left the instructions at the top, not far from where I buried my excess gear. That's untouched. Which means they're either not curious, or not good at sign, couldn't see it.

Rayburn's cutting the times, stretching the distances. It was a mistake, arriving at that first one early. Gave him a hint of my outside edges.

Those are narrowing every second.

The next mapped point is even farther north than the last was. Into Yellowstone country. Have to cross what I already did twice before. My strength is failing. I'm staying hydrated, dressed for it, eating on time not cue, building rest stops into each upward movement, taking the descents slow and steady, reading the turns far ahead and cutting them slow. Doing everything as right as I can to get it all fixed, but still I'm fading.

~

There's no fixing things in this life, not really, Lanes—you know that, don't you?

Can't fix pain or sorrow, regret. I understand now that the nightmares will only leave here when I do. The white flame tells me this. But tonight I won't see it, won't yield. Out here it would be far too easy. No Pony to kick me back into living. No Bess to shout me home.

~

Aside from Adele, who's disappeared, only the animals are keeping me company now. Picked up sign for wolves a few hours ago, and an ermine, a moose.

Wish I could've seen more than their tracks. Why, I don't know. Something to take my mind forward, away, maybe. Here is too troubling, by far.

Three years, gone so fast. Most of it spent with me standing head bowed, missing every sign that could've coaxed me back in. Pony, Jed, the crew. I walked out on them all, not in fact, but in spirit, which is worse. Only Laney wouldn't let go. No matter what, she held firm. While I groveled in the pain, woke myself up nights, calling for Paul and cringing from Foy and that damn little girl crying for her daddy in my dreams. Who the hell is she? Sure can't be me; I've never cried for John Nowata in my life, never will. Can't be Bess; I know her voice too well. Besides, if it was Bess, she'd be bellowing. This little girl sounds so lost, so far away, so small and hurt, I know I should do something, quickly. And would, if I knew what, where, or how. I hate this unending dream; it makes me crazy, takes over my days; I slip away from work and hide from everybody, afraid they'll see the guilt in my eyes.

Paul wouldn't have done this. He wouldn't have let go. He'd have sucked it up and gone on. That truth of him is in his journals, I think, his steadiness. Love for me, my yes, love for Jo and Bess if he could've known her, but not so deep he'd have let go of his life if he lost us. Paul knew how to dream without it tripping his feet on the road. Maybe that's why I quit reading his journals. More truth there than I could handle.

Until now.

When I get the girls home, I will read. To them, to me, to the night, to the day.

And I will live. Fully, from this moment on, no matter the cost. Zero sum?

I think not. This is fullness, all the numbers one can reach for.

Something large moves off to my right. I stop, alarmed. Too much thinking, not enough—

And then I hear the familiar crunch, and smell the musky scent.

Relax, TJ, it's just a moose. Neck deep in a snowdrift, chewing on bark. What a way to make a living half the year.

The moose doesn't bellow, doesn't rush away. That'd be too much trouble, burn too many calories, food's too hard to come by. I ease on off, almost smiling.

So that's the difference between seeing the tracks and the beast.

Everything. And nothing at all.

There is no zero sum except in the games of the mind. Here in the arms of the world, life is fuller than that. Even the simplest of things, like a footprint. Connecting with nature cancels the zeros.

If Paul were here, he'd write that down. Once upon a time, I would've too. That's how we met, writ-

ing in our journals during breaks on a climb. I haven't
touched mine since the day I found him dead.

I whisper the words again to myself. No zero sum
for the living, here all's full bore, toes to the road and
you sing or shut down. There is no middle of the road
for existence, Taliesin. No time to scribble now, no
means to either, but when you get home, you have a
habit to reclaim.

And a brand-new journal Josie sent me for my
birthday to start in.

I feel stronger now than I have in days. There is no
magic, no prayers, nor need for either.

DECEMBER 20

The fall came at the worst possible moment. Near dawn I crossed behind a large boulder, not realizing the snow masked a deep drop. I heard the loud angry roar as I fell. Straight down—not far, only ten or fifteen feet. No mountain fussing at me this time, none of Rayburn's doing.

Bear.

Griz, denned up. I'm just inches from the opening. A warm, rank smell rises. "They're not true hibernators," I hear Laney tell the tourists. "Not like the black. Grizzlies have been known to come out charging, if disturbed, even in the dead of winter. Which is why they den in such remote areas. Humans seldom ever stumble over them."

Oh really.

All the years I've spent here, being careful not to disturb one of these creatures, going acres out of my way to avoid it at times, and now, here, middle of December no less, when I can absolutely least afford it, I am doing it anyway. Big-time. Nose and knuckles to nature. The bear roars again; I try to roll to my right side, breaking my borrowed skis loose, the hell with them, I'll worry about mobility when my hide's in the clear, trying to get a foothold to scramble upward, forgetting my injuries for one clean split second, this bear connects it'll make my arm look—

Just move, Tally. No time for analogies. UP. Now.

There's one last roar, I make it to about six feet higher on the slope, and then everything lets loose.

NIGHT

The dreams run unbranded, Bess never here, always just out of sight, around the next corner, then the next, or is it one I can't see? The little girl calling for her dad, I should find him and bring him home, but can't. I'm not on the search.

I see places I've been, but unlinked, no reason, no time, no sounds. For a while I'm burning cold, heart dead as a stone, and then too warm, white hot, yet no sand, I keep looking for the sand, where the sand is, he'll be. Nothing hurts, that's good. My boot hits his neck, I hear her call me to stop so I do this time, drop his arm, walk away, my hands clean. So he comes for me like before but I don't resist, fingers close on my throat, heavy, fleshy fingers, strong in his need. His ring, hard pressed steel, leaves its mark on my face like always but none on my soul. It's all going to be okay, Tal, it really is. Bess is ahead, in the light. Don't say her name. Baby feet bound to now.

~

I wake unable to move, wrapped in something heavy, neck to toe. And warm. I cannot hear the wind; I'm inside, but where?

The light is dim, flickering from beyond a slab of wood laid flat on the floor. A long-bladed knife gleams from the slab. There are other things too, but I can't make them out. Am I tied down? My arms won't move. I try to raise my head, feel faint; the edges of my eyesight blur and blacken.

The corners of the room are too dark to make out. Is Rayburn here, then? Waiting for me to wake up so he can put me to sleep again permanent? Silent, mind racing, I wait. Listening for clues—Bess or Josie, the sound of a breath, a footstep or sigh. Nothing.

Easing into a sitting position—I'm not tied down, just wrapped in thick furs—I scan the room again, head so heavy I can hardly hold it up. There's only one door, less than six feet from the pile of bedding, and it's closed. The fire vents through a small hole in the low ceiling; heavy timbers line two walls. Underground. I'm underground. In an old mineshaft.

The Sullen Slipper? Hardly. It's sealed off tight, just a few feet from the entrance.

Then where?

How could Rayburn find this place?

And how did I get here? More to the point, how can I escape?

I crawl for the door and drag myself up, press my ear to the heavy wood, nothing, so I lift the crossbar and push. It doesn't budge. I'm trapped in here until whoever brought me comes back. Suddenly the air feels muggy and leaden, not warm and comforting, I throw my right hip and arm into the door, trying to break it free, I'm suffocating, have to get out, but nothing gives. In the door, that is. In me, everything.

So I crawl back to the bedding, curling up against the wall, head on my pack, breathing fast, trying to collect myself, slow down. There's a fire, Tally. He'll be back. If you pull yourself together by then, you'll have a chance. Continue this—

Forcing myself to calm down, I start over. You breathed fine when you didn't know where you were. Carry on. Carefully I creep around the room, missing nothing this time. Well used. Lived-in. There's a strong smell of wood smoke and food seared over the fire, and the pit beneath it is cured by long service, rocks charred many times over, one or two split from cooling too fast. A battered kettle sits on a stone warmer. Neat stacks of firewood and kindling line one wall, a set of skis, boots, and several packs hang from the other, the third wall embedded at intervals with heavy hooks, for snowshoes maybe, a rifle. Two wooden traps and three rusty metal ones hold down one corner of the room. Hunter? Escaped con or just Rayburn? Who lives here?

On the only shelf, a set of camping pans, one fork, one spoon, another long-bladed knife. Two tanned deerhides rolled up beside the wooden slab in the center of the floor. On it, another knife and an old mason jar filled with odd things—a handful of nails, spent shells—one more knife, this one I know. It's Foy's, the one Rayburn left at the Sullen Slipper for me, the one I buried in the wood in a rage, now it's here. Along with the package I left on 8276—Rayburn's first note, our photos, I should've burned all that too. A small object gleams from the center of the pile, and I bend to pick it up, realizing too late what it is. Recoil, drop, the ring rolls toward the fire and spins down on its side.

On instinct, my fingers find the scar on my face. That ring put it there three years ago.

But how did it get here?

Same way I did, it seems. Dragged in by this person, who has to be working for Rayburn. How else would he have the ring? I remember falling at the bear's den, scrambling, trying to escape, and falling again. Then this room. Nothing in between.

~

I want it to stop now. I'm ready to be done with Australia. Surely this has gone on long enough.

It is time for it to stop.

Not by me following the white flame either. This is *my life*; I will not relinquish it by my own hand. Ever.

So I must read the spoor. Cut for sign. Follow my own path home.

~

I start with the feet. Feet, always, I know best.

The soles on the two pair of boots hanging near the skis have the same wear pattern, long to the inside on the left; their owner tends to toe inward on that side. Inner heel of the hiking boot's worn harder than the outer, ball of the foot almost clean, though these boots have covered some miles. Rugged miles. Right foot toes out, heavy wear on the ball. Maybe an old injury of some sort? Touring boot pattern's less obvious, but still shows deeper wear toward the insole on the left, outsole on the right. Confirms initial assess. He comes down hard on the heel, toe-in, possibly flat arch, for one foot, and the opposite for the other?

Well, that axes Rayburn. He toes out on both and limps on just one, thanks to me. And his feet are four sizes larger than these.

Next I reach for the skis, lifting one down first, then the other, standing them belly out and propped against the wall. Good skier. Corrects for stride, no sign of toe-in or -out on this surface. The skis are old, waxables, but in excellent shape. The binding clip—

I've seen this pattern before. But where?

From outside, I hear footsteps. Descending to the door. Whipping the skis back into their places, too slow, just one arm, I sink to the bedding, kneel, lie down. Flat on my back. Same as when you left, whoever the hell you are. Sleep, Tally, be asleep. Gives you a chance to gain some info while he's not aware.

There's a clattering outside, things being dropped, heavy things, maybe wood, what else? I've seen that binding pattern before. Just can't think where. It's so close, tip of my synapses, was it recent?

As the cross brace for the door swings up, I remember.

That's the mark made by the bindings at the last kill.

The poacher.

We found your guy, Laney Greer.

Or rather, he's found me.

~

For what feels like forever, we hold the standoff. Me "asleep," him staring, I can feel it. Every cell clamors to make a break for the door, run away, but to what? I'd die in minutes out there without my clothes, no gear to boot. And my left arm's too banged up for hand-to-hand combat. So no, wait and pray there's another way out. One that doesn't involve too much activity on my part.

When the door finally swings shut, the man hangs something on the wall, quiet thuds—another pack? Snowshoes? And then drops something heavy between the fire and me. Heavy like a body, small. Bile rises in my throat. It's a wood fire. People have to eat, Tally. It won't be human, it'll be an animal. Another wolf? Laney Greer will have my hide if I don't figure out how to arrest you pretty quick, sir.

I stir, as if in sleep, make a small sound, inadvertently, I hope, then settle back, still, aimed straight at the fire. Lashes down, I use them as a screen. Can't see well, but enough to make out the lower half of a figure, kneeling at the fire, knife in hand. It is an animal, between us. Small, furry, not a wolf. Ermine. Jeez.

The poacher moves backward and stands up. Eyes closed, no lashes for screens now, can't afford it, I lie immobile. He stops near my knees, says nothing. I want to scream, What the hell do you think you're doing? But don't. Words make you vulnerable, open windows to the inside. As things stand now, he doesn't even know I'm conscious.

The poacher steps away, takes something off the wall shelf, something metal, it clinks, grinds, turns back to the fire, I hear his feet make the half-turn. For one brief second, I open my eyes fully. Then snap them shut.

Why the hell didn't I put that together?

Not a him, it's her. Nez Perce, Choctaw, and English. She's warming a can of beans. Pork 'n beans. Stirring it with another knife. She is well supplied with the tools to make short work of the living. Laney's poacher is a *woman*.

"Relax, Potawatomi, you're safe," she says, not turning around, hair shining silver in the light.

I stare back at her, openly now, but say nothing, and she picks up a small tin cup and brings it to me. I have no sense of time, night or day. How long have I been here? Long enough to warm through completely, at least. But how long beyond that?

"Gave us a scare, you did. Here, drink this."

I take the cup, but don't drink. "Who's us?"

"You think I'm with him, don't you? Your Mr. R. S., the one who's set all this up."

"Are you?"

"No."

"Then what do you know about a Mr. R. S.?"

"Only what I deduced from these." Adele bends to finger the items on the wooden slab. The package, Rayburn's note. "So he is a Mr. then?"

I sit up, too quickly, sloshing warm liquid. She reaches for the cup, says, "Easy now, Potawatomi, with that head you can't afford to move very fast. I worked on your arm, but I can't do much for the rest of you."

"Where am I? And why do you have my things?"

"Didn't seem you needed them anymore, though I see now that's not the case. Not didn't need—couldn't carry. Am I right?"

"Yes," I admit, irritated. "But you still haven't answered my question. And why were you following me in the first place?"

"I've already answered that, I believe, and sufficient the first time. I'm not in the habit of repeating myself. Dulls the mind."

"Because I was in your backyard," I say, beginning to get angry, remembering. "Did you bring me here?"

"That I did, Potawatomi."

"So you heard the bear."

"That too."

"And pulled me out, dragged me here. Wherever here is. But *why?*"

"Who's the little girl in the photos?"

I can't explain Bess, just can't. No reason to, either. If she's working for Rayburn, she already knows anyway and is just toying with me.

"And why is this Mr. of yours leaving you presents?" she asks, reaching for the ring.

I start to correct her, but stop. "How did you get that? It wasn't in my things."

"No, it wasn't."

"Then how did you get it?"

Adele looks at me and sighs. "Your road would be much smoother if you weren't so rude, Potawatomi. But never mind. I'll answer your question. I got it from the place you were heading when you came upon the bear."

"You went through my things?"

"That I did. Your pack, your pockets. Who do you think undressed you?" She's right. I am undressed. Wearing just my silk long johns. My clothes are stacked in a neat dry pile near my feet. The contents of my pockets, Paul's knife, my feather, the mulga, nightshirt, and ashes are placed neatly on top. Well, now's a fine time to notice all that.

"So you went to the next point and got this ring from there?" She's the poacher, Tally, why don't you bring that up, throw her off guard? No, keep your trap shut. Don't muddy the waters. We'll work on the wolves later. And the ermine. How can you kill such a gorgeous creature?

"I did. Long haul, that was. About fifty miles. Turned my yesterday into more work than I had planned."

Yesterday? So what is today? The ring. *Rayburn means me to quail. Eventually to break. Today must be—*

"What is today?"

"Today?"

"Yes, date and time! What is it?" I ask, suddenly frantic, searching the room for something tied to the temporal but coming up empty-handed. Except for my things, every item in this room could be twenty years old. Or fifty.

"In about ten minutes, we're coming up on the twenty-first, I believe—

"The twenty-first! No! You've kept me here this long? I can't—

Adele ignores my outburst. "So you'll be wanting this." She takes an envelope out of her shirt pocket and hands it to me. "More instructions, I believe."

There's a single piece of notepaper inside; another tiny map square flutters out as I unfold it. Bess's handprint, in a dark muddy color to match the blood on her nightshirt. Sick. Tired, overdone. Ridiculous, it'd be, anywhere else, but here—with her baby fingers trapped on the page—it makes me ill. To make sure I don't miss the obvious, Rayburn has penciled in a caption.

B+, courtesy Josephine

How can he know Josie's blood type? Full name? Does he really have us so neatly tagged? Mind dull, I reach for the topo square. Another deadline missed: 20.12 2200. Ten P.M. Two hours ago. Dragging out my maps, I start looking for the location. Maybe I can still get there.

Adele bends over and stabs at the map with one finger. "Forget it, Potawatomi. That spot's a hundred miles away."

She's right. I match the square to a point back south, down and across the valley, out beyond DuBois. There is no way to get there today. Even by snowmobile, from here, it'd be tough. By car, from home, I could do it, providing Togwotee Pass is open, but the site itself is still set about twenty-five miles off road.

Is that it, then?

I lean against the wall, eyes closed, wetter than they should be and it's not from the wood smoke, can't think about Bess and what he made her see before he took her prints. Adele says nothing, the hell with her for now. What now?

~

Without a word, I reach for my clothes, swallowing back the salty taste of nausea. Time for me to move on.

You don't like it, have to stop me, Miss Youngblood.

She doesn't try. As I drag a fiberpile sleeve over my busted arm—splinted now almost professionally—she stokes the fire and lifts the beans off with a pair of tongs. "Care to share?"

"Not hungry," I say, though suddenly I am. The knowledge alone makes me mad. I tug a side pocket open on my pack with a little too much force and feel a twinge in my neck that wraps around my shoulders and eyes. More than dizzy, it's almost a disconnect. There may be a little more wrong with me than just a sore arm.

So what. Still have to move. If you've got the money for pork 'n beans, why the hell do you kill wolves, moose, and ermine, old woman?

"I'm not in with your Mr. R. S., Potawatomi."

"He's not mine, quit saying it like that. His name's Rayburn. Rayburn Smythe, Australian. He's got a bone to pick with me."

"I'd figured that much. One bone at least, maybe two. Are you sure you won't have some food?"

When I hesitate, Adele reaches for a bowl. "You can have your own dish. I'll eat from the can."

"If you've no connection to Rayburn, why get involved at all?" I ask, accepting the bowl. I'm starving. Haven't had warm food in days.

"Like I said—"

"Your backyard. So you live here?"

Adele's eyes catch mine and lock. "You know the answer to that."

"Full-time?"

A nod, careful, deliberate. She knows I know about the wolves. What now? We both tense, not sure of the other's intent.

"Since when?"

"Since I turned eighteen. Sixty years next May."

"Alone?"

"Ah, now you pry," she says, a smile flitting across her face, quickly disappearing. She's still uneasy, doesn't know what I'll do. Should be. Poachers burn my hide. She's just lucky I'm too cornered on my own account.

"So your story about being in town and hearing the news on me?" I ask, opting for low-key. The fact is, I suddenly realize—a lifetime's earnest environmental commitments gone irrelevant in an instant—I don't really give a rip what animals she's killed at this moment.

"Just that, a story. I keep up with the news," she says, leaning backward and pushing some wood aside to reveal a small trapdoor. "With these." Two small radios. "Above the outer tunnel, the reception's good. Get the Falls some nights. Public radio and the park channels nearly always. I can even dial up the police band both sides of the range, excellent."

And what do you use for power? I almost ask, but stop. I'm getting sidetracked here. Just because she's the original mountain woman or something's no reason to dawdle, Tally. Move on. You have to try for DuBois. "Look, I need to be going, but thanks for the food. And for warming me up, fixing my arm, saving me from the bear, I'm sure he wasn't very happy about me dropping in like that."

"He's a she. Mama bear, getting on up there, like me. I've known her a long time. I call her Wylene. But yes, she wasn't very happy. Neither was I. Thought I might have to shoot one or both of you to get you out."

"Well, that appears to be something you don't have a hard spot with," I say, eyes on the ermine. I wasn't going to bring that up.

Adele measures her words, staring into the fire. Her rifle's back on its iron pegs on the wall. The wood on the stock gleams, well worn and well tried. "True enough. It's eat or be eaten out here. No 401K to fall back on."

"That simple?"

"That simple."

Oh, really? Something about the line of her jaw, her certainty that she's got this all figured out, sets wrong. "Do you have any idea how hard we—no, *Laney*, that's the ranger in charge of the wolf reintro program, the little short woman with me when we've been at your kill sites, you saw us, I'm sure—do you know how hard she's worked to bring the wolves back to this country? Let them thrive?"

"No, no idea. You people hunt them out, pay hide bounties for years, and now you want them back? That's what I was afraid was happening. And you go along with that nonsense, Potawatomi? White man's poisoned your brain?"

She has a point. A good one. The culture is insane.

Rip it out, plug it in, call it good. Whatever we decide is best *is*, the hell with—well, everything.

Adele's waiting for an answer, staring intently at me. The firelight warms my face. She didn't bring me in here to harm or trap me; she fed me instead, kept me warm, made the long trip to that next point and back. She's not with Rayburn. Too independent for him. He wouldn't be able to control her. So it's like she says. I just got into her backyard, and she kept track of why. Lucky for me. What she does to survive is none of my business.

"I have to go. Where are my skis?" My head still isn't quite right, but I've wasted far too much time here. I have to leave.

"Just outside the door. You aren't going to try to ski to DuBois."

I nod.

"You should go to his main camp instead."

"Would if I could," I say, pack slung over my right shoulder, reaching for the crossbar, which opens easily now. I've stepped out into the corridor, heading up a rickety flight of heavy beamed stairs, skis in hand, when everything stops. I turn quickly to stare down at Adele. "You—"

"Yes. I was over there just now, in fact. I've been keeping track of him and his bunch for two weeks. He has two kids with him, both red curly heads, and a woman."

DECEMBER 21

From the slow, grueling pace of the last few days, I dropped my skis and barreled down the stairs to Adele. Rayburn's *here*.

The next few minutes are a blur. Many questions, more answers. She talks while I unload and reload my pack. Event's changed, so does the gear.

"Watch your topknot," she says in farewell, waving me off, promising to wait here and not follow or intervene. No one else needs to die. Besides, with the information she's given me, there's every chance I can get in the back and bring the girls out undetected. Not that it'll be easy, in my condition. My arm's the weakest link—if I had my druthers I'd have it stacked on ice somewhere, but I don't, so it isn't. Can't call for help, which is too bad. I could really use Pony's about now. Especially with those sag-lines.

Rayburn has trip-wired the approaches with small explosives, two full perimeters of the camp except for the one entrance they're using. Adele says he and his men—down now to two—are heavily armed and have night scopes on at least two of the rifles. They trade watch at four-hour intervals, day and night. But there's a side entrance to the shaft they're using to hold the girls that they probably haven't discovered. It was closed off years ago. Adele stores her bait in there to keep from drawing attention to her home. So if I can make it through the trip wires, I can reach Bess and Jo. Some day, when this is all over, I intend to be amazed at Adele Youngblood, how she survives—no, thrives—up here, but right now, all my energy's aimed at two little redheads. Five hours till daylight. Before the sun comes up, it'll all be over.

The camp is less than a mile away, which is what got Adele's attention in the first place. Seriously on her backyard. Four men snowmobiled in two weeks ago, off-loaded supplies under cover, and left again. Adele inspected the boxes, decided they were up to no good, and began shadowing the site. Then Rayburn showed up, with only two men along. They erected a small portable yurt, a low-profile canvas hut, near the mine's mouth, and then laid the explosives, taking time off to kick-start the avalanche on me and plant the next instructions. Audra and the girls arrived two days ago.

When I asked about Jo and Bess, Adele said they looked scared and hungry, but that both of them were paying attention and that Josie in particular was scanning the surrounding area every chance she got. Looking for me, has to be. Good, kid. That's my in.

"And Audra? Have they hurt her?"

At this Adele hesitated, grimaced, and finally shook her head no.

Grateful, I continued unloading my pack. Had to go in light. Once I get the girls out, Adele insisted, I am to bring them to stay with her while I go for help. That's the ribs of the plan. Her last words, though, stunned me.

"I believe the young woman works for them."

As I sidestep down the rough wall of the canyon on this side of the mine, I hear her again, see her eyes as she sat there breaking the points off a set of leg irons with a maul, and yet I don't. Nothing I know of Audra squares with what Adele just said.

I don't believe she would betray us. Doesn't make sense.

And yet I can't afford to go in assuming that what I know is right. There's too much at stake.

Don't believe it. Won't. But I'll act as if I do until the girls are safe and I can figure out what Rayburn has done to get Audra to cooperate.

I'm down to hands and knees now, counting the paces but not with my feet. Passed the outside perimeter ten minutes ago and dropped the snow-shoes Adele loaned me there, the trip line right where she said it would be—run low through the middle of a small grove of aspens. Now on to the next one, and I can't afford to find it with my feet either. The first was beneath six inches of new snow, except where Adele's tracks crossed it. With the drifts at this lower level, the next could be much deeper.

Gloves off, I'm moving snow a few inches at a time, sweating despite the cold, full into my second wind, all thoughts of being tired long gone. My daughter's less than thirty feet away, the entrance to the shaft she's in is somewhere just ahead. The taste of old silver's back in my mouth. Good. I can use it. Better than a toothache for keeping me awake and on track. Feel nothing now but a buzz on my skin. Every hair at attention. Bess is in *there*. Josie and Aud. And there's nothing between them and me now but the ground I have to cover.

Rayburn's sentry smokes. I catch sight of him for a moment as I ease down the hill and around the back. I'll have to watch Jo and Bess on the return—they're both allergic, get coughing spasms, lungs shut down, we have to stay ahead of that smoke on the exit. Shouldn't be too much problem. We'll be moving fast. Our path's a good thirty yards away from the front, without clear line of sight, too, till we get back out here among these wires, and the sentry stays near the main opening anyway. They probably don't dare risk patrols, might set off their own explosives. Probably think it's not needed either.

None of them have much wilderness experience, or they'd have detected Adele. She's been close on their heels the whole time. But then she's been living right under the noses of the feds for six damn decades, they built a park and a wilderness area right around her, so she's got skills. I probably only saw and tripped her the other day because she wanted me to.

Pony's like that. Able to see and not be seen. Wish I'd had her teach me—

There it is. The next wire. Quickly now, I clear beneath. It's strung a foot off the ground, would've hit it sure coming in blind. The surface is icy, can't risk slipping, so I toss my pack over and step onto it. Leave it behind, Tally, to mark the spot. Next time you come through you'll be hoofing. Carrying Bess. From the side pocket, I retrieve Adele's parting gift—three sticks of ancient dynamite she scrounged from a road crew older than me. Hope I don't have to use it, it's liable to blow me into next year, all Rayburn's hard work down the drain—tuck it inside my parka and hurry on.

The two boulders are just ahead; my vision's well adjusted, which is nice because the leap down between will take faith, Adele said. You can't see anything, but the ground rises to meet you.

I cut my eyes at her on that one and was rewarded by a pain in my temple. And then felt silly because as long as she's been out here, she probably never heard that trite old saying. It's got to be twentieth century, teens or twenties, came along about the time people got romantic about my kind, I bet—which of course couldn't really pick up speed till they killed as many of us off as possible, and hobbled the rest—then somebody nabbed it from the Irish and attributed it to us. Had it printed on saucers and cups they sell to tourists in trading posts. Like a real Indian don't have sense enough to know that when the road rises up to meet you, it means you're about to get smacked in the face.

But then again, Adele listens to NPR and uses words like *deduce*. She's probably heard that trite saying and just about everything else dissected by scholars and elders alike longer than I've been alive. She grinned at my look and said, "I mean it literal, of course."

And sure enough, my feet find the flat stones, just as she said they would. Crouching into the opening, I switch on the headlamp, red-lensed to save my vision, leaving the outside behind. A narrow tunnel leads toward the mine, a heavy metal grate over the opening. Above and to the left, though, and well hidden from view, is an open chute. From this I can enter the main shaft from the side. One corridor lengthwise, one across, and I'll be above the room they're holding the girls in.

It's probably three. Still some time before they'll be getting up. Hunched over—they didn't build this place for tall people—I hurry on. The air isn't as stuffy as I'd expected, nor as damp, though there's seepage in some places. It's much warmer in here than out-doors, fifty degrees maybe, instead of two.

If Paul could see me now, my, what he'd think. You've lost your mind, love, he'd say.

You knew that when you signed on, O'Malley, I'd tell him, like always. In a way it is always. Minus the spark of light that he was in the world. And yet, now that I've let go, I'm beginning to see that again, too.

Rein it in, Tally, focus. As I make the final turn, I click off the headlamp. There's a dim yellow glow just ahead. That'll be the battery-powered lantern Adele said they're using. Heart pounding so hard I can't hear anything else, I crawl toward that light.

~

There are times when time steps aside, and you slip off the now like a grain of sand to the ocean.

Everything recedes when I see Bess. Everything but salty tears. They rain down my frozen face.

She's sitting on a pallet, wearing the same clothes she left home in last week, face dirt-streaked and thin-ner, I think, but not hurt bad anywhere I can see. She's just sitting there, quiet, playing with her toes. Does that all the time, has since she first sat up. Fascinated by her feet, I thought at first, but then later realized it's not fascination, it's a calming thing. Meditation, baby style, I once told Audra, who agreed.

Audra's here, too, asleep, bruises on face and arms but otherwise okay, it seems. I can't believe she'd betray us—no way, Adele's got it wrong—and those bruises argue my point. If she helped him, he made her.

And there's Jo, curled up behind Bess on the pallet, pale as a ghost, always was, and taller than I remember her being. It's been six months since I last saw her. She may be taller than me now, catching up with her dad in that way at least, as she always vowed she would do. Her hair's cut short, but still curly, and it's washed with the sun, streaked pure gold in places. Looks more like Paul than she ever did. Move on, Tally. You can look at them later.

Aud's on a cot in the middle of the room. Very small place to keep three people, even little ones. No openings but the door. And this secondary shaft, about eight feet off the floor, which appears to be grated and closed off from below, but Adele chipped the grate off thirty years ago, in case she ever needed quick access to this room, planning ahead for a federal assault that never came because we aren't as thorough as people think. While I was still asleep, "healing," she said, she brought soft skin rags here and wrapped them on the grate's edges. All I have to do is lift it back and climb down. Get the girls up here and gone.

This was too easy.

How can I be sure Adele's not at the front entrance now, informing Rayburn he's got a guest at the back door? Was it all just a big plot? A little too convenient that she'd be here and know all this and not be involved, isn't it? Be on my side in a battle to the death?

When has the universe ever favored me that well?

When it gave me Paul to love for a season, and his child to raise for life. Adele's on the up, Tally; don't squander your energy on doubts. You've still got some instincts. Trust 'em.

But what about Audra? I trusted her.

And have not a smidgen of proof that was in error either, not at this point. So I won't bail on that instinct either, not yet. Can't. Instincts are all I really have anymore.

As I watch, Josie stirs, reaching for Bess. When she realizes Bess isn't sleeping, Jo sits up and pulls her into her lap, rubs her back—Bess loves that, always has, it's genetic, I think. I grab the grate and drag it aside, good thing for those skins or it would've scraped sure, especially with me one-handed. Easing into the opening, I prepare to lower myself, but stop. The girls are awake, Bess will surely call for me. I need to get Jo's attention. She'll have to keep Bess quiet while I deal with Audra.

Two soft flashes of my headlamp, red sputters from the dark. Josie, look up. *Look up.*

Again.

This time she sees and inhales sharply, reaching too late for Bess's head, which swivels my direction.

"MomMommy!" she shouts, leaping from Jo's arms and landing on the floor in a heap, hands still reaching for me. Audra stirs and sits up, I ease back and drag the grate into place, can't risk them seeing it gone, peering from darkness to them, praying that Bess gives it up.

She doesn't. "I want MomMommy, aaaw—"

"It's the O'Malley gene," Jo says loudly to Audra, barely clearing Bess's wails, pulling Bess to her and holding her tight. Keeping her from looking my way. About to smother her in the process. Bess fights. Jo hangs on. "She had a nightmare."

"Well, quiet her. You know—"

Audra's words die in her throat, terror leaps in Jo's eyes, as the heavy door swings open with such force it bangs the wall.

Rayburn. He steps inside.

What have I done? Made it worse. Much worse.

Josie shrinks, Bess keeps yelling. Eyes cold steel, Rayburn bends over them, raising his hand as if to slap Jo. If I just had two arms, I'd land in the middle of that man this second. Maybe I should try anyway. The palm of his hand connects with her cheek; Jo's head flies back, Bess stops screaming, snuffling quiet, patting Josie's cheeks with her hands, flattening herself against Jo's chest. Rayburn raises his hand again, Jo stares him down, pulling Bess closer and her hand away so she won't get hit, doesn't flinch. That's it. I reach for the grate. I'm going in—

Stop, Tally.

Just stop. A couple slaps she can survive. A bullet she cannot. If you blow this now, you're all dead.

Pressing my back into the stone wall, I hunch on my heels and stare through the grate from the dark at my girls, willing them to know we are near the end of all this.

Hold the course, Josephine. We've survived him before, we'll do it again. Just hold steady, be you, feed the fire, kid, don't let it die. Don't you dare get agreeable now, it'll make him suspicious. Hold the course.

His hand connects once more.

~

"She had a *nightmare*, I said!" Josie shouts, between slaps, furious. The sound echoes through the mine.

The sentry comes to the door, pokes his head in, nobody I've ever seen before, rifle slung over one shoulder. "Need anything, sir?" Stateside. Not a hint of an accent. Another man joins him, eyebrows raised in a question.

Rayburn almost smiles, shaking his head. There's a look of near admiration in his eyes for Josie and disdain for the men he's paid to keep him safe. Can we use that? "Return to your post. Now. Both of you." Doubtful. We are all pawns. It doesn't matter if Jo holds her own.

Audra is standing, shoulders loose; I've never seen her like this. Hints of it, maybe, in the sadness, but never this. As if she's come unmoored. Maybe Adele's right, technically, that she's working for him, but it's not her idea. What did Rayburn use to suck her in? Money? Can't be. She lives too simply, has too few needs or wants. Family? Has none, she says, so not that. Then what? She would not have sold us out on her own, that's all there is to it. Means she's in as much danger as we are. Maybe more—

Rayburn turns to her now, brushing his forefinger down one cheek lightly. She shudders. "See that I'm not disturbed again tonight, my dear—"

The words hang in the air as he leaves, closing the door gently behind him.

Bess cries into Josie's shirt. Jo glares at Audra, who wilts, it seems, and returns to her cot, saying simply, "We need to get some sleep. Tomorrow we all go home."

As soon as Audra turns onto her side away from them, Josie's right hand and middle finger fly up. Not once or twice, but three distinct times. So much for my worries she'd get agreeable.

Satisfied she's made her point, her eyes fly to me. Louisiana's on third base, toes turned for home. Wyoming, get into play.

Grate aside, once more, we wait.

0315

Thirty minutes later, Bess is sound asleep, curled up on the pallet by Josie's side. I flash the headlamp twice, preparing to crawl down. But instead of waiting for me, Jo reaches for Audra, taps her shoulder. I freeze. "I'm thirsty," she whispers.

Good idea, kid. She hasn't just been watching,

she's been planning—the Tanami hardened her, prepped her for this—it's clear from the way she stiffens even when she looks at Audra that she considers her an enemy, someone who has to be gotten out of the way, if we're to escape. I pull my legs back into the hole and wait.

As soon as Audra agrees to go for water, Jo crawls onto the pallet by Bess, knees up, encircled with her arms, apparently simply waiting for her thirst to be slaked. But when the heavy wooden door closes behind Aud, she puts one hand over Bess's mouth, whispering into her ear, then drags Bess up, raising her as high as she can reach. I stretch one leg out of the opening, straight down, Bess sits on my foot and grabs hold, and I slide backward, lifting my daughter to safety. When my knee clears the lip where the grate used to be, I reach for her with one hand, and it's done. Pulling Bess to me, I heave and sob, then pry her fingers loose and set her aside with an inaudible shush, stretching my leg back down for Josie. You have to understand this, Bess, I think in my head, eyes locked with my daughter's in the dim light. You can't throw a fit now.

Then I turn toward the room and reach for Jo. Feet to the wall, Josephine, I say silently, locking my fingers around her wrist and holding on, breathing hard, deep, controlled, don't lose your grip. Nose over your toes, kid; I stare down at Jo. Tripod, remember the tripod, only move one foot at a time, keep the other three points stable, thank God you like rock climbing, or this'd be a hell of a lot harder. Bess crawls in behind me, clasps her hands around my waist. We are the anchor. I stretch as far as I can and grip the rock so tight my arm cramps.

Seconds later, seconds that feel like hours, Jo clears the opening. No time for celebration, Audra will be back any minute, we head for home.

~

"She'll tell him, the bitch," Josie whispers as we round the first bend. "I hate her."

Reaching one hand out, I stop. Maybe I've missed something in Aud. Both Jo and Adele can't be this far wrong. But I just can't see it.

Beside the point. If Audra's working for Rayburn, she'll tell him, and we'll never clear the perimeter of the mine. If she's not, he'll kill her, and I'll never be able to live with myself. Either way, I can't leave her behind. Pulling the headlamp off, I cinch it up and set it on Josie's head, pointing toward the end of the tunnel, drawing her and Bess close for one last hug. Bess clings to me; she has an inkling what's coming. People shouldn't have to do things like this.

Get over yourself, Tally. Fair's not the point. You're here, you're breathing, that's as fair as it gets. That they're still breathing with you is gravy. Now put on some damn biscuits. "To the end, turn off the light, and wait. Two clicks like this," I click my tongue, "turn it on, but no matter what else you hear, don't come back, understand?"

Both girls nod. I try to think what to tell them further, for if I don't come back, but can't. There is nothing to say. I *have* to return.

Jo settles Bess on her hip, crouching to keep from hitting her head, and starts down the tunnel. Bess reaches one hand toward me but doesn't cry out. Somehow she understands.

I can't watch, I'll fall apart. Turning, I head back to the room. This has to be silent and quick. Nonlethal. I'm still not convinced Audra's with Rayburn of her own free will, but I can't afford to let her warn him. Can't afford to have her die on my account either. I have to take her down and convince her to cooperate. One-armed. This is why you study jiujitsu, Tally. Pretend it's a drill at the dojo. Easy as one hand tied behind my back.

A truer analogy than I'd like just now.

I've barely dropped to the floor when I hear footsteps outside, and it begins to swing open. Flatline, TJ.

~

She's not resisting. At all. With me in my shape, Audra could've made this much harder, but she's making no attempt to fight back.

She dropped the cup on the cot when I hit her from behind, going for an armlock that would immobilize her mouth, and raised both hands instinctively. As soon as she saw it was me, she slumped. In relief, I'd like to think, but I don't dare ask now. We have to get out of here first. Left arm raised in warning, an effort that draws cold sweat and makes me sick in the knees—it's just rebandaged, not fixed—I loosen my neck wrap and hand it over, motioning her to cover her mouth with it and turn round. There is no fear in her eyes; she seems resigned. That makes a certain amount of sense.

Audra knows what I'm capable of, has stopped in at the dojo several times to watch us spar and once commented that my arms and legs should be registered as deadly weapons.

"Except I don't aim to kill," I replied, and she shook her head.

"And how much would it take to change that, eh?"

It was my turn to shake my head; no good answer for that one.

Now she runs the kerchief through her mouth, making an effective gag, and ties it in a double knot at the back of her head. I stand beneath the opening, point toward it and bend, bracing my right knee and arm tight against the wall, indicating that she should use my knee as the first step, my arm as the second. She doesn't hesitate, quick moves up, I barely feel her weight. At the top, she looks down, our eyes lock; here's the moment of truth.

If she goes on ahead, I'll have to rig the cot and pray it doesn't shoot out from beneath me, then run like hell to catch up before she reaches the girls.

But she doesn't leave. Instead she lies flat on her stomach and reaches both hands down for mine. Fingers laced and locked around my right wrist, the young woman who's cared for my daughter like her own for two solid years but who may now have sold us out to Rayburn supports my upper body as I plant both feet on the wall and climb. She could drop me, and there's not a damn thing I could do about it. In light of this, the gag seems unnecessary.

~

I hit the opening on my knees, whispering, "Down and left." Audra crouches into a run ahead of me. Seconds later we turn the bend, lose the light. I click twice; a red beam shines just ahead. So far, good.

When we get to the girls, I reach for Bess and the headlamp. Can't miss the look in both Jo and Bess's eyes when they see Audra. Pure fear. Even from Bess.

For the first time, I falter. Maybe I did the wrong thing, going against everybody's gut but my own. But there's absolutely nothing to be done about it now.

Reaching for Bess with my good arm, I hoist her to my hip and crouch, move forward, with Audra in front and Jo just behind. Very exposed here, if she really is our enemy. What else would explain how close in they got? The cameras? Who else had access?

No answers. No time. We reach the end of the chute, and Audra steps down, into the outside air. With Bess still clinging tight to my sore ribs, I manage to swing Josie down with my right arm. Audra reaches to help steady her as she lands, but Jo jerks free. Then I hand Bess down, and Jo pushes Audra's hands away to take her. A couple minutes later we come up under the two boulders and scramble out, headlamp switched back to off.

Only to see lights sweeping the perimeter. Flash-lights, and shouting near the mouth of the mine. We all back up, and I feel Audra tapping my hand, giving me my neck wrap.

She has taken it off. Is that it, then?

But Audra shakes her head in the dim light and whispers, "The cup had to be returned."

The *cup?*

The cup that she brought the water with. Should've known Rayburn would have that kind of control at this point.

Nothing for it, we have to go on. Putting Josie behind me and Audra just in front, I hoist Bess onto my hip. Dodge the lights and the explosives, just make it back across this little canyon to Adele.

Suddenly Audra stops, says, "Go on—I'll give you some lead time, eh?" And with that she leaps back down beneath the boulders, me whispering for her to stop in vain. Seconds later we hear her yelling from inside the tunnel. Calling to Rayburn loud and clear.

"See," Josie says, disgusted.

There's no time to even agree, much less go after Aud or come up with another plan. All instinct from here on. Holding Bess tight against my side, I plunge into the snow, Jo close behind. The light's still weaving, but only one now. Maybe someone went back in to check on Audra. Run, Josie, run. Over my pack, leave it, can't stop. On to the next sag-line—don't trip over it, Tally, count out the steps, thirty-seven exactly to it, moving faster now, drop that to thirty-two, thirty to be safe. There. As soon as we clear the hill, I'll drop a couple of these charges, and we'll have a chance.

Just clear the hill.

~

Rifle shots, semiauto, ring out as we scramble upward. Not too close in, though; they're guessing. Strafing the area, trying to put us to ground—better look out, they'll hit their own trip wires. But they'll have direction of travel in no time if they come through that tunnel. And if they've got nightscopes on those guns, we can't be on this side of the hill when they do.

They're in far less rough shape than we are. Not carrying a kid, either; they'll move much faster. Three of them, one of me—no, make that four with Audra. Why would she do it? Go back inside like that? To give us lead time, she said, but that doesn't make sense. We *had* lead time.

She has to be working for him. The girls have no doubts, and they should know. Then why didn't she just yell from where we stood? That would've ended it all. Come *on*, Tally, *move!* I wrap the last strap of the snowshoes Adele loaned me onto Jo. My legs are longer, not by much, but enough to break trail, and I've been in deep snow enough to know how to work it, so I'll go bare. Jo needs the traction more than me. It's still not good odds.

But at least we're outside their wired perimeter. I

reach for a tree branch to pull up on, my shoulder fusses then bends to my will, Bess tightens her legs on my waist, her grip on my collar, and whispers, like she always does at home, "MomMommy, me too."

"And I love you," I whisper back. Jo pats my lower back, reaching for the branch as I move beyond it. "You too," I hiss to her, and she pats again. Girl's from Louisiana. Been on snowshoes twice in her whole life. Hardly ever sees snow. They let school out when one flake is spotted. But she hadn't seen much sand before the Tanami either, and look what we did with all that.

Let's go, O'Malley girls. We got us a date with a mountain woman. Ten feet more, we can blow this popsicle stand. Literally.

~

Got two charges lit and thrown, hard as I could opposite directions. Both right in the middle of the sag-lines, though, I hope.

Confirmed. All hell breaks loose on this side of the mine. We duck and hold, count to ten, then start clawing upward, war zone behind. We have a window, that's all. When the mud settles, those men will be hot on our trail. Even if they don't know beans about tracking, they'll use the charges as a center point, ride a perimeter on this quad, and trap us inside. It'll only be a matter of time before their trail crosses ours. The question is: Can we be to Adele's before then?

How much ground can you cover when your whole world's at stake, Taliesin? A bullet zings past, they're shooting again, still guessing, I think—we've dropped behind the hill now—but it's pretty damn close for a guess. Move out. No time to philosophize when you're being shot at. Light on—we need all the help we can get while we're ahead—I plunge forward and sink in to my waist. Very hard to break trail when you keep falling beneath it, but there's no time to moan about that now. Just cover what you can; as soon it quiets over there, we'll have to go full dark again.

Josie looks at me and grins, face caught in the dim red beam, struggling with the heavy shoes, but game for the effort. "I *knew* you would come."

Bess hums, just one beat. Her happy hum. The thing she does when the hissy fit didn't work but she's ready to claim me again anyway.

I look at his girls, and see Paul in their eyes. And this, I finally see, isn't a bad thing. I'm not wishing to be looking at him anymore, not aching for his hands to take mine, his arms to hold me close, keep me safe, push back the world and the pain. He went on ahead, and left me them.

So be it.

I'm as safe as I'll ever be right this moment. I can live forward from here.

~

If they let me.

We're inside their new perimeter. Not deep enough in to maneuver much either. Headlamp off, tucked in my pocket to avoid a reflection, but they've got nightscopes, so we're grounded too. Tucked in the snow on a side hill.

They're in close. Real close. Both snowmobiles. Two people on one machine, one on the other. Does that mean they left Audra behind? Adele's still half a mile away. We couldn't move fast enough. Just couldn't. They have us cornered now and are working to close the gap, paralleling each other about 200 yards apart.

I have one last card to play. Taking out the final stick of dynamite, I bite the fuse off short. The girls huddle together while I crawfish about thirty feet down the hill, darkened headlamp in hand. Looping it over a tree branch, I click it on and start crawfishing backward. See it, please, see it now, don't pass, you'll see us instead.

The growling machine comes to a halt on the hill above. Rayburn or the sentry, don't know, can't tell, doesn't matter. He has to stop to scope. *Yes.* Crawfish on deck, crouch and light. If he scans to me before I get this fired and thrown, it's all up.

A blinding flash and boom tear the hill between us apart. I got that toss. There's a loud, angry roar behind the explosion. Human roar. Male. Has to be. The light got to his eyes inside those night goggles so he can't see. I didn't kill him, he just can't see for a while. Another window.

Scrambling back to the girls, I grab Bess and we scuttle on, bellies to snow. There's shouting behind us, that's fine, the second machine cuts across within yards of us, the two people on it zooming up to the first or what's left of it. I sure hope the flash blinded him, or there'll be all hell to pay if he catches us. And he'll be bent to do it for sure.

There's yelling, two directions, both men, can't make out the words over the buzz of the snowmobiles, but they're angry.

Suddenly the night goes unearthly silent. One machine switched off, then another. No words. Have they spotted us then? Pushing Jo and Bess to the ground, I lie flat over them, just as the dark is split by a rifle round. And then another.

Rayburn. Has to be. And he's not shooting at us either.

One of the sentries failed, became a liability, and Rayburn put him down. He has no tolerance for weakness, will not accept it.

So their numbers are down by one, and I know the country. Our odds just improved.

~

We struggle on toward Adele's, snow to my shoulders in places. Both the girls are shivering badly; I've given them my parka and lining, but it's not enough. Neither has complained. Or said anything since the last shot. Even Bess seems to understand the need for silence.

The machines have not restarted, so they must've left them to track us on foot. I don't know Rayburn's skill level at that. Foy was good, the others were decent, but their boss never got a chance to follow us in the Tanami. With us unarmed, in snow, at night, he's got all the advantages. Snow's easy to track anyway, hard to conceal your own trail even if there is time, impossible when there isn't. And since he has night goggles, we can't move on a straight route either—have to dodge, don't dare double back, but break line of sight however and whenever we can.

So I know the country, yes, and I have the skills, but I also have a busted arm, two kids, not enough equipment, and no backup plan at this point. And he's in too close. With extra sets of eyes. Is Audra helping him? One of the snowmobiles just chugged its way by, up ahead. The other hasn't moved.

Flatline—no. Think this one through, Tally. Every step's another chance to slip from their noose. It's not over till the neck swings. Jed would understand. No normal rules will work for now.

Surely we haven't been through all this just to die out here in the cold.

~

But then again, maybe we have.

Face lit by Audra's light, I'm staring into the barrel of Rayburn's rifle. Bess on my hip, Jo next to her, hanging on to me. We're several feet lower than them, too far to connect even if I was whole enough to try something. They circled around on the snowmobile, got ahead. Had to be the night sights. Followed us easily till Rayburn knew he didn't have to struggle and stepped just ahead, to the top here, watched us come on. There's no other way through to Adele's.

She's not a quarter mile away. Maybe I shouldn't have been so adamant about her staying put. Forced her to promise, argued that we needed her alive and that I could get us through. The only exception to our deal is the callout: If I don't return by noon, Adele will ski to Moose and call in the troops.

Rayburn says nothing, motions for us to climb up. When we reach the top, I stumble backward a few feet, trying to give us a window—if I can get the girls out of the line of fire, I can move in close, try to take him on.

He closes that option immediately, walking after us, but maintaining an eight-foot space. Unhurriedly, setting his rifle in the lee of a tree, he takes out a handgun. Beretta 9mm. Still favors that make and model.

He has said nothing—neither have we—but the pale light of predawn seeps through the pines as he motions to hand Bess over. She clings to my neck so tight, I can't breathe. Can't do this, won't. You'll just have to shoot us here, where we stand, I think, and plant my feet. And if you set one foot closer, you'd better watch it, because I'm not out of this game yet, and I won't get out easy. Audra clicks the light off, looks away.

So that is how this is to end?

"Josephine, go to Audra," Rayburn says.

Josie squeezes my waist. He's trying to split us up. We won't comply.

"I said go to Audra."

"No."

Raising the Beretta to a line with my forehead, Rayburn looks calmly at Jo. He could be offering her anything, a snack, a toy, a day at the zoo. He's full of empty. This is the killing time, we're in his sights. He raises the revolver, steady, cocks it, and reaims at me. "I said go to Audra."

It's for effect, I think hard toward Jo, willing her to stay put, holding tight to her hand. Too easy. Come all this way just to shoot me? No. He wants me to die slow and in pain, wants me to feel what I did to him for hours at least, if not days. He won't take me out clean, not now. So as long as we don't make any sudden moves, don't get inside his space, he'll string this out to the bitter end, just as he's planned it. We'll get another chance at him, Josephine, stay put.

And then Rayburn smiles, and lowers the gun. Aims it straight at Bess.

The day I found Paul flashes through, his head blown apart because of this man. He'll do it. He'll kill her right here in my arms. The pain in my head becomes a loud roar. No.

Breaking my fingers from Josie's grip, I say, "You must go."

Jo hesitates, reaches for my hand again. Rayburn's smile deepens. He nods.

Sobbing, Jo stumbles toward Audra, snowshoes crossing up and tripping her once, then again. She fights to regain her feet, clawing the snow. When she reaches Audra's side, she turns to stare back at us, then Rayburn. "I'm *here!*" she yells at him, standing as tall as she can make herself.

Rayburn doesn't acknowledge her; she's still no more than a pawn to him, it means nothing that she obeyed or spoke. He smiles at me instead, sure of the outcome, confident of his control.

"Now for the little one. Audra," he says, nodding toward me.

She is to take Bess. I should've known. Audra begins walking toward us. No. I won't let go. Bess starts to cry, I back away—if I break for it he'll just gun me down, then the girls; you have to do what he says, Tally, for now. Just for now.

Then Audra is here, taking Bess the way she's done a hundred times before, but never like this. Never grim, never ripping her from me, baby fingernails scraping my neck from hanging on so hard, Bess screaming in terror and rage. I limp after them two steps, but Rayburn eases the gun around to follow Bess and puts out a hand to stop Audra from going on, then raises his eyebrows at me. I freeze.

Rayburn nods and draws back the hammer on the Beretta, places the gun's muzzle on Bess's head.

Straighten up, Taliesin, inhale, you have to get inside his head, break open empty, or it's over. You are the daughter of John J. Nowata—*live it through*. Reaching into my pocket for Paul's knife, never breaking eye contact, got to get inside, I flick the blade open.

Turning it against my own throat, I say, hoarse, "If you kill her, it ends now."

No thought, no sound. Just my eyes locked with his.

0736

By noon, when Adele heads to Moose, it'll be all body recovery over here. Three at least, maybe four. Two trips in the helo. Only one if they can get the Huey. Five to six hours for Adele to make the trip, maybe a couple more depending on how fast she skis, thirty to forty minutes to scramble the helo and crew, fifteen to reach the mine. Somewhere between six and nine tonight, Windy Point will arrive. But we'll be in rigor mortis by then, or gone well past it and simply frozen.

That is what I think as I drag myself down the hill toward the mine entrance. Stumbling, falling, rising again, every step a nightmare, I've crawled as much as I've walked. Following along in the tracks of the snowmobile.

Both Josie and Bess went silent when Rayburn tossed a watch at me and said, "If you aren't walking in the door when that chimes, they'll be dead when you do."

Forty minutes. I've used thirty-eight of them up. Watch in hand, I struggle on, too cold to shiver anymore.

As he turned to leave, giving Josie an unnecessary shove toward the snowmobile, she stared back over her shoulder. Empty eyes. I feel sick, me using the knife that way—it might've brought back memories she can't handle. I didn't know what else to do, Josephine. Please understand. Don't give up now, kid. You can't give up.

Thirty feet from the mine opening, I fall again, scrabble back to my knees, can't go on, can't move anymore. The watch hands sweep gracefully around. Bess and Josie watch from the door of the yurt, holding on to each other. Audra stands beside them, Rayburn next to her. The other man stands there too, silent, one gun held loose in both hands, full auto, I'd guess if I was guessing. Knows how to use it, too, it's clear. And I thought it was bad when it was only semi.

Stand up, Tally, walk forward. Your daughters are watching. Yanta. *Go.*

This isn't about outlasting him anymore, Pirli. It is to walk and not flinch. You are here.

Under the numbing cold, I feel the heat of her campfire gather, collect, roll into a ball, and enter my feet with small explosions. Suddenly strong, I stand and walk toward the mine. Maybe there is more to this healing thing than I'd reckoned. Josie smiles and nods at me, Bess claps. The watch begins to chime as I walk through the door.

Straight into as bad a beating as I ever took.

So if the healing stuff works, it sure picks its battles, and it left me to sink or swim on this one. Mostly sink. Gulping water and slush like a fish.

He took a stick to me, the first swing when I stepped in the door. The warmth I walked in on fled as I landed face down, bleeding, into the mud. I registered Jo tearing into him and getting knocked aside, Bess screaming at the top of her lungs, Audra grabbing the girls and holding them back, Rayburn almost hissing, no words, just sheer rage. He always had somebody else to do this part of the work for him before, somebody paid to batter and kill, but now it's just him.

He still has the skills.

~

Before it was over, both girls intervened. Or tried to. And when Rayburn threw them aside, Audra flew at him in a rage and wound up taking the brunt. Now she and I are both locked in a small earthen pit, crumpled side by side in pitch-black ooze.

On a body. Dead. Has been for a while. I can't smell a thing, but Audra can and is still vomiting periodically.

Other than footsteps closing in for Rayburn to shout out the time lapses—0915, 0930—and then retreating again, we have heard nothing. No sound from the girls. No way to even know where they are.

"Has he killed them?" I whisper, unable to keep the thought in any longer.

"No. And he won't. Not till you're there."

I crouch against the wall, this all feels surreal, the body beneath shifts with my moving weight, I fight to stay conscious. Who is it? Somebody else, like Trav or the sentries? How many men did he start out with here? Five or six? Unlikely ever to know, no use wondering. Complete waste of time.

What do you think about, then? Just before you die? What did Paul think about, racing through the desert to me, with them close behind? Is there a way to make sense of leaving when you're not getting to choose the exit? Some split second of clarity? The meaning of it all?

I draw a blank. Audra's heaving again. Rayburn calls 0945 and leaves. Zero-nine-forty-five, I don't think so. Translate it out of the killing, surviving mode, Tal. 9:45 A.M., morning still on our world. We won't submit.

But we will die, it is clear.

Audra whispers, "We didn't know what he had planned."

"We?"

"Andje—his son. Here. He's in here." She heaves again. Rayburn has a son? "He killed him." Rayburn killed his own son.

How can you do something like that?

Threw his body into this pit, and now us in after him.

"We didn't know. He—"

Audra breaks into tears, muffled. I have never seen her cry, not once in two years. Be sad, yes, but cry— no. "He was always so different to us, so *decent*. Paid for everything from since I can remember. School, college in London, music lessons, trips with the swim team. Helped my grandmother back home when she got sick, reined in my mum when my dad was gone. Like an uncle, Uncle Ray we used to call him. Even Andje called him that, made his dad laugh; we had no idea, Tally."

"It's fine. Done now," I say, surprised to hear no anger in my voice. Probably lost the physical ability to express it some time back. So there is a decent side to Rayburn. Where does it go when he looks at some-body like me? Or Paul? The girls? Even his own son— something must've happened to make Rayburn snap on him, too, but what? Andje's body lies stolid beneath us; I try to shift off it again, but cannot. The feel makes me seasick. It's like Hal or Rosemarie, Darren Oley, all the people we couldn't save. "All done for. But I would like to know how long you were in on it. And why."

The darkness swells around us, I try not to think about the body in here with us anymore. Try and fail. Eyes closed, I lean my head against the dirt wall, sud-denly realizing that I'm not afraid of the closed space. At all.

"Can you just tell me that much?" I ask.

"I was in from the start," Audra replies, her voice so low I can barely hear it. "He paid my way here. I was supposed to stay in close, keep an eye, collect information."

"So you took the photos?"

"No, he had other people for that. I just told them where we'd be. And when."

"And let them in the house to install the cameras?"

"Yes. I'm sorry, Tally. I was angry with you, so angry for such a long time—"

"Whatever the hell for? I never did anything to you! And I don't even *know* Andje."

"My father—"

And there it is.

The little girl I always hear in my dreams. Here. It's Audra, sitting across from me now in the moldy dark. I am not dreaming this. *"What?"*

"Earl Foy was my father."

Yes, there it is, the outside edges of my nightmare all this time. A child standing far away, calling for her dad to come home, hurry home, and me holding his arm up behind his back, stomping on his neck, once, twice, three times, and then four. That awful gurgle. He *did* have a family. I knew it, knew it then, for damn sure knew it later when I tried to find them, kept telling myself I had no choice, but I did. I feel sick, the smell of death overrides my sore nose, I feel it to the bones on the small of my back and start to suffocate, I need air.

The weight of a life not valued one whit by me while it still mattered. I took it. And brought his daughter—and us—to this.

All for what? "Oh, my God, I am so sorry," I finally manage.

"It's not as if I knew him well, I didn't. I was raised by my mother, like Andje." She stumbles over his name, holding his feet to the ground of now without intent. It's clear she loved him, still does. "In New Zealand, same neighborhood. Like I said, Uncle Ray paid for everything, both households, best schools, even college, until my dad died and he lost his business. When he told me what you'd done, how you'd attacked them, no warning, I couldn't see it. I wanted you to pay, wanted him to make you pay and let me help. Andje's my friend. He dropped off an expedition when his dad said we needed a climber."

So this dead man beneath me is the man from the ledge? The one that brought Laney off? Andje. Rayburn's son. I keep repeating it in my mind, like a mantra.

"But we didn't know what he had in mind, he said he'd only be teaching you a lesson—we didn't know. Not until Travis stabbed Laney. That wasn't supposed to happen. We thought we were just supposed to scare you, but Travis had different orders."

"To kill Lanes."

"That's what he was trying to do when Andje cut him loose—finish her off. After that Andje panicked, he said, dropped off your gear and pulled up on the

other route to wait till you went by. He knew he had
to get her down because you couldn't in your shape.
He's not a mean bone in him, Tally. Not one."

"So he brought her down?"

"Yes, then tried to call to warn me, but—"

"You'd already taken Bess."

"Yes."

"And the business about Dix and the Coors?"

"I needed a reason. I'd waited too long, kept
putting it off. I was supposed to take Bess as soon as
we reached Las Vegas, but couldn't. Almost backed
out. But then I saw them feeding her beer, and all I
could see was my mother falling drunk into the house
and me praying for my dad to come home all those
nights and you—"

Audra pauses, and I say nothing. This is what lay
beneath her quiet surface. The young woman paid to
care for my child carried her own measure of pain.
And, except for that one time at the hot springs, I
didn't even attempt to allay or understand it. Until now
I had never paid Audra that much attention, truth tell.

"So I took Bess and started home. We were to hide
her for a few days, that's it. I actually thought we'd be
staying at my cabin in Kelly, but when we arrived, it'd
been cleaned out, the lease closed."

"What about the condo in Wilson?"

"What?"

"The condo leased in Wilson under my name, with
Travis—with all of my things there. Even some of
Bess's toys. Did you do that?"

There's genuine confusion in Audra's voice. "No, I don't know anything about a condo."

I'm quiet, digesting. So this part of the plan Rayburn kept from her. What else? I lean my head against the wall, so very tired. Weary of it. What does it matter anymore? The details are moot at this point. "I didn't know he meant to kill you, Tally, not even when I made it back here. It took Andje, seeing what he did to his own son—he tried to save us, you know, the girls and me—came back here and fought to get us free—"

Audra's crying so hard now, she makes a gurgling sound. Uncanny, familiar. Like her father. "It all happened so fast," she whispers.

Yes, that it did.

10:30 A.M.

So Rayburn murdered his own son, enraged about the betrayal, no doubt. His plan shot to pieces by his own blood kin. His decisions challenged.

And Laney would be dead without this man beneath us?

No wonder he was weaving about out there on the flats; he had to know that changing the plan would get him killed. At the risk of his own life, he saved Laney. Tells you something important. His body lies motionless beneath, only moving when we do. I feel sick at the waste, the extravagant pain. So many people hurt over all this.

No one else, please. No one else needs to die. If somebody's got to go on this thing, let it be me. Let him take just me, at least leave Audra, Bess, and Josie alone—they deserve a chance at a life, please. I've had mine. A good fast run at it, and so much packed in it might count for two or three, truth tell. So if somebody else has to go to even the numbers, take me. I reach for Audra in the dark. She squeezes my hand.

"How bad are you hurt?" I ask.

"I'm fine," she replies as she always has when asked how she is, but now the break in her voice belies her words. "You?"

"Leaking brain cells, but that's just old age." Audra doesn't laugh like she once might've, she just sits quiet, holding onto my hand. "We'll make it through this, kid. How, I don't know, but we will. The road will rise to meet us."

Footsteps from above, close. Audra is silent, breathing heavily. Rayburn calls 10:45. The time intervals must be his way of trying to break us further, illustrate his total control. There is no sound from the girls. He leaves.

"We will, Audra—"

"I don't want to make it through, Tally. I've seen all I want to see of this world."

"Don't say that. It looks grim from here, but that's only because you're locked in a damn dirt toilet! I know what I'm talking about. You *can* make it through this."

There's silence now, her hearing me, I hope, me fighting to stay conscious. Body parts are starting to hurt again, come alive with a vengeance.

"I don't think your brother meant anything by the beer," she says.

"You don't?"

"No. It was all good fun, and I used it as an excuse. But I shouldn't have left like that, should've called at least so they wouldn't worry."

"No worries now," I whisper, echoing a phrase she used to say all the time, feeling sick to the stomach about Dix in the dryout. Will he come through this time? He's fought so hard for so long, tried God in every form, tried work—hard enough to break a lesser man—tried everything. Shamans and healers, medicine men, Sun Dance and sweat lodges, prayer sticks and ashrams, free love and safe sex and celibacy, too, you name it. I removed myself from all that, refused to participate, barely listened. Dix would pray for me when he'd go to one of his gatherings, make tobacco ties for his war-hardened sister, and I'd tease him about it. What the hell was I thinking? If I'd gone to Sun Dance with him this summer, maybe he wouldn't have broken in Vegas when Bess went missing? Or maybe I'd have been there so she couldn't in the first place.

Moot now. There is only the sound of Audra's soft sobs in this pit. I feel helpless.

"I am so sorry about Andje," I say. "And your dad." Bears repeating. "I've been sick about that for three years, wished over and over I could take it back." My voice trails off into silence, how do you explain the inexplicable? It's like slapping a Band-Aid on a severed head. Do I tell her I tried to find her, to apologize, to seek forgiveness? Paid a small fortune to an Aussie equivalent of a PI for two months—while she was working for me, no less? Kept my guilty secret locked away from everyone, used what money I had to find a way to fix what I'd done? But would that confession be for me or for her?

Audra asks softly, in the voice of the child she still is, will always be, waiting for her father to come home and be a dad. "Would you please tell me now why you did it?"

When I pause, groping for an answer, wondering if I should clean it up—she clearly doesn't know the truth about Foy—she asks, "Did he have something to do with Paul dying?"

"He shot him."

"Oh," she replies, wounded, her child's dreams of a daddy shattering, as she dully adds, "Then he deserved it."

"No. Nobody deserves that."

"Then why? You always say you don't believe in violence. So was it self-defense?"

The truth, Tally, now. No more denials. "They called it that. Me too, for a while."

"Oh. Then I understand—"

"No, Audra. I wanted him dead. It's that simple. I could've done different, could've left him alive, but I

was hurting. Angry. Scared stiff. And I wanted somebody to pay for all the years of that. Your father paid
with his life."

Audra doesn't say eh, she doesn't say anything.

Rayburn calls out 11:15, 11:30, before she speaks
again. My time to be here is shrinking.

"I am glad to've known you, Tally."

"Don't say that. Don't talk like you're leaving,
you're not." The words churn in my stomach, deny-
ing the calm tone. We're unlikely to leave here alive,
and we both know it. *You're just not.*"

She doesn't respond. I have to reach her. It's the
least I can do.

"I mean it, Audra. When he lets us out of here, you
have to stay alive. *Must.* He won't make it easy, he'll
think of some new awful thing for you to do, you can
count on it, something gory and gut-sick—may even
make you finish me just to prove the point that you
can't bail out on him like his son did. *Do whatever he
says.* Do you hear me?"

She is silent.

"Just do whatever he says. Then, if you make it
through, live on past us all. Past Rayburn. Past me.
Past your dad. Make this horror count for something
good. Or mediocre, your choice. Just live on past us,
Audra, so it's not all for naught."

"For a Yank," she says, and I know she's smiling,
"you sure—"

"Talk funny. Yeah, I know—some foreigner keeps

reminding me. That's okay, just so long as it sticks in your skull, eh?"

At that she chuckles, low and faint, and it's broken by a sob, but she laughed, and that's something.

Minutes later, the trapdoor swings open. Time to move up, into the down count.

11:35 A.M.

They took Audra away and left me here. Rayburn held the hinged door up, the other man reached for Audra's hands. She managed to stand and nod at him.

"Hi, Keith," she said, as if she were greeting him at the local café. Except duller. The lilt in her voice that was always there, even as quiet and sad as she was, is gone.

I've strained to hear something, anything, in vain. At least there hasn't been a shot, or a scream. No yelling, no talking. I'll take that as a good sign.

Soon it will be your turn, Tally-ho. I like the sound of the nickname, turn it over in my mind, hold it close, words running like a gentle river through the now. All the names I'm known by, a list as long as my arm. Taliesin, Tally, Tally-ho, Tal, and TJ, Knothead, Nowata, Knucklehead, and Boo, and a few more too colorful to repeat. Each given by someone who loves me.

And then there are those from the girls. Mommy Two, for Josephine. And MomMommy, for Bess.

Who will I be when no one remembers my name?

~

She speaks from the fireside, always from there. It's not memory that matters, Pirli. Nor speaking. From that side, *we are you*. Never forget.

From that side, they are us. Me, here now. I've talked to them, harangued and sassed them back, begged them for help all my life. Turned the dead people in my life into my gods.

Until a couple days ago. When the little nightshirt that's still pressed to my stomach fell out of that package. I lay one hand against it now, touching it through my shirt, feeling as if nothing intervenes. Or ever has. Ever could.

In itself it means not one thing. No one alive—not even Bess—would know its significance. But it's the defining moment of my life.

Not Paul's death, not my mother's or grandmothers', either one, not even Foy's. Not seeing my father go to prison, get out, go again, not hiding from him or hating him, wanting to make him pay. Not climbing the Grand or rafting the Snake. None of those. If I had to pick one moment of the last thirty years that slapped my world into perspective, it'd have to be the moment I found this nightshirt.

I didn't put it into words when it happened, couldn't have. Would not have known how. But when this shirt fell out of that envelope—

All my gods died. Even the ones I'd handpicked.

Haven't said a prayer to a one of them since. Never will.

I understand now, finally, what she meant. *From that side, Pirli, we are you.*

I carry everyone I've ever loved within. There's no need to pray, unless I just want to. They know me. *I know me.* My only job is to be fully here while I'm here, and walk on, no regrets, when I'm not. Live till you die, then die and be done with it.

Another version of zero sum? Oh, no. This one brims full, not empty. With the courage to do what you know to do, no matter what comes.

The trapdoor swings open again. This time, only Rayburn. He stands tall, one hand motioning me to stay put. The other hand cradling an urn.

Paul O'Malley.

My eyes land on Andje. Smythe, I suppose his last name must be. Blond hair like his dad, and tall. Crumpled now and gone, but he had the courage of his convictions to the end.

Will I?

11:40 A.M.

"I'm a man of few words, Miss Nowata," he says, at last. "But you know that by now, no?"

I nod, staring straight ahead, all nerves on edge. Some have dropped clear off it.

"Do you know what you've cost me?"

Shaking my head, I press the nightshirt to my skin, draw strength from it. And from Andje. He did it, I can too.

"Him, for one. And her, Foy's little girl. Her grandparents. I supported these people, with money, things they needed. Them and others. I was a regular contributor to the biggest homeless shelter in Sydney, did you know that? And the Arts Board, that too." So that explains the expensive clothes and wine, the book he was reading way out at that desert camp when we first spotted him. It was the weirdest thing, like a duck nesting on a sideboard at the Biltmore. "I did all these things, happily, I might add, until I lost my livelihood. Gratis you."

Gratis me?

"Ripped my business one side, the other. Most of my assets frozen or seized. Audra's people have to fend for themselves now. What do you have to say to that?"

My eyes drawn to the urn, I force them to look up at the man holding it. What do I say to him?

He limps a few steps away, calls for Keith. "Marston, get in here."

This may be my only chance to get through to him, touch the empty, get him to see us. Say something, Tally, quickly. Not just anything. Say what you mean. "I didn't want to hurt you, out there in the Tanami. I wish I'd never stumbled into your camp. Wish Paul hadn't. I hate violence, hate what it does to people—

what it did to my family, to all of us, to your son here—"

"How *dare* you speak of *that* as my son? Marston!"

Don't stop, Tally. "I didn't want to hurt you, didn't want any of this—please believe me. I'm sorry."

"My, aren't we touching?" Rayburn laughs, the flash of anger gone. He seems now to be enjoying himself. "I would've expected more from you than this pitiful plea for nonintent. Feeling your mortality, hmm?"

I shake my head. It's no use. I can't reach this man with words. He's like my father, all empty, no ears to hear me anymore.

"Well, *I'm* not sorry. Not in the least." Rayburn is staring at his son. "Andje always was a little weak. He got that from his mother." There's a long pause. "And my father."

More family history, playing itself out every tomorrow that comes.

"It's a big world out here, Miss Nowata. Eat what you kill, stay one step ahead."

And more survival. In the Tanami, just before the end, it came to me strong that survival's our best excuse for our meanness. That wasn't from my elders, dead gods, Paul, or the poets. It came from me, out there at the end of my rope. I'd forgotten it till now, never wrote it down. "The true survivor is one who has finally learned that survival itself is beside the point," I say aloud.

That, at least, he heard. He blinks once, twice, glancing down at the urn as if he's never seen it before, at me in the pit, his eyes darting away, then back, helpless somehow, and afraid. That's the core of the empty. Speak now, Tally—it's your last chance to make him see. "I had choices in Australia. I am sorry that the ones I made caused you harm."

There's a moment of complete confusion in Rayburn's face. I hold my breath; he walks away two steps, wheels, comes back. Does it again. Stares at me, Andje, the pit, around the mineshaft, breathing hard.

Suddenly he turns on his heel and leaves. This time he doesn't come back.

11:45 A.M.

"Outside with them," he says to Keith Marston, voice colder than when he started. The confusion is gone. "I must take this man to his girls." Patting Paul's urn, and smiling at me, Rayburn leaves.

Keith grabs my right arm and yanks me out of the hole, pushes me into Audra, and trains his gun at our backs. We stumble toward the sunlight.

11:50 A.M.

While we were locked in the pit, the men were busy. The first thing I notice as we are herded outside is the charges they've placed in the mine. Rayburn intends to blow any evidence off the map.

They've also packed the snowmobiles, not heavy but leaving no room for more than one rider each. I glance at Audra; she nods. She won't be leaving with them.

As we clear the opening, my heart pounds in my throat to see the girls outside, then falls fast and heavy like a stone.

They are tied together back to back, but Rayburn motions Keith to stand guard. One man and a machine gun for two tiny girls. Has it trained on them, no less, feet apart for solid stance. One wave of that gun with his finger on the trigger and everybody here goes down.

Josie and Bess are seated on the snow, naked, shivering, encircled by a line of gray ash. Rayburn is shaking what's left of the urn's contents over their heads, then tossing the heavy container aside and moving toward us. Paul, he just scattered—

And the baggie is still in Bess's nightshirt. How can he ever be whole again now? I was supposed to make him whole, take him to the ridge above the lake. I promised. But how can I do that now? The girls are shellshocked, faces tearstained and filthy, eyes bloodshot, bodies touching but each looking lost and alone. Jo has a bruise on one eye and shoulder, Bess on her cheek and left leg. The ashes coat their faces and hair.

How long has he had them out here? Not long. They're still shivering. Stay alert, Tally, don't get sidetracked. Watch for your chance. The girls do not speak when Rayburn walks us past them, but I fight through the muzziness to say, "Hey, kiddos."

That earns me a swift kick in the back of the knees. So be it. They needed to hear I'm okay. Stick with me, Josephine, watch and wait, I think, but Jo's head is bowed, she cannot hear. And Bess stares at the sun-drenched snow with glazed eyes. What did he say to them, or do? The ashes, is that it? He used Paul. Said or did something that bent them inside. Even Bess has gone quiet. I tremble, my knees give—don't let go, Tally, now. Stay with him. Watch their edges. Bide your time.

A single chair, with several lengths of cord draped over it, sits a few yards away. So this is it. There is symmetry to Rayburn's revenge.

Turning every ounce of my self behind, toward my girls, I walk on to the chair, chin high, trying my best not to limp or faint. We'll live beyond this, you two, I promise. If not here, in this place, then in the very next.

The words sound hollow; a sob catches in my throat, guttural like Audra and Foy. I swallow it down, but it rises again, primal. At base we are all the same. Fragile, small, unsure. Dix believes in an afterlife. All my people do. Grandmother Bess was a healer. I was always more pragmatic. Sometimes bodies are meant to wear out, move on, make room for the next generation. Fine by me my whole life. Suited my sense of balance. We're here a while, then not. Who the hell cares where we go as long as we get to leave?

Now I listen for something within to leap to claim an existence. Here, there, somewhere. Wait for the anger to erupt, an all-out death struggle to stay in this one—or take somebody with me when I go as it did in the Tanami. Nothing comes. Nothing speaks. Nothing moves.

So I turn on will alone, reaching for Rayburn's arm, but there is no substance, he slams his gun against my shoulder, I can't see. Face down in the snow, his boot on my neck, can't breathe, it's dark, she cries for me, "Mommy!" A single name, a new one, heard for the first time ever.

I slip into the abyss, long known. All is still.

Except the us that we are.

In the gray light I feel Bess in my skin, in my breath, I hear her laugh last week at Dix, see him smile and give her an airplane ride over his head, both whirring for engines in tandem. Paul's in the taste of the wind, kind and warm off the snow. My mother in those scraggly pines she loved so well—she never saw trees like these, but I have seen them for her. All my grandmothers in this sun. Ducket in the moon that rides unseen. Audra and Lanes, Pony and Jed not yet with us, but one day they too will come.

So this is the end.

I don't need more. Don't need healing or saving or listening to from beyond. I carry all I ever touched or thought or loved deep within.

If I die here, that much will live on, afterlife or no. It is peaceful now, and warm.

So very soothing.

There is nothing to fear.

~

Roughly, I come to, sputtering, spitting snow, Rayburn's hands dragging me into the chair, lashing me to it. Shoulders, one knee, one ankle, leaving one leg loose; it is all so familiar. I don't resist; there's no point, that split second beyond made it clear. I feel nothing, grieve not at all, there is a peace to what's coming that I welcome. No fear. Not for me. Not for Bess, or Jo, or Aud. I look at each of them now, steady and calm—they need to know it's all right. That's a mom's job. I might've flubbed some of that on the road to here, but I intend to nail the end. Cold.

Rayburn steps back, revolver in hand, and tosses a long knife on the ground. Crude, homemade, deadly, it looks just like Foy's. The metal gleams, a world under water, I hear voices, faint, indistinct, see Audra say something back and him throw her down, kick her forward, once, twice, then bend to smash her face with his gun and force the knife into her hand, drag her to her feet. Turn eyes to the girls, Tally, catch theirs and hold on, then look at Audra.

To do this thing, she needs my help. When her eyes meet mine, a child seeking her father still, for always, I nod.

She holds the knife out in front of her with both hands, shoulders quaking, tears pouring down her face, the tears of a lifetime. Rayburn yells, impatient—I hear him from far away, muffled, and keep my eyes on Audra. *Do whatever he says.*

The sound comes from the top of the pass. Rayburn turns slowly as Keith's knees buckle, he spins backward, red spray against the snow, another jolt, he's full down; somebody's shooting. At the top of the hill, a snowmobile, paused, crosswise of the trail, two figures, one with a long gun, aiming.

Pony Sutton.

Another round, Rayburn recoils, hit, he falls to one knee, dropping his Beretta in the snow and then rising to reach for it, but Pony clips the snow with another round and he pauses, moves toward us, then quickly away, toward the girls for two steps and then veering off, to the snowmobiles now, crouching, trotting, he's getting away.

Audra stands transfixed, knife loose in her hand, staring first after Rayburn and then up the hill, then at me for a moment before she bends to cut me loose. Suddenly a round catches her in the chest and I scream, "Pony, *no!*" leaping for Audra, but missing, still lashed to this chair, falling onto my side. *"Not her!"* Sutton, *stop.*

Another round, Audra goes down, close to me, I try to cover her body with mine, the best I can, grab her head, Tally, hold it up so she doesn't strangle, come on, kid, not after all this. The chair bores into my back, holds me too fast, I can't reach her, I'm tied.

"Don't you dare die on me! Come on, Audra, *please*. We can make it."

And then Pony and Adele are here, lifting me up, pulling me away, that soft gurgling, I can't bear it. Adele loosens my ropes, I claw my way toward the girls. "Can you fix it, *do something?*" I plead with Adele, gesturing at Audra, hurrying on to Jo and Bess, dragging the cords off, pulling them close, trying to warm them with my body. "Please don't let her die!"

Pony bends over Keith, tosses his gun near me and, nodding toward Audra, says to Adele, "Stay away from that bitch. She's kidnapped her last kid."

Then she starts toward her snowmobile, saying to me in passing, "You're welcome. I'm going after the goon. Y'all send me some backup when the troops get here." As the whir of the machine closes in the distance, I hear Audra's struggle end.

An unearthly quiet hangs over us now. Josie and Bess are clinging to me, we shudder as one.

"I'll go inside, find some covers," Adele says, touching my shoulder, and I flinch, still staring after Pony. I can't move. How on earth did I walk out to that chair?

Jo pats my arm, pointing toward Adele. "Lady! Tally—stop her!"

The mine. Wired. "Stop! He's wired the mine! Get out—"

She turns around just as the hillside explodes. Holding onto the girls, I tumble into snow, rocks, rubble.

Rayburn had the last shot after all, maybe it was zero sum.

The loud *thud-thud* of a Huey wakes me up. I'm flat on my back, on a Stokes. Jed and Wes have the head, Vince and Nels my feet, they're carrying me to the bird. The girls? Where are—

"Lay the fuck down, Nowata," Jed yells, roughly, "before I slap the crap outta you." In all the years I've known Jed Timmons, that's the first cuss words I've ever heard him say.

"They're fine, Tally. Already in," Wes shouts. Sure enough. Jo's bundled in a sleeping bag and strapped to a seat. Bess is strapped into a small litter on the floor. Both look cold and miserable, but somehow okay. Josie's happy to see me, Bess is just mad at being held down, screaming her head off. When she sees me coming in beside, but strapped down too, she redoubles her efforts. Right now all the adults' names in her world are mud—mine high on the list— because we have her pinned to a board, and if I'm not here to rescue her, I'm clearly part of the problem. That's Bess O'Malley for you. Can't be hurt too much if she's acting so normal.

She's liable to hold some of the last week against me for a good long little while.

I believe now I can live with that.

"Audra?"

"Dead," Pony yells flatly, from the side rail. She's got one foot in to steady herself as she helps situate my litter, but her hands are shaking, and it has nothing to do with the rotors. I start to ask about Rayburn, but she interrupts, "Him too."

"Adele?"

Pony points outside, and sure enough, there she is. Sitting on the chair. Hair's a little mussed, and she's a little banged up, but nowhere near what it could've been. Just ten more feet—

When we're all secured, Wes and Pony step back. Pony thrusts her hands in her pockets and stands tall, yet hunched. She doesn't look at me as Wes waves the pilot off. Despite all her talk, she has never killed anyone before, and I see this new thing settling about her shoulders. The path ahead for her will not be kind or easy.

Wriggling one arm free from the tie-ins, I reach for Bess's hand. Jed's on a jump seat near our heads, his own head cupped in both palms. Hard day on the people that know me. Hard week. Hell, hard couple of years.

As we putter above the snowfields, turned south at last, he leans over me and yells, "At any point in the last five days, did you ever consider sitting your ass the hell down and calling for help from your friends?"

I grimace. Actually no, I did not. It was all moving too fast, like a river in spring thaw; there was no time to pull up in an eddy for reflection and planning. Put that into words, Tal, exactly like that, he'll have a hissy but it might do him good—like Pony says, he's way too uptight sometimes—but I don't get the chance.

Jed yells, "You little shit. We've been trying to catch up with you for days!"

I try to smile, say, "I know."

"No, you don't. Pony saw your neck wrap at Kemp's place the night you lit out—did you know that? And, believe it or not, Vince'd already had some doubts—couldn't raise your prints on ordinary surfaces at that condo, for one thing, then Audra's cabin turned up empty for lease—she was in on it all along—and we've been busting our nuts trying to find you, trying to figure out where you went and why and what it all had to do with Travis turning up dead and then Laney's dog. But you didn't slow down long enough to know any of that, did you? Or let us catch up?"

Jed waves one hand in dismissal and sits back, shaking his head, looking everywhere but at me. Probably doesn't need a verbal answer, reads it in my eyes. Good thing, doubt I could talk.

"That's what I thought, Knothead. You just wait till you're mobile again. I'll deal with you then."

I try to shrug. A soft twitch at the corner of Jed's mouth belies his stern words. Bess squeezes my hand. Maybe I'm forgiven. Josie winks at me with the one eye that's not swollen shut. Yes, clearly I am.

We make a wide turn for home, finally, already there.

DECEMBER 31

The days after the rescue ran long, into each other and beyond—Bess and I not quite home yet, as we'd hoped, but we're both safe now, Josie too, and that's the whole sum of this year in my life.

On the mundane side of things, I'm not wanted anymore, not by the law anyway, but by almost everyone else for a variety of reasons.

Loose ends to tie up, Vince said, but I think, from the laconic way he asked his two or three questions, that it was his way of apologizing. Not necessary, I told him, and meant it.

Rayburn and his crew did a good job. Very good.

Except for not being able to pick up any of my finger-prints on ordinary surfaces at the condo—things like the sinks or the tub, the tables and lamps—they had me down cold. Prints on drinking glasses and plates, several changes of clothes, books, and papers. Shoes, even a toothbrush. "If it'd been me, I'd've done the same," I told Vince, and he nodded, earnest. He really does try to do the right thing. And we do tend to get a little off the beaten track up here at Windy Point sometimes. Can't blame the man for attempting to rein us in.

The loose ends, though, are still loose, and may never come fully together, though both Vince's office and the park have sought help from Australian, British, and Swiss authorities. It appears from bank accounts that Travis was receiving money from a shell company for almost a year before he showed up in Moose. This means that Rayburn set his plan in motion before I ever left Australia. Keith Marston was actually Dale Munson, a petty thief from Phoenix who went to high school with Travis, but the man I blinded in the night goggles remains unidentified, his body unclaimed at the morgue.

No one knows who killed Ducket, who took the photos, or who the other associates might have been, and the men whose names Pony took down last year seem to have trouble enough elsewhere not to've been involved here. Two are in prison; another's on his way there: only one is in the clear with the law, but he's been in El Paso working for the last three months and, according to his employer anyway, hasn't missed a day. Many loose ends like these.

On two points, though, the case is exceptionally clear: Audra and Andje really are Foy's and Rayburn's children.

Audra grew up in Auckland, just as she told me at the mine, but after her mother died eight years ago, she did move to London. Her college expenses there were all covered by a corporation in Sydney until it was dissolved, three years ago, leaving her unable to finish her final year. Soon after, she came to the States, and it seems clear that someone helped with her initial expenses. The bank account she left shows no signs of anything beyond the salary I paid her, but she couldn't have afforded to live in this valley entirely on that. I always assumed she was wealthy, had a trust fund or something. Which is partly true, I suppose.

Andje was schooled in England as well, to be a doctor, and had served with the Swiss Disaster Relief Services for two years before taking leave to climb Kangchenjunga, the world's third highest peak. According to another member of his team, he had already arrived in Nepal, with plans to spend three months traveling prior to the expedition, when he received an urgent call from his father. From Laney's notes of the week prior to December 14, Wes was able to deduce that he was her thousand-dollar client. Somehow on the day the two of them did that climb, they connected well enough that he risked his own life for hers—and again for Audra and the girls—when he realized what his father was up to.

It is not the whole story, but perhaps it's all I need to know. I want the Tanami to be done with me, and it seems, finally, it is. And yet the lessons keep pressing homeward. Father and son, Rayburn and Andje. Father and daughter, Foy and Audra. What each of them was will always elude me, but I see strong evidence in the children that their fathers were more than I knew them to be. This makes me think about Dix and me. And our father, the fear and fury I've always carried for him. When I remember Audra crying for her dad, not knowing all of him but wanting desperately to—having enough faith to see toward what she believed him to be—I wonder about myself. When I think of Rayburn hurrying away from that exploding hillside, wounded and surely afraid before Pony's last bullet claimed its ground, I wonder even more. Clearer heads than mine might be able to draw neat lines of good and evil in all this, but I cannot. Or won't.

Maybe I'm just getting too damn old to be comforted by lies.

Or been busted up so much the last few years that my body won't carry a single extra weight. Grandmother's feather and the mulga were still in my pocket when they brought me here to St. John's. Zee recovered them from my clothing and set them on the nightstand after I got out of ICU. She said she burned my clothes, and gave orders that no one bring me any more until the doctor has already signed my release.

"I'd do the same thing in your shoes," I said.

Zee stopped her bustling then, came to a full stop, and looked at me. Tears sparkled in her eyes before she spoke. "Paul's gone, Tally. For good."

"I know."

"If I could bring him back for you, I would." Zee stared at the floor and then out the window, hands in the pockets of her scrubs. "I took something from your clothes and hadn't planned to give it back. Keep thinking you must start living again. But then," she said, walking to the bedside and handing me a sealed envelope, "who am I to say when?"

After a quick squeeze on my wrist, she nodded and left.

In the envelope is the small plastic bag of Paul's ashes.

It will have to be enough.

~

Home once was these mountains, a place where I rested secure. Windy Point, my house. The mountains are still here, but somehow I am not. I have already left in my heart.

And Windy Point is coming apart, definitively. Not on purpose, but long overdue. Our team's down to Jed, Wes, and the seasonals now. Laney's out of the coma, but unresponsive. Near catatonic. Says nothing, to anyone. They're feeding her through tubes. In my mind I walk to her room every day, many times, and sit by her bed, talking about every ordinary thing I can think of—everything but what happened to us on that mountain, and what happened to Duck—but she just sits there, staring. Empty, it seems, but not the kind that turns outward. This empty is all turning in. The doctor says trauma can do that, and she'll come out of it when her mind feels safe again. As soon as I'm well enough, I will go to her. Surely then she'll know everything is okay. Pony goes every day, Jed says, but she hasn't been in to see me yet, so I don't know what she's learned.

Apparently that's not personal. Pony's not seeing much of anybody else these days. They put her on admin leave, which is standard procedure in any shooting. She's spent some time in the mountains—doing what, no one knows—and a lot of time at the Cowboy Bar. I do know the why of that, but wish I didn't. The only reason I didn't get sot drunk when I came back to the States was Bess. Well, that and the fact that I can't drink much without falling asleep. Jed says he doesn't think Pony's even drinking, but she sits in that bar for long afternoons, saying nothing to anyone and wearing an expression that suggests she'd rather they not say anything to her either. He is worried. I promised to do what I can, as soon as I get out of this hospital. "Which won't be early this time," according to Zee, who went so far as to have Jed threaten to post a guard in my room once I was no longer in ICU. Then she decided that controlling the clothes was just as effective.

Speaking of Jed, he never got around to lining me out about things, but he's stopped in a couple times a day for the oddest excuses. Even brought me a gift yesterday, way too pretty to open, with a huge bow as big as his head.

"JT, why're you doing all this?"

He hemmed a bit, hawed some more, shuffled his feet, and almost left, but finally blurted out, "In case you decide to up and die on me."

"Good Lord!" I said, with as much force as I could muster. "All the hills you drug me up all these years and now you worry I might die from a straw in my head? What about flatline, eh?"

He threw up one hand and left, promising he and Lisa would bring Bess by tonight at five. I reached for the journal Josie brought to the hospital before heading home with her mom, vowing to start it for the new year. With an entry for how a half southern, Okie Indian came to be saying the word "eh" on occasion. More occasions, sometimes, than she likes.

And then I sneaked a peek inside the wrapping.

Jed had my light climbing boots bronzed, and set in a glass case that won't open.

Engraved with a small silver placard that leaves no doubt as to his motives.

> *Never again—in winter.*
> *Love,*
> *JT*

Well, O'Malley, there it is. I suppose now I'll change shoes.

JANUARY 2

A new year, and reason to celebrate. I am finally home.

With a permanent shunt in my head, the modern equivalent of a straw leaking spinal fluid on purpose; a drain in my brain. The permanency part I won't accept yet, particularly not from a medical science that still uses staple guns to close head wounds. When Dix gets through rehab, I intend to ask him to take me to Sun Dance. Sweat lodges. Vision quests. Whatever it takes.

In the meantime, since I can't climb, I'm on medical leave. Which means I have all the time in the world to spend with my daughter—a very interesting first.

Bess seems no worse for the wear, aside from a few nightmares, which subsided last night to her simply waking near four to shout, "Bad man!" once or twice. When I reached her bedside, she was sound sleep, self-sufficient as ever. But she needs me for other things. Audra, for one. She still asks about her every day. And Ducket. I've started looking for a Newfoundland pup for Laney, and possibly another for Bess. She won't ever have a sibling—lucky for the unborn, I believe. But a Newf might do her good.

And anyway, we may soon be living in a place where water rescue's a bigger deal. Dix has transferred to a rehab clinic in Minnesota. We haven't really gotten to talk; he only called briefly last week on his way up there. Shelby's folks are helping her close the house in Oklahoma and move to Duluth while he's gone. We are all hoping that a new start—in a state with no ties to the past—will help with Dix's recovery.

I have turned my mind to leave here and join them. Taking Laney home to her parents as I go. The Greers are poor, but as generous as humans come. And Episcopalian. Fourth generation. Go figure.

~

I went into her room yesterday, in a wheelchair—not because I couldn't manage on my feet but because Zee wouldn't let me.

I arrived with all faith. Sure that just seeing me would snap Lanes out of it, bring her back. I was bursting with things to tell her that would reassure or entertain, not just inform, and several to hide: she could know about Ducket later. Much later, after we find her a puppy. And I wasn't sure I'd ever fill her in on the details of what went down at the mine. Some of that just doesn't need telling. When you speak evil, it corrodes the listener too, colors how they see the world from then on in. So no, that will all go to my grave with me.

Zee parked the chair at Laney's bed and left, closing the door. "Hey, Knucklehead, it's me," I said, leaning forward and reaching for her hand.

Laney did not move.

So I tried again. "Lanes, we made it through, see?"

But she didn't, it was clear. Her eyes were open, but she wasn't seeing. So I sat quiet for a while and then told her about the rescue and how Andje brought her down and saved her life. "He was a good man; your instincts were right. But your poacher's a *woman*, Laney. Which explains why she outsmarted us every turn. But she helped me through out there last week, so I think you need to cut her a break when you're back on your feet."

At that Laney started to cry. I stood up and tried to hold on to her so she wouldn't be afraid and talked the kind of nonsense we always talk to keep her tethered to the now. Said things about how Adele might kill some animals to survive, but surely no more than the folks in their big houses and cars through this valley. Looped around, made connections I'd never thought to make before, about Eco-Jim and Adele and how they're fighting for the same thing, same as us. Wound up telling her about the moose eating bark and the mama grizzly's den, and finally about Adele breaking the points off those wolf traps we'd found. "She didn't kill them, Lanes—same rancher laid traps and by the time Adele came along the wolves' legs were rotting. It wasn't all that it seemed from the sign." At that she finally quieted, and I sat on the bed beside her, sure she would speak. Whisper. Something. *Anything. Just look at me, please, and let me know it's all going to be okay.*

But that was it. She lay still with her eyes open for the longest time, staring at the ceiling. I finally moved back to the chair and sat watching her, telling myself she had to be relieved someone was watching out for her wolves. When she fell asleep, I leaned back despite my protesting head—any pressure shift thunders through like the whir of an ocean inside my skull and down my spine—and stared at the ceiling myself.

Pony and Zee have been busy.

Photos of Ducket and Lanes, Rosemarie, Jed and the crew, all of us. But there's only one each of all the people, and at least fifty of D. Every pose imaginable of that dog. From baby to now. In the center hangs the oversize shot I took last year of him and her and Rose and Bess on Blacktail Butte. It used to hang at the foot of her bed: Pony brought it here. Trying to pull Laney back into her life. It was a good try.

When Zee came for me—signed release orders in hand—it was dark. And when Wes drove me to Moose and pulled into my driveway, holding open the front door so I could go inside, I saw my path from this place.

JANUARY 7

Neither Dix nor I spoke at our father's parole board appearance this morning. Neither of us could go.

I'm not sure now I would've even made the effort, given the means, though I had prepared long and fiercely for just such a thing through November. Now I wonder about my motives, my certainties that I am right and he is wrong. And anyway, I can't fly either. So I'll leave John Nowata in the hands of his new-found gods.

But I can drive a car, so I am on my way now to the Cowboy. Rounding the square with its antlered arches on each end, catching a whiff of the Original

House of Sourdough as I park and cross the street. The snow crunches beneath my feet, and then the boards of the sidewalk, as I walk toward a part of my life I disavowed after Paul.

The bar scene in Jackson was never about drinking for us back then. We'd gather to talk and warm up and dance, living down together whatever hard thing we'd done or seen that day or week. Laney made a handwritten sign for her desk years ago that just about said it all:

SAR

Acronym for search and rescue,
Rhymes with bar.
Where we usually end up when we're done.

That was the sum of us at Windy Point back then. We worked hard and played hard and fought hard, every day, to call it good.

Square, Pony would say.

~

The heavily varnished wood doors open, and I step into the foyer, the darkness ahead warm and beckoning. The long bar to the right and giant burlwood railings polished by countless hands over time always draw me in, but when I reach the center of the room I always stop, and today is no exception. The famous stuffed, snarling grizzly is still captured in its tall glass box, and I can't pass without noting his existence. No one notices me, or calls hello, like they used to. This is a new crowd, no one I recognize. I weave between the bar and the tables, heading for a far corner above the dance floor. The smell of popcorn, peanuts, and beer hangs close; I remember dancing so hard we sweated ourselves into dehydration a few times. Downing glass after glass of water we paid for to keep the waitress in rent money every month. Letting the pounding rockabilly music eat through to our bones and fix things for a couple hours.

I hear they've moved away from country-western some now to compete with the Rancher's touristy rock fare.

That is change for you. Human.

Before you know it, they'll change back again.

Pony sits with her back to the bar, staring at the stage behind the dance floor, one foot propped up on a chair. A glass of white wine sits untouched on the table next to a stack of bills and some change. She's set for a long afternoon, doesn't acknowledge me at all.

"Mind if I join you?"

"Yes."

"Well, too bad. I need to sit down."

"Should've stayed home. You're wasting your time here."

"That's something I've gotten pretty good at the last couple years. Wasting time."

Pony doesn't respond, or look at me. There's no point in trying to fix anything or reason with her now, I recognize the signs. She's where I was last year, and the year before. I'll just have to talk and hope something connects. Sort of like with Lanes.

"Do you intend to die here?"

At that Pony picks up the glass and takes a long drink. Not neat, the way she used to drink wine, but greedy and thirsty, with anger behind. When she sets the empty glass down, the waitress swiftly shows up with another and collects the correct amount of the tab from the money still on the table. Pony nods, but when the girl walks away, she calls, "Bring me a double of Jack too, would ya?"

So she's moving on to the hard stuff now. On my account? Talking can wait. "I'll leave you to it, then," I say, intending to leave.

"Seen Greer yet?"

"Yesterday."

"She say anything to you?"

"No."

Pony stares at her hands as the waitress sets a shot glass on the table. The whiskey gleams gold in the light off the dance floor. As the waitress starts to leave, Pony reaches for the pile of money, crumples it up, and gives it to her. Must be thirty dollars there, at least. "Let's settle me up for today," she says to the girl, who immediately starts to count out what's due her for the drink. Pony waves her to stop, saying, "We're square."

"*Thanks so much,*" the girl beams. The tourists here, though typically well-heeled, tip like most people with money to burn: poorly or not at all. Pony waves away the thanks, frowning, and the waitress leaves. I sit quiet. It's her turn to talk.

"Got somethin' for you in my car." Pony lifts the shot glass and stares at it, then sets it down hard. Liquid sloshes over her fingers. "Let's go get it."

Without a word I follow my old friend out and down the boardwalk to the alley where she always parks the Sub. She starts to say something to me, but opens the front passenger door instead. Inside is a cardboard box. "It's heavy. Where're you parked?"

I motion toward the square, and Pony says, "I'll carry it for you." She walks steady and sure, not even remotely drunk, probably didn't have but that one glass of wine all afternoon. But she's cloaked in a towering silence, so I follow suit. More slowly, though. I'm still not myself.

Pony slows to match my stride, and I catch sight of her bootprint in the snow. It is exactly the same sole as mine, but bigger. She places the box gently on the seat of my car and taps the top twice, says, "Got as much as I could."

I reach to open it, but she shakes her head. "Go home, Knothead. Take a load off before you pass out and I have to tote you off the street. I'll be fine." And then she swings away and starts back across the square. Near the elkhorn arch, she stops, though, turns toward me, and shouts, "Make that Pinhead for now. I never knew anybody with a straw through their skull."

~

Somewhere soon she will come through the darkness, and I will be waiting for her.

I understand her path. Understand but don't judge. Killing Rayburn and Audra did something she didn't expect, broke her deep inside. She was sure of herself before, sure of right and wrong and how both should be dealt with, pretty much like me three years ago but without a Joy Nowata to've brought up other options ahead of time. Pony's mom left when she was two. The only girl in a house full of Marines, she had to fight her way up in the world. Got pretty good at it along the way. Much deadlier than me, even with my jiujitsu. The first years we knew each other we argued like cats and dogs—her sure "eye for an eye" was the only way to go; me sure it wasn't. But neither of us had ever killed anyone, so we were just woofing, and we knew it.

That all changed with Australia. And it has changed again now.

Pony is ashamed. She knows the whole story, that Audra wasn't trying to stab, but free me. That she was in on it, yes, but not in on what it became. That Andje saved Laney's life and tried to save the girls. So she is wondering now if there was another way. Waking in cold sweats and fighting back nausea and seeing in everyone's eyes a creeping judgment. Especially mine.

But I do not judge you, my friend, I think, as

strongly toward her tall, proud frame as I can. One day you must let me say this aloud. But for now I will think it and pray—yes, *pray*—for you, Pony Sutton. I'll pray that you find peace and know quickly this one thing: you did the best you could do with what you had on your plate the other day, and that's all any of us can ever hope to do.

As I bring the car to a halt in my driveway, Pony's Sub passes, looping around the narrow street to her own house.

Paul O'Malley, you were right. It's all going to be okay one day soon.

~

Too curious to take the box inside, I sit in the car and use Paul's knife to slit it open, hearing again her brief words of explanation. *Got as much as I could.*

Inside is a beautiful burnished urn.

Paul's ashes.

That's what she's been doing in the mountains. Collecting him, bringing him back to me. I cry all the way inside and when Bess folds her arms around my neck in a tight hug and asks for Audra again, I just cry harder. The doctor said I should expect the head wound to make me more emotional for a while, but I don't think that's it.

Jed's wife Lisa points to a sheet of paper on the counter, "From Wes," and then gives us both a hug and leaves.

It's a list of Newfoundland breeders expecting litters

this spring. California, Colorado, Michigan, Wisconsin. And two in Minnesota.

"I'll take that as a sign," I told Bess as she asked for sweet corn. Her favorite food.

Only at bedtime do I notice that the answering machine's flashing. One message. John Nowata has been released on parole.

FEBRUARY 21

Jim Kemp is dead. I'd only seen him once since all this happened. Over at the chapel.

He came to pray. I came to sit and think.

I told him about some of what had happened on the mountain. Adele, mainly, since she's the big mystery now. Nobody has seen her since the day of the explosion. They brought her in to the hospital, but she disappeared, and Jed's turned the range upside down trying to find her, or her camp, someone who's seen her. To no avail.

"Are you sure you didn't just make her up?" he finally asked me last week.

I said no, but I really don't know. How does an old woman walk unseen for sixty years anyway? I thought, but didn't say. Jed has enough on his plate for now. Eventually I'll be well enough to ski, and I'll go look for her myself. If she's there, maybe she'll come out. Then when we get Lanes back on her feet, I'll take her too. Let her meet her poacher in person.

One thing's interesting, I told Jim. "No more animals have gone missing. At least none that we know of."

"So you see us as similar, her and me?" he asked.

I nodded. "Would've liked you to meet."

"Maybe we will."

"May be."

Less than a week later he was dead, and the little I knew of him slipped into memory. But if this life is unending, a continuing thread from here to beyond, as I saw it so clearly at that mine, perhaps he really will meet Adele.

I'd like to think so.

MARCH 12

Pony is gone. Transferred to the Border Patrol in Nogales. Didn't tell a soul she'd even applied, just announced her resignation two weeks before she left.

I've seen her a couple times since the Cowboy, but we didn't talk. She's still not ready.

Neither is Lanes, it seems, though she's out of the hospital and staying with Bess and me for now. Unresponsive, not a single word yet to anyone, but she's able to swallow and manage basic body functions with help. We're on a waiting list for a Newf this summer. And Dix says he'll introduce us to a healer he knows up in Canada who claims she's seen me in a dream and is supposed to work with me. I don't know exactly what to think of that.

Paul's things are gone too now, except for the box on my dresser and a few things I saved back for Jo and Bess—his journals and a couple of his shirts apiece. Soon I will open the box, but I'm not ready yet. I know what's in there; he told me when he gave it to me: so much pain. I need time to prepare for it.

We have scheduled the memorial service for early August, while Jo's out of school and Miriam's not teaching. By then the snows will be long gone from the ridge, and my head should be better able to make the hike.

There has been no word from my father.

For this I am grateful.

Wes is coming for dinner tonight. In spite of my reservations, I may be grateful about that, too.

AUGUST 2

We scattered his ashes today, on the ridge above the lake, just as promised, though a little late.

Everybody came. I was surprised. Many people from the park, the whole Windy Point crew, even the seasonals. Even Pony flew in for it. Not Laney—she's not up to hiking—but she was with us in spirit. And the girls sneaked Bess's puppy into Jo's daypack, so he was with us too. Howling to be let out before we reached the trailhead. Jed agreed to look the other way and not give us a ticket. "This one time only, young lady," he said to Bess and she laughed and said to the pup, "Did you hear that—*really?*" That's her new sentence. Says it all the time.

In lieu of a service, Josie read from one of Paul's journals, a short piece about the trumpeter swans on the river and the way some of us mate for life, and we all stayed and listened to the wind for a long while after. I didn't cry. My tears are gone.

Pony must be, too. She stood at the edge of the group with her hands rammed into her pockets, shoulders hunched. So alone.

She is still on her path.

The only time she said anything was when Bess got to her on her rounds, stopping in front of each person with the puppy clasped in her arms and saying, "Pet him."

Everyone else had complied, so Bess was practically strutting when she reached Pony. "Pet him, you," she said, as Josie bent to help keep the pup from sliding free. Baby Newfs are chunky. Bess will have muscles to rival mine before she's four if she keeps this up.

Pony's eyebrows shot up at the command, her arms crossed in front of her like a flash, and she backed up two whole paces. Bess followed.

Trapped and frowning, Pony said, "Why? Why should I pet your dog? Why don't *you* pet him?"

And then Bess pulled out her big guns, the word trick she's just learned to deploy. She leaned her head way over on her shoulder and stared up at Pony, little arms hanging onto the wiggling pup. In her sweetest (and rarest) voice, she asked gently, "Pretty please?"

"Son of a—"

I smiled then, as Pony bent to pet the dog, her normal choice of words dying in her throat.

She is on her way back to the light.

It was then that I saw the cardinal again. One quick flash of red among the heavy greens of summer. Suddenly I realized it wasn't just Pony, but me as well. I, too, am on my way back.

Birds every which way I look.

AUGUST 8

We leave tomorrow.

The movers have gone, taking everything with them but his journals and the small box that was on my dresser. Paul gave it to me seven years ago today. It was a gift, but one I rejected at the time. Couldn't take it, thought it gruesome, too hard to contend with. But since he'd given it to me, I couldn't dare throw it out. I've dusted around it ever since and never once looked inside.

But now it is time. The journals are ready, five entries, from four different years. I've never read them like this, back to back.

A candle's lit. We always did that, nights.

August 8

Today's especially bad for flies. Buzzing things. Honeybees and hornets, yellow jackets, bumblebees, ants. Insects of every sort. Impaling themselves on the desperate need to mate and live a full life in the few days before they die.

Tal's been stung three or four times already. "I've about had enough of your Buddhism shit," she declared a while ago. "Fixin to go buy me a flyswatter and swing it, bub, if you don't convince these beasts to procreate someplace else!"

All talk, she is. But very entertaining. I'm enjoying getting to know this woman from the Plains.

Though she denies that, too. "I'm from here." As if saying it firmly, with a soft stomp of the foot, makes it so. History's in the making; Tal's outwitting her past. But she seemed serious enough about the flyswatter. So I redoubled my efforts at coaxing them elsewhere, and that's when it happened.

A fat bumblebee, fuzzy jet black and bright yellow, got caught between the storm windows, so I tried to rescue him. Her, actually, I see now. As I lifted the inner pane, the bee made a small hop upward and I lost my grip. The windows slid closed, in an instant

that I couldn't take back, and cut off the bumblebee's head, so neatly I felt sick. Only her
head. Clean. Her body fell to the sill, the head
too, a few inches apart. Then—and this I still
cannot fathom—

The bee's front legs, moving like fingers,
reached up where her head used to be, feeling
for it, finding nothing. Over and over, again
and again, reaching for what should be there
but isn't. For almost a full minute.

Suddenly her body fell on its side, and was
still.

I called for Tally, sure she would want to
see this, but she'd already headed to town, for
the swatter, I think. So I did the next best
thing: found a small empty box, lined it with
cotton, and carefully placed the bumblebee's
body and head inside. Then I wrote a note for
this woman I love, got the words the way I
want them and copied it onto a tiny scrap of
paper, folded inside the box. I doubt there's
another soul alive who can understand why I
would do this.

But this one can. That much I know.

August 9

Well, maybe not.

Tal never even opened the box. Last night

before bed I told her the story and gave her the box. Without a word, she stood up, stiff as a board, tears in her eyes, and set it on her dresser.

"You don't want to see what's inside?"

"Absolutely not."

"There's a poem—you don't want to read it?"

"Nope."

"Shall I take it back, then?"

"No—go away! It's mine. You gave it to me. So now you just leave it alone!" she said, sassy, the way she is, but serious, we both knew.

Honesty. That's a smidgen of my reason for being here.

August 8

It's been a year now, and the box still sits unopened. I don't dare ask about it. Or touch it. Tally means what she says. True as the sun. Don't touch means don't touch.

I wonder when she'll ever open it?

August 8

We're in the Boundary Waters today, plagued by hordes of buzzing things. Biting, buzzing, sucking things. Have to take refuge in the tent by nine or they'd suck us dry.

Reminds me of the bumblebee. The box is still on her dresser at home. Two years it's been. Unopened still. And untouched, except for dusting. Tal faithfully keeps every speck of dust at bay, twice a week wipes it off with a soft cloth, sets it back in the exact spot. She has yet to say a single word about it.

I don't understand this woman yet, and wonder sometimes if I ever will. Perhaps understanding eats away not just the mystery, but the joy.

Either way, I'm home.

August 8

Tomorrow I leave for Australia. Nothing more to do, but be here this one night. She'll join me in a few months for a long, leisurely stay, but my heart is heavy watching her sleep. If she is.

That damn box is still on the dresser. Four years to the day. Have given up on living long enough to watch her open it and find the poem. Somehow now, I doubt she ever will. Too much pain of innocents, she said the other day. Too much pain in this one world.

Maybe the box holds the pain, and she can't throw it away because it's from me. That makes me sick inside, worried. Not for me, for her.

We said I do on the chapel stoop years ago now, and meant it. I've watched her grow since then, and laugh, feeling safe. But I've worried too that because of me her life is smaller than it could be, or should. This time apart will give her a chance to stretch her wings. I have no fear that she'll leave me, leave us. We're hooked at the hip for the duration.

But, just for once, I would like her to have the chance to

Love me without need.
Live not just through the fear, but beyond it.
Know that now never dies,
And that I will never, ever leave.

If I had one wish for this love of my life, it'd be for her to open the box and find no pain.

And so I finally open the box, to find the severed creature. Dried still, beautiful, as Paul knew it would be. Beneath the cotton, his poem.

> *It is not about pain, Tally dear—*
> *Not about loss, or departure—this life.*
> *It is about having the courage, once beheaded,*
> *To go on feeling for one's head.*

AUGUST 30

So that is it.

Australia finally lived through. Bess is well, I'm healing. I've taken the leap and will attend my first sweat lodge this weekend. We'll see about that.

On to a new life now, flatter shoes. In a place as level as the sea. What they call hills amount to speed bumps, and there's more water than you can shake a stick at. My biggest challenge at the moment is my daughter. Bess isn't all that happy with the move yet, wants to "climb on mountains" when she "gets big," and thinks I've blown her chance at it for life by coming here. So she shouts at me once or twice a week to "go climbing!"

I figure she'll get over it when she dies. Maybe.

One thing I realized last night—just came to me, no reason, no connection, things do that these days—is that I'm no longer afraid of heights. Still. Haven't been since the night Pony and I went back on that peak, looking for Laney. So much was going on then that I missed it clean. Only in living beyond—constant feeling for my head, I guess Paul might say—did I remember it.

So, there it is, Tally J. Permanent straw in your head, or semipermanent, if the sweat lodge works like Dix says. Permanent bump on your arm, and limp on the left. Permanent snit for a daughter, who thinks her current mission in life is to scale K-2 . . . and your job as mother is to get her there now. While under doctor's strict orders not to fly or climb. When—for the first time in your whole blessed life—you could be doing both without fear.

So be it.

Sure the hell beats zero sum.

Or that's what I think until Bess tackles me again, and then I wonder some days. I really do.

POCKET BOOKS
PROUDLY PRESENTS

LEAVE NO TRACE

HANNAH NYALA

Available in paperback
from Pocket Books

Turn the page for a preview of
Leave No Trace. . . .

DAY 1

I worked my first search for the National Park
Service the day I turned nineteen, and found my
first dead body three days later.

Her name was Loren Blair, young and athletic
and as good on a mountain as anybody ever gets—
a first-rate climber in a class of her own—but she
wasn't climbing the day she disappeared. She was
simply out for her morning run, tall and blond and
beautiful as always, looking more like a model than
a nature rat, when she stepped off the trail,
slipped, and fell to her death. Five days passed
before anyone even reported her missing. I didn't
get to her till two weeks later, far too late to do anything but call in the 11-44 and bag the body for
transport and try desperately not to throw up in
the process. Loren no longer looked like a model
or a climber. She belonged to the dead, not the living. Nothing and no one could bring her back.
This is the bitter edge of the work I do. The smell
of death never lets up.

The next day the Chief Ranger made me a permanent part of the Windy Point Search and Rescue

Team, and since then I've been stationed in the Grand Tetons, mountains that draw plenty of people who are a lot less prepared and fit than Loren Blair was. I've been trained to rescue these people, dead or alive, clothed or not, in all kinds of situations and all kinds of weather. I can rappel off a rock face carrying a grown man and do a solo rope rescue without backup, if needed. I can ski an injured climber off a pass in a blizzard and control the descent. I have been well trained to do these things.

But I have not yet been trained to deal with myself at the smell of a three-week-old corpse. They can't train you for something like that.

And I certainly wasn't trained for this.

Nobody can train you to die.

My name is Tally Nowata and this morning, for the first time since I was ten, I remember my dreams.

———

I dreamed of rain and then of dying and then of rain again and woke in a cold blind sweat, reaching for my half-finished net like a drowning person lunges for a line except my net was on hot sand instead of water. Red desert sand that hasn't seen rain in at least a year to boot—which puts the lie to the wet part of my dream and punches the death part home. Hard.

It's the bird, the songbird, that brought me to this, not the situation, not the sand, not the fear, not even the raging hunger. It's just the bird. My very own personal last straw.

Two months ago I wouldn't have eaten a songbird to save my life. Today I did exactly that. Stranded in a strange desert 10,000 miles from home, starving, alone, and beginning to come unraveled at my seams, and still, the worst of it is having to eat bird.

"When you get down to the end of your rope, tie a knot in it and hang on," Grandmother Nowata used to say. She never said what to do with the nausea that comes with hanging onto your own rope that tight. Or what you're supposed to do if you discover your neck in the noose. Pray for double joints from the waist up and squirm free if you can, I suppose. That is Oklahoma's answer for anything a gun won't solve.

Never was much for a gun. Ropes are more to my liking, but a rope here would be overkill. The best tool I have for this job is a hank of flimsy hemp twine, and its rough edges did a number on my fingers this morning. Every knot I tied in my homemade net left its mark on me, but I squared them off anyway, four by four out from the middle until it was the size of a small tablecloth. My hands are still raw and shaking and look like they belong on somebody else—one of the dead tourists we pulled off the Skillet Glacier last year maybe. Minus the bloated pallor, mine look just like theirs did when we zipped them into the body bags: blue-gray, chapped, and battered from the struggle to survive.

On the carryout, Jed quipped that if only they'd prepared their *minds* for the backcountry as well as they had their fancy, color-coordinated, Goretexstudded gear, we might not be having to tote them and it out.

"Any man who can say tote *and* hold up his end of a litter at the same time might be worth keeping around," I muttered, easing my way down a section of scree while trying to keep my side of the litter stable, and Jed shot me the bird with his eyes and almost tripped in the process.

"People pick some of the most inconvenient places to die, don't they?" Jed grumbled, regaining his feet and making do with a gloved finger my direction. I grinned and winked at him. Jed's been my best friend, colleague, and climbing buddy for nine years. We've shot each other the bird so many times we can do it without moving a muscle, so one of us going to the trouble of raising a finger is like shouting through a bullhorn. (And winking back is the rough equivalent of poking the bullhorn inside his eardrum and hollering at the top of my lungs.) I could feel Pony Sutton grinning at the back of our heads. The Windy Point Search and Rescue crew has been together so long now we know each other's every last quirk. That is handy for the kind of work a SAR team does: total equality, total comprehension means we don't have to waste words unless we just want to. Jed shook his head. He could feel Pony's grin on us too.

Laney Greer piped up from the head of the second litter. "Bet the jackets these blokes're wearing cost $500 apiece. Pay my rent and part of the super's with that kind of dough. And just look at all the good it *didn't* do them."

We got quiet then, the way you do on a carryout sometimes—not tense, just focusing on the job, no longer able to leave issues of mortality to someone else.

Pony broke it up. "New gear's a dead giveaway, Lanes," she deadpanned, and we all groaned at her bad pun, then laughed not just because it was true but because every last one of us needed a break from knowing what we were toting right then.

It's a fact. People who pitch up in the wilderness sporting the latest outdoor fashions are a SAR team's surest customers and biggest nightmares. We used to bet on how fast it would take them to need rescuing after they left the visitor center at Moose and how big the callout would be for each one. Ten dollars a head for every SAR crew member called in to work the gig; two for every body put on standby. Since a big search can sometimes have more than a hundred people on the ground and that many more packed and ready to show up, our bets got lucrative fast. I paid for a two-week vacation in Yosemite that way one time, and the rest of the crew groused about it for three years in a row, but that didn't stop us betting on the tourists.

Paul once said it was arrogant the way we did that. "Save people's lives and bust your sides laughin' at 'em all the way home." When Paul is annoyed, the Louisiana bayou baptizes every word.

I tried to explain it—how if you don't laugh when you're scraping somebody's body off the rocks and hauling it down the mountain you'll go right round the bend in your own head—but couldn't, so finally agreed, "Hell yep, it's arrogant. Got a right. Let me tell you one thing for sure, O'Malley, one thing for damn certain. You ever see *me* needing the services of a SAR team, you can count on it—bet the farm you don't own and your next girlfriend's pretty blue eyes too—it'll be a cold day in hell proper. *Very* cold, like switching that brimstone for this blizzard, poof!"

"As if one little Indian girl could change the whole ecosystem of hell," he drawled, and I retorted that if you spend enough time anyplace you eventually get around to working on the decor.

"And please don't call me Indian because I am only half." This has always been a sticking point with us. Paul puts more stock in ethnicity than I do. He can afford to. He's Cajun and Irish. I am something a good deal more complicated.

So here it is. Midsummer in the Tanami Desert of central Australia and hell gone twenty below zero. Paul has disappeared and I am alone, have been for fourteen days, eight of them without food. Hence the plan to trap that lonesome little bird. Necessity is the mother of everything.

He started whistling from his favorite perch just inside the supply tent at dawn. I heard, tried not to, and kept layering in the knots. Soon the blistering summer sun ricocheted off the sand and parched every single inch of my exposed skin. At 11:00 A.M., the ground thermometer hit 124 degrees Fahrenheit. I tried to ignore it, kept working.

Around noon, I finished the net and stood up, startling the songster into leaving—by the exact same route he always used, I noted, with a certain amount of grim satisfaction. It's our loyalty to routines that makes us most vulnerable to predators. Balancing on two metal crates, I stretched the snare across his flyway, lightly hooking the middle and one corner between the tent frame and canvas, and stepped down trailing a long piece of twine. Then I crawled back up and readjusted it four more times before I was satisfied it was ready—in theory. There was nothing else to do but wait.

The pores on my sunburned neck seeped sweat, I could feel it rise, but the hot winds off the spinifex plains sucked the salty mist away before it even broke the surface. Heat shimmers rose and wavered. Tussocks of yellow spiny bushes marched endlessly to a lost point where this aching empty land finally meets the endless sky. My skin was taut and tired, stretched over my bones like a dirty piece of old cellophane, my long hair heavy with grit, my throat scoured by dust and thirst. My stomach bucked and kicked every few minutes from hunger pangs or the knowledge of my situation or both. Breathing hurt.

Red sand stretched like an ocean every direction as far as I could've seen had I been staring at it instead of the net, waiting for the bird to reappear. Clumps of acacia and other trees whose names I neither know nor care to dotted the swelling sand, struggling to recover from the bushfires that swept through last season, hardy shoots of pale green poking out through hectares of charred stubs and roots. A few mulgas, so dry their leaves looked silver, hugged the drainage near the waterhole. Fire does the spring cleaning here. It's the desert's housewife, more interested in culture than ecology.

But I wasn't looking at the scenery or paying much attention to the Tanami's living arrangements this morning. I've spent too much of the last couple weeks doing just that. The view never varies. Nor do the facts. I'm still stranded over 300 kilometers from the nearest human settlement and it's still gone twenty below blessed zero in hell. Half-breed Okie lost in the heart of a continent that's losing its ozone—now there's a bit of cultural data for you. It's easier to get skin cancer here than anywhere else on the planet today. As if I didn't have enough to worry about already.

Worse yet, none of my skills as a wilderness ranger back home in the Tetons make one whit of a difference here. It doesn't matter that I'm an experienced climber with peaks like Denali and Rainier scratched off my Must Climb Before I Die list. Doesn't matter that I know how to dig a snow trench with skis and wait out a blizzard in relative comfort. Build a warm fire out of wet wood, spot an avalanche slope and grizzly spoor. Rig a Tyrolean traverse and guide a loaded litter to the ground on it. Doesn't matter that I've worked with a SAR team in the Rocky Mountains for eight years, helping to save the lives of 47 tourists who got themselves lost or injured in the backcountry. Or helped schlep out the bodies of a slim dozen more who didn't survive despite my crew's best efforts. Doesn't matter that I've stood at the feet of way too many three-week-old corpses, preparing the body for transport and reeling from that terrible smell. Doesn't matter. None of it matters here, and that makes me sick to the stomach. Literally.

Anyway, enough of that. The bird finally returned. The trigger loop of twine sat limp in my fingers. I waited, nervous, sure he'd see the line snaking its way from the saggy tent above his head down to this woman below and depart by the back way on principle if nothing else. I could see it in living color, him somersaulting backward off the perch, neatly avoiding my trap, doing some solo avian version of a Flying Garibaldi move, way out of reach or need of a net.

But he didn't. He just sat there, trusting and simple, surveying his little world, scratching his head. I wanted to leave and started to. He opened his beak to sing me off, in a routine we've pretty much perfected over the last month, and somehow, accidentally, I yanked the line. Tripped over it, I believe.

Then I simply stood there, trapped as a deer in headlights, shocked that my hairbrained plan had actually worked, not knowing quite what to do next. I've never killed an animal before, not even for food. None of my years of training are worth one red hill of beans here. Working search and rescue has nothing whatsoever to do with this level of survival.

Park rangers, it hit me dead center, as the bird

struggled against the coarse mesh, fluttering and chirring in terror, are just as mortal as any tourist on the planet. Skills be damned.

Especially if they're the wrong ones.

When that thought landed on the warm feel of the suddenly limp, feathered body in my hands, I pitched forward, heaving, crying, and the fingers that just wrung the tiny neck went numb and clutched at my stomach. The songbird, still secure in the knotted twine, tumbled to the sand and lay still, quiet at last.

Last straw. I, Tally Nowata, smell death. Again.

Only this time it is my own.

DAY 2

This wasn't supposed to be about dying. It was supposed to be a vacation, a four-month furlough
from a stressful job, joining the man I love in a
place I knew nothing about on purpose. I came for
fun, relaxation, sex, and companionship—and not
necessarily in that order, either. Before exiting the
plane in Alice Springs, I'd never set one foot in a
desert, never had a hankering to, wouldn't ever
have done so if it hadn't been for Paul. I like trees
and mountains and cold, rushing rivers. I like val-
leys tucked away in the shadow of tall granite walls,
plants without spines, and freezing wind and rain.
Deserts were too much like the plains—you can see
for sixty miles any direction either place and that's
just too damn far—so I intended to leave them well
alone and die someplace temperate and green and
preferably wet. Now here I am in the middle of a
hot, red, sandy land, staring death down the nose
and gagging so hard it hurts, and all the stuff I
came for is gone like it never existed. Even him.

What I know about desert survival you could
put in a thimble and still have room for a big man's

thumb, so what I think about my chances of surviving here are unthinkable. But I'm not a needy woman, clutching at any man in sight to help steer my boat or shoo the mice off my terrain. I'm as capable of taking care of me as anybody, more capable than most. I'm worried about Paul, yes, but I can stand on my own two feet till he gets back, and he knows that as well as I do.

This is something I've never said to another living being, but here I've taken to saying it right out loud several times a day. Convincing my own self maybe. Talking tough to keep the truth at bay.

Truth is, though, it's not working, because in spite of all my talk the last few days, I am a little unnerved at this exact moment.

The worst of it, I think, is that after all the trouble I went to yesterday—snaring, strangling, plucking, beheading, gutting, skewering, and roasting that damn bird—I still haven't managed to keep a single bite of it down. Tried again last night and erupted like Mount St. Helens minus the ash. My unfinished dinner went flying into the bushes and I tumbled onto my hands and knees, sick as a dog. Sicker, actually, than any dog I ever saw.

Back where I'm from they shoot dogs that get this sick. It's the Okie version of the good neighbor: put the unfortunate out of their misery so the rest of us don't have to watch 'em suffer. That way we can all pretend we're exempt from the rules, forget them a little while longer, play God with a stick and a smile. But, then again, maybe that's not quite right.

Grandmother Nowata used to say, "Life's a terminal disease and nobody's gettin' out of it alive. Okies are tough, but Indians are made of four-ply steel granite. They have to be." I never crossed horns with my father's mother over that. She was dead by the time I was old enough to have the nerve to cross her. But, for my money, genetics are almost beside the point in the Sooner state: the whole damn population takes a stiff upper lip to the extreme. That used to bother me. I felt trapped by all the adults' strength.

Today, though, I wonder. Maybe their forgetting is done to remember and they aren't so much playing God as figuring out how to survive *and* not kill him— or anyone else—off. Maybe the thing we all know best about death is the one we lie about last. Maybe, when you get into the business of saving lives like I have, you forget the most important point: we none of us are gettin' out of this gig alive. Maybe people like me fight too hard to beat the odds and people like my grandmother walk nearer the truth.

May be.

Can't say. Wouldn't know.

All I know is my own truth: If you're still breathin', you're still a candidate for my services. SAR isn't a job so much as an attitude: So that others may live. Save a life no matter the cost. We come onto every gig willing to give our own lives if necessary. There's a certain folly in that, but we're well trained, well equipped, and deadly effective when we show up, so people rely on us. Even *we* rely on us, me perhaps most of all. But then, I'm usually on the good side of bad situations in the outdoors. Here everything's changed, like a pair of die flung high and no telling where they'll land.

Enough. Just work the gig as if you picked it, Nowata, and keep your head in the middle of now.

It took a long time to pull myself together enough to retrieve the bird's carcass and begin brushing sand off the greasy meat with fingers so dirty the effort itself was moot—but necessary. When a person shrinks inside herself, effort alone becomes part of the point, a big part. If you can still struggle you know you're still alive, that sort of thing. Lies become articles of faith.

Spoken aloud, truth.

Where are you, Paul O'Malley? I've run it down in my head a hundred times and am no closer to knowing now than I was the first time through.

Supply run to Alice Springs, four days tops. You were supposed to pick up your daughter at the airport, get that worthless base radio repaired again, buy another month's stock of food, fill the water dolly, and come straight back here. You are the most reliable human being I ever met. Never late for anything, not even by a few minutes.

But you're overdue now, for the first time ever—and by way too many days to count yet again—and I don't know why. And the worry is starting to eat at my edges.

LEAVE
NO
TRACE,
Hannah Nyala's
fiction debut, is an action-packed thriller!

Tally Nowata has saved many lives as a search and rescue worker. In the mountains of her home, she is an expert at survival. But in the Australian outback, she is only a tourist—a tourist whose boyfriend, Paul, went to pick up his daughter and never came back. He has been missing for six days, leaving Tally stranded in the unforgiving wasteland of the Tanami desert.

She sets out to find him…only to discover that he has been murdered and his daughter left to die. Tally knows that it's only a matter of time before his killers find the camp she left behind and the arrow pointing out her direction.

She is grieving, tired, and bitterly aware that she knows too little about this land, only bits and pieces of information that Paul had given her. But there is nothing to do but go on, carrying Paul's memory and his daughter with her in a desperate struggle for survival.

Publishers Weekly praised *Leave No Trace*:

"Nyala's intimate knowledge of survival tactics and her informal yet stylish prose make this one of the year's most noteworthy suspense novels."

Available from Pocket Books

10930

Don't Miss

POINT LAST SEEN

by HANNAH NYALA!

Nyala's passionate immersion in the art and science of tracking leads to the first safe place she and her children have known. Point Last Seen *is a wholly original account of one woman's life and an intriguing glimpse at the meaning and power of following footprints.*

Escaping an abusive marriage, her children abducted by her violent husband, Hannah Nyala was left alone to pick up the pieces of her life, to heal physically and spiritually. She wanted her children back...but first she had to fight for her own future by teaching herself the skills of tracking in the Mojave Desert. She became a search-and-rescue tracker dedicated to saving the lives of the lost and so attuned to nature's messages that she can read the history of a footprint, the clues in stone and desert sand. That's just the beginning of her incredible story. For Hannah would soon make the most chilling discovery: someone was tracking her on a vicious quest to do her harm.

Praise for *Point Last Seen*!

"This is an unusual book. Indeed, it reverberates like a nightmare, as memorable for the lessons it embodies as for its terror. An arresting tale of courage and hard-won wisdom."
—*Booklist*

"In this beautifully rendered narrative, a woman reveals the art of tracking both in the wilderness and in autobiography."
—*Kirkus Reviews*

Available from Pocket Books

Visit
❖ Pocket Books ❖
online at

....

www.SimonSays.com

....

Keep up on the latest new
releases from your favorite
authors, as well as author
appearances, news, chats,
special offers and more.

SIMON & SCHUSTER
A VIACOM COMPANY
www.SimonSays.com

Pocket
Books

2381-01